Deadly
Stone Bags

Deadly
Stone Bags

A. D. Russo

To order additional copies of this book, contact:
Xlibris Corporation
1-888-795-4274
www.Xlibris.com
Orders@Xlibris.com

1

John Wilson was happy doing his ten laps in the quiet
of the Olympic swimming pool. Actually he was happy
to be alive at age sixty-four doing anything. Eight years
had passed since he'd been diagnosed as HIV positive. Taking the mounds of drugs was a good trade-
off for being able to enjoy a busy and full existence.
He dog paddled over to a metal ladder and climbed
out of the pool. The former Secretary Of
Commerce's trim muscular body and handsome Yankee face masked both his advanced age and medical
affliction.

Wilson removed the water goggles from his sky
blue eyes, which he rubbed before looking around
for the pool attendant. "Clyde," he shouted toward
a small room used as a storage area and hangout by
the pool attendant.

Wilson looked around. He wasn't accustomed to
waiting for anything or anybody. "Clyde, where are
you? Must be on one of his prolonged breaks." He
grumbled, "Those people—prolonged breaks are

their thing." There was some of the old starch in his voice. He turned toward the main entrance to the pool area. "Sure could use a towel."

He thought he was talking to himself until the door opened behind him and a voice said, "Here. Here's your towel, John."

Wilson smiled. He recognized the husky voice. "What are you doing here today?"

Before Wilson could turn around, his smile was erased by a sharp blow to the back of his head.

"Gotta get back to the pool." Clyde Gomez was growing tired of the small talk even though he was good at it. He slid to the edge of his seat and shook his head at the rap music blaring out of a radio on a shelf above his head. "Crude dude in the mood for some bitch food? Crap. Why you listening to that crap rap stuff, Louie? Salsa's our music. Besides, rap ain't even music."

Louie snapped, "Says who?"

"Guy who teaches my psych course at Community says rap is the result of a sick society. Rap's nothing but clang association. Bunch of inane rhymes. Stuff connected with schizzy behavior, a serious mental sickness."

"Clang ass what? Since taking them courses, Clyde, you been talking another language. I suppose he don't like Madonna even?"

"How'd you know? He says she's helping to corrupt America. From middle America down, she's a star. From middle America up she's a slut."

"Sounds like you're really caught up in that college stuff. So you're still going nights."

"Yep." Clyde stood up and stepped toward the

door. "Taking more courses now. Only way for me to get out of this joint."

Louie shrugged. "This joint ain't so bad, 'cept they're keeping it open for nothing today. Ain't nobody here. Hell, this gotta be the deadest place on the planet this time of the year."

Clyde appeared glad. "I know. Had only one guy so far today and he's probably gone by now. Better check, though." Clyde stepped into the corridor. Two heavyset individuals coming toward him with their heads lowered slowed to a halt near the entrance to the sauna.

Clyde knew that if they used the steam room they'd need towels, so the conscientious attendant shuffled his sore sandaled feet across the tiled floor to a towel closet. When he returned to the sauna with the towels, Clyde's mouth opened wide, exposing a row of large crooked teeth. He grew increasingly alert as he looked around the steam filled room. "Wha, where did them two go? They come here?"

Two friendly businessmen doing some business talk in the sauna smiled patronizingly. One of them said, "Who?"

"Two gentlemen. Must've decided to leave. Saw them and went to the towel closet." Clyde smiled politely. "You fellas don't need anything?"

"Nope."

Anxious to be free of the steamy sauna, Clyde sped down the tiled corridor to the cool high-walled confines of the Olympic swimming pool area. There he could sit and daydream away the remainder of the dull afternoon.

Clyde entered the pool area and was looking around for a place to park his tired body when he saw the large object at the water's edge.

Clyde leaned forward to take a better look and froze, his normally sleepy eyes widening alertly on a suddenly blanched mulatto face. The floating object was an extra large transparent plastic bag that appeared to be loaded with a fleshy material. He took a step back, his slender body recoiling when he thought he saw the buoyant thing move. Clyde's bony knees already wobbly almost caved in. Though violence had produced a lot of unsavory stuff in his Bronx neighborhood, nothing could match what he was looking at now. He scurried out to the wide corridor.

Even before he reached the main lobby, Clyde called out to the security guard who was seated like a satrap holding sway over a battery of television monitors: "Benny, Benny. Hey man, I need your help."

The security guard was too caught up in a talk show. Even his surveillance monitors were being ignored. When he looked up, the many years of practiced arrogance among his peers exaggerated the annoyance on his flaccid face.

"What's up, Clyde? You look like you seen a ghost."

"I don't know what I seen. It's not quite human looking. It's—hell, I really don't know." Clyde's sleepy eyes had grown into giant white marbles covered with swelled bloody veins.

The Spa guard grumbled, "You couldn't have seen a flying saucer inside this joint. Where is it exactly?"

"Floating in the pool."

"Floating in the pool? Let's look see." With a ho-hum expression, the guard checked the pool monitor. He shook his head. "Can't see anything with this. May as well take a good look see." He gave the pool monitor one last glance before rising and adjusting his standard cadet blue uniform while paying special attention to his gun belt and revolver. "C'mon."

The guard brushed by the clearly shaken swimming pool attendant, almost knocking him over as he walked briskly toward the Olympic-sized swimming facility. Clyde followed reluctantly, cautiously. He was curious about his find, but he didn't want to take any chances.

The security guard stopped in the entryway. "Hey, how'd that get there?" The guard grabbed at his thirty-eight and pointed it at the partially submerged, plastic-encased object. He approached it with the same respect and caution previously exercised by the pool attendant. "Holy shee-it. What in hell is it?" He would have preferred having someone else find out, but he'd been acting too macho around the pool attendant for that.

The security guard reached down and nudged gingerly at the buoyant object with the nozzle of his revolver, causing the object to sink, then bounce and roll in the chlorinated water. The Spa guard recoiled and quickly withdrew his hand. "Whoa! You was right, Clyde. This ain't nothin' to fool with. I better call the po-leece."

The security guard rushed back to his post in the lobby with Clyde following more closely behind him than his shadow. The guard dialed 911 as fast as his quavering fingers allowed. He waited. "Where are they when you need them most?"

When two uniforms arrived, the one in charge nodded toward his associate. "Let's pull it out, Joey."

Joey didn't look too happy. "Never expected to be doing any fishing today, Sarge."

The uniforms tugged at the buoyant cadaver until they had pulled it over the limestone coping at the edge of the pool. The police sergeant looked up. "When did you discover this thing?"

"Clyde, he discovered the thing. He works the pool."

The sergeant turned toward the pool attendant. "Funny you work here and don't notice how the guy ends up like this."

Clyde said with a tremor in his voice, "I do double duty between pool and steam room. Real slow day today for the pool."

The sergeant grumbled as he stood up and faced the security guard. "You got a log of all the users of this place?"

The security guard appeared helpless. "We don't got such a thing here. Just monitors for security."

While sizing up the security guard, the police sergeant grumbled, "Joey. I better go get some crime scene tape and call homicide. Make sure no one touches anything." He nodded toward the hallway. "Take them two out there and get their names, addresses."

The cop reached into his pocket for his notebook. "Okay youse guys, your names, where you live."

The confusion of a crime scene began to take shape when several crime scene technicians arrived and started looking for evidence. A coroner and his assistant immediately began the task of removing the heavy-duty plastic bag, which the coroner carefully folded. Then he cleared his throat and spoke nasally into a small recorder. "The victim is a white male. His upper torso was enclosed in a clear plastic bag, super heavy gauge plastic, type of bag used in industrial or commercial settings for heavy duty application. The plastic bag has a nylon cord manufactured into its outer brim which someone pulled and tied and which I untied."

A homicide detective asked, "Think it was a suicide, Morris?"

"Don't know what to think. Not yet." The coroner shrugged his fat shoulders. "I'll tell you more after I've examined the corpus."

Another homicide detective ushered the still clearly shaken swimming pool attendant and security guard into the poolside area. "You guys recognize this individual? Know who he is? You must. He's gotta be a member of this club."

Both men looked incredulously at the victim's face and nodded.

"Mister Wilson," the security guard said softly; all the macho juice had been squeezed out of him. "Nice sort of guy. Real important, I guess."

"Not any more." The homicide detective turned to the pool attendant. "Was he swimming at any time while you were in or around the pool area?"

The pool attendant said, "Like always he was doing his swimming exercise, as he called it. I just somehow forgot about him." The pool attendant appeared to be in a trance.

"You forgot about him?" The detective tweaked his bulbous nose. "So you saw him alive?"

"Yep, I did. He was just starting to do his usual swimming exercise. Did it a lot, almost every week of the year."

"You notice anything else? Anyone else go near the pool around that time?"

Clyde's eyes said he remembered. "Saw two guys in the vicinity, short while ago. Heavyset types."

"They didn't use the pool?"

"Nope. He was the only one."

When a tall wiry looking individual entered the room, all eyes turned toward him.

"Hi Murph. Clyde here was just telling me about two fat individuals being at the scene here around the time of the homicide. Him and his buddy found the body, wrapped in a plastic bag."

"I know. The M E and his assistant told me about it; bumped into them on my way in." The chief detective of precinct seventeen studied the faces of the two still visibly shaken Nordway Health Club employees. "Did both of you see the two men?"

The spa guard looked at Clyde who nodded and said, "I saw them. Didn't fully recognize them at the time."

Murphy's smirk broadened. "And now you do? They had to be members. Can't come into this place unless you're a member."

"True, excepting that you can come with a member." Clyde's face said he remembered more. "I'm not that sure, but one of them looked like a member who comes here mainly with his boss, Mister Stone, when he does come. And now that I think of it, use the steam room together. Other guy, him I'm not absolutely sure of, although I'm pretty sure I seen him before too."

The inspector wanted to know more. "Mister Stone?"

"Yeah, he came with Mister Byron Stone."

The police inspector appeared surprised. He turned toward a homicide detective as he enunciated, "The Byron Stone?"

"Yup," Clyde answered wide-eyed.

"We'd better take a look at the club roster."

A tall man toting a black case tapped the inspector on the shoulder. "I'll take it from here, Murph."

Murphy turned toward the precinct's head criminologist. "Where've you been?" He glanced at his watch. "You're a bit late, Morin. Coroner's already left with the most important piece of evidence, a plastic bag. Not much else, besides the victim."

"We'll make a thorough check anyways."

"I'm sure you will, Morin." Murphy's pronunciation of Morin was closer to "moron". This "criminalist" had never impressed him.

2

"Mister Stone? Mister Byron Stone?"

"Yes. Who's this?" It was late. The voice at the other end of the line sounded tired.

"This is Inspector John Murphy, homicide. I was wondering if you could answer a couple of questions for me."

"About what, inspector?"

"About John Wilson, his homicide."

"John? Dead? When?"

"This afternoon. His body was found in the Nordway Health And Athletic Club pool."

"That's too bad, but I hardly knew Jack."

"Wilson's partner, Nicholas Stockton, I was just talking to him; he mentioned that you've used their law firm, Wilson-Stockton, for some of your international transactions." After awaiting a response for a few seconds, the detective said impatiently, "Mister Stone, I know for a fact that your company uses Wilson's outfit. That was borne out by Wilson's partner, Nick Stockton, who is a very close friend of yours as anyone who reads the financial pages knows."

"Financial pages?" Byron Stone paused to consider the police inspector's contrived connection. "Stone Holdings has used them on occasion."

"On occasion?"

"Yes, only occasionally, as in not very often. We have our own legal staff."

Sensing that there would be no further response, Murphy said, "I understand that you're a member of the Nordway Health Club, a director. Stockton told us."

"That's true, as is Stockton."

"One of your employees, a Doctor Cameron Blake, is also a member. Isn't that so, Mister Stone?"

"That's true also." There was a pause as Byron Stone yawned. "You're calling at an awful late hour, aren't you, Inspector? I just arrived here from a trip to Europe. Couldn't you have waited until tomorrow morning?"

"Sorry about that, Mister Stone. I didn't realize how late it is. I must've been on the phone with Mister Stockton longer than I realized. By the way, Mister Stockton said that you may have gotten Doctor Blake his membership into the Health Spa?"

"As a matter of fact, I did get Cameron his membership. There's usually a long waiting list. Why? Why do you ask about him?"

"Just checking. Thank you, Mister Stone. You've given me all the answers I need, for now at least. Just one more thing. Have you gotten any other people into your health spa?"

"Several. Can't remember their names right off hand, except Boris Kleptokoff, my administrative assistant."

"Boris Kleptokoff?" Murphy paused. This was some of the information he sought. He had just attended a seminar on Russian Mafia. "Sounds Russian. Could you spell that for me, Mister Stone?"

Byron Stone spelled the name for the inspector. "Thank you. That's all for now, Mister Stone."

3

Sue Brown slammed shut the apartment door with the heel of her tired foot. The climb up the three flights of rickety stairs was almost too much. She plopped the newspaper, briefcase and herself onto her bed. Oh how she ached. She lay back and scanned the front page of the newspaper.

When the degrading and repugnant picture of a dead man caught her attention at first, she read the caption under the photo. Former Secretary of Commerce, John Wilson, who specialized in representing foreign corporations doing business in the United States, was found dead at the exclusive Nordway Health And Athletic Club in Manhattan.

She wondered where she'd heard that name before. It came to her as she read further: According to his partner, Nicholas Stockton, Wilson was well liked by his colleagues and had no enemies. Although suffering from a chronic illness for several years, the mild mannered bachelor was very busy doing a lot of work overseas for his firm, which specializes in international law and commerce. Stockton himself had just arrived from a trip to Ireland to watch the Irish Derby with his close friend and business associate, Byron Stone, when he got the bad news about the other senior partner of their law firm.

Sue stopped reading. "Byron Stone." She whispered the name reverently. She knew she should have called him about his dad's serious illness. Stroke. Damned shame. He was a great guy. Time to be assertive and call. Owe him a call out of respect, common courtesy. A crooked smile crept across her pretty face. She knew full well she was rationalizing. She really just wanted to see Byron again.

She stared at the photo on the front page of the Daily. "Gotta call." She thought of how generous the Stones were, providing her with a full scholarship to grad school. She thumbed through the newspaper. "What a coincidence." After turning some pages, she found what she wanted.

Sue scanned the racing results and entries charts in the horse racing section. Then she switched to the overnights to see if there was any mention of Byron's outstanding filly, Samsona. If the filly were running over the weekend, it would be something to look forward to. Sue's father had trained the filly's dam.

Sue found the handicapper's column and read it. There was nothing in it about Old Stone Stable's horses. Sue stood up and placed the newspaper on top of the bureau and checked her watch. A rerun of all nine races from Belmont would be shown on Sports Channel in less than half an hour. That would break the monotony for a short while. Her pretty face cracked a wry smile. "Give or do almost anything to see Byron Stone again." She made a distorted face at herself in the mirror hanging over the bureau. "For a budding expert on assertiveness training you don't show me much. Call the guy. You've got an excuse." She hissed like an angry hag: "Damn it all, do it. If you were really assertive you'd give him a call." She shook her head helplessly as she glanced at the TV sitting on its stand against the wall. The TV was another reminder of Byron, whose dad had sent it to her as a Christmas present during her first year at the university. Unfortunately, nothing of interest on the damned contraption Friday nights, she thought.

Air. Suddenly she felt suffocated by the stale air in the room. More air was needed. She dragged herself over to the window and tried to open it. She finally got the dilapidated window open, not without cost. "Damn." She sucked at the finger with the broken fingernail.

When Sue left sunny southern California to do her graduate work in New York with the help of a scholarship from the Stones' S and P Foundation, she never imagined that she'd have to put up with a one bedroom so-called efficiency apartment no larger than a mare's foaling stall. There were times when she would have preferred a mare's foaling stall. No matter how she'd tried, she could never get rid of the acrid smells of cat urine and roach powder deeply embedded in the rickety wooden floor and the sweating plastered walls behind which an army of roaches and an occasional rat resided.

After quickly stripping off her blue jeans and blouse and revealing the curves disguised by them, Sue sat nearly nude on the twin bed. Nudity along with the added reinforcements of open window and fan were hardly enough to do combat against the unbearable heat and ennui of another Friday evening. "Dull, dull, dull," she moaned.

She coughed, a dry gagging cough. Mold spores, chemicals in the roach powder and plain old dust had to be conspiring to choke her to death.

Sue eyed the newspaper. She pondered the fate of the unfortunate dead man pictured on the front page. Things could be worse. Ugly, horrible way to die and one of Byron Stone's buddies was closely connected with the man. There might be more about Byron in the remainder of the article.

Sue checked her watch. Plenty of time till a rerun of the afternoon races at Belmont would be shown on Sports Channel. She grabbed the newspaper.

"Holy crap." Sue read aloud, "Head detective John Murphy revealed that Byron Stone was questioned also. As recently as last week Stone Holdings Corporation was named in a Federal investigation, which also involved Wilson and his partner, Nick Stockton. Stone said that he'd had little or no contact in the past two years with Wilson except indirectly through Nicholas Stockton, Wilson's close associate."

The article continued to say much more about Stockton, nothing more about Byron. So she let the newspaper drop to the floor.

She pictured Byron Stone when she'd last seen him, so sophisticated, so mature. "He doesn't even know I exist."

Sue reclined on the bed and shut her eyes. She tried to relax by using a simple relaxation exercise she'd learned in a stress management workshop. Her faint smile erased the small web of wrinkles from her sweating face. She tried thinking about something pleasant.

Jim Morrissey said he might pop in on her, as he did last Friday, after he was done with his work at the university. They could try C A T again. She pictured his amazed green eyes devouring her body the last time he had opened the door of her apartment and found her nearly nude.

Sue sat up and glanced at her watch, feeling a tingly sensation in her crotch and belly. C A T, the Coital Alignment Technique, worked big time. They tried it after they'd both read about it in an article written by one of their grad school advisors. It described the two thousand year old Tantric exercise for helping one to achieve orgasm.

Sue ran her hand over the soft mattress of the twin bed. She vowed that some day when she got some kind of monetary windfall, she'd treat them both to a king-sized bed in a resort hotel somewhere in the Poconos.

Sue checked her oval face in the mirror above the bureau. A little more make-up would help. Even though Jim Morrisey told her once that she was the prettiest girl he'd ever dated, she wasn't all that confidant or satisfied, especially when it came to her firm, though ample breasts.

Sue looked down at her bare, shapely legs, almost the color of cooked egg white. Discouraged, she heaved a sigh. She needed a tan real bad. She ran the back of her hand over her large sensuous lips and small turned up nose sprayed with the only things on her face which occasionally got her to put on more makeup, her freckles. After flicking a few stray strands of her straight sandy brown hair from her doe-like hazel eyes, she stared at the wall.

She felt caged. As a psychologist and sex therapist in the making, she knew full well where her mind was. Drive reduction was needed and not with just any guy who happened to come along. Certainly, Jim Morrissey would do tonight. Loads of fun and somewhat intellectual. Too bad he wasn't like the prince charming she would have liked when she was growing up and reading romance novels in which the heroine always ended up in bed with the hero of the story. Byron Stone would be more like it.

She glanced at the clock on the bureau and debated her call. Jim may have forgotten. If he were home, she could ask him if he planned to come back to the university to work on his research during the weekend and get him to come sooner than later. Sue reached into her briefcase and found Jim's phone number. She dialed and what she hoped wouldn't happen, happened.

"Hello," a husky female voice answered.

Sue didn't dare respond.

"Hello, hello." Silence. "Who the hell?"

Sue put the receiver down. Another confrontation with Jim's mother wasn't needed. She sat dazed and numb for a moment while picturing an overbearing, oversized, mustached and matronly appearing woman at the other end of the phone line. She had never met the woman in person, but that's how she pictured Jim's mother, and fairly or not, it didn't matter to her.

"You tried, girl." She reached into her briefcase for a notebook.

The phone's ringing made her drop the notebook.

Jim? Could he have been home and guessed it was she who'd called? She cleared her slightly above alto voice and grabbed the phone expectantly. "Hello."

"Sue. How are you doing?" There was a slight pause. "Hope I'm not calling at a bad time?"

The mellow male voice at the other end had a numbing effect.

"Who's this?" There was no mistaking the voice even though she hadn't heard it for more than a year. Her heart started racing.

"It's me Byron Stone. Sorry I haven't called you sooner, as promised. Been extraordinarily busy past year or so."

"Byron." Sue stammered, "It, it's great to hear from you. What a coincidence. Was just reading about you and your friend in the newspaper."

"About Nick and John Wilson? Too bad. That was one horrible way to die. Plastic bag, just like out of a movie."

"Just horrible. Who could do such a thing? Was he a close friend?"

"I knew him, but more at a distance you might say, mainly through business. As the newspaper said, he was a partner of my very close friend, Nick Stockton. They were in the same law office. You're right, terrible way to die, although a lot of people are being killed every day, everywhere these days."

"Tell me about it."

Byron Stone said quickly, nervously, with an impatient quality in his voice, "Sue, I didn't call you to have a philosophical discussion. I'm calling about a personal matter."

Sue heard Byron sneeze. While she waited, Sue pondered the why of the call. Her first reaction was that he had called to tell her about his father's death. But she wiped it out quickly with the thought that he would have called her dad about that kind of news and not her. A hope entered her mind. Knowing how much she loved horses and horse racing, perhaps he was inviting her to go to the races with him.

"Sorry about that. Must be my allergies acting up."

"I've the same problem this time of the year. Before I forget, saw where your filly Samsona won a big race couple of weeks ago. Saw the race. She really looked great. Another big horse for Old Stone Stable."

"You saw the race? Belmont? Wish I knew. If you were there you should have come down to the winner's circle. You could have taken the picture with us."

"I saw it on television. By the way, I was talking to my dad. Even though he's stayed retired since he stopped training for your father, he's been keeping up with what your stable's doing. And he saw the race too, on TV. But he called me also to tell me about your dad. Sorry to hear he had a stroke. How's he doing? I've meant to call you."

"He's hanging on, barely though. But he's a fighter and according to his doctor may still make it, although he hasn't regained consciousness yet." Byron's voice sounded burdened with sadness.

"I hope he does. He will. He's such a dynamic type of guy."

"I don't know; even if he makes it, he'll never be the same vital and dynamic person he used to be." Byron paused. His voice sounded more upbeat and in command when he continued: "Say, enough sad talk, I'm really calling to see if you could join me this weekend for a happy trip to our place near Mystic and Stonington in Connecticut. I've been meaning to do this for a long time. It'll give us a chance to get caught up on what's happened to us over the past two years or so. Boy, they seem to have flown on by so quickly. And there's something I want to run by you. But that can wait until we're at my summer place."

"I'm not doing anything special, although I'm not entirely sure." Sue's voice trailed off. She suddenly felt shaky and inadequate, even intimidated. Yet this could be an opportunity. She'd often wondered what it would be like to interact with him in an intimate social situation. She didn't want to sound too anxious. "Such short notice. Let me check my schedule."

Byron waited.

Sue tried to catch her breath, but she nearly hyperventilated. She really wanted to go. What a godsend, a short vacation, something she sorely needed. And he wanted to discuss something with her. She felt her heart pounding away. Byron Stone always had that affect on her. She waited, hoping that he'd say something. In all of her prior experiences and contacts with him, no matter what she felt about him sexually or socially she had to maintain the same level of positive response and interaction. He represented wealth, prestige, ownership; she and her family represented service to that ownership. This call from out of the blue did suddenly create a new, though not totally inexplicable, excitement and hope.

Byron broke the silence. "Sue, hey, are you still there? You've got to go with us. I've invited some great guys and gals."

"Okay, what the heck." Sue conjured up the words as calmly as her excited and stirred up state of being allowed.

"I'll have you picked up tomorrow morning at nine. You're still at the same place, I take it?"

"Yep."

"We sail around ten, so that we can enjoy the entire day. Supposed to be a great day for being out on the bounty. I'm using Dad's new boat, one built less than three years ago. Hardly used. You'll like it."

"What'll I wear?"

"You'd look good in anything. Plain old jeans are okay. Same as you'd wear around the horses. Bring a swimsuit. We'll see you shortly after nine." Byron hung up abruptly.

Her heart still thumping like the hoof beats of a horse, Sue slowly placed the phone on the small corner table next to the bed. She wiped the new sweat on her brow with the back of her quivering hand. A strong current of excitement surged through her as she contemplated what had just taken place. Life was strange. Barely minutes before Byron called, just getting her self to call him seemed futile, and now the unexpected. She couldn't wait to see him again. She appeared confused and grim faced as she studied herself in the mirror.

"No way," she said as she thought: He's just doing it out of friendship, and whatever. Not a chance fickle woman. No, it's just another family related thing, a friendly gesture. She made a funny face at herself in the mirror before turning away. Even a tout at the race track would say she was a hopeless long shot. She looked back at the mirror. She knew she could be better looking than she appeared in the mirror. How? Having her hair done professionally? She checked her watch. It was way too late.

Sue shut her itchy eyes and rubbed them. When she reopened them, they became fixed on the unseemly photo of the dead man on the front page of the Daily. Sue shuddered, realizing suddenly that she hardly knew Byron Stone. They lived in totally different worlds. Her thoughts became muddled. Was it possible that a person of his stature could be involved in some way with the man's murder? According to what she'd read in the newspaper, Byron and the dead man's partner, Nick Stockton, had to have been close to the dead man.

"Doesn't affect me. Got to think positive." Sue turned on the TV set. It was time to watch the rerun of the afternoon races at Belmont.

4

Murphy heard the footsteps. Frank Marone was usually late. The office door swung open, revealing a paunchy, medium-sized man whom Murphy respected even though Marone was rough around the edges and could be extremely abrasive at times.

"Sorry I'm late, Murph. Traffic."

"Late? You're never late. Besides I've nothing else to do but wait around for you all day."

"Yeah, yeah. So what's the latest on Wilson? You said over the phone it was no suicide."

"According to the M.E. it had to be murder. Just finished talking to him. Although, whoever iced Wilson wanted it to look like a suicide, for whatever reason." Murphy handed a forensics photograph to Frank Marone.

"Yeah, I saw the newspaper photo. It's even worse than women boxing. Funny you guys are still letting those tabloid twerps take such a picture. Grotesque."

"Right now I'm more concerned about who murdered him. Even though I remember reading when

Wilson was Secretary of Commerce that he was a homo, and rumor was that he got AIDS from having an affair with some guy in his law office."

"So he could've wanted to commit suicide."

"Had good reason to maybe, except Morris is pretty definite Wilson was murdered."

Frank Marone's middle-aged face clouded over. "Still can't figure out why I'm being brought into this one? Sure ain't because of my superior good looks."

"Ain't. It's only because you're still on the joint crime-fighting thing and your boss wants to keep you busy. Nah. I just happened to be talking to him yesterday and he said you weren't working on anything right now and he said he'd assign you. And we agreed this investigation's going to go way out of my jurisdiction before it's done. Not out of yours, of course. It's common knowledge that you're connected." Murphy put his hand over his big mouth to muffle a mocking sound.

Marone didn't laugh. "Mafia, me? C'mon, Murph. We've gone over that ground before."

"Not Mafia. The Feds. Maybe even CIA."

This time Marone did laugh. "Or 007. Get real Murph. I was sent to a special training school once, run by the FBI. How many times do I have to tell you? You're just too thick."

"I know, I know. Anyway, with your experience and exposure to Interpol, you'll be able to deal with the guys we're dealing with in this case. Wilson's law partner, a Nicholas Stockton, and his buddy Byron Stone."

"Nicholas Stockton? I believe he's the one who was involved in that rumor about AIDS. And Byron Stone? Him I've heard of too. Big time operator in the business world. Still, it sounds like you know where you're headed."

"Don't think so."

"What else can you tell me?"

"All we know so far is that the outfit Wilson headed up has done some work for Byron Stone, and that one of Stone's top guns, guy named Blake, was at that Athletic Club about the time Wilson croaked and another guy who works for Stone was with him."

"Heavy stuff."

The police inspector laughed as he sized up his state police counterpart. "Heavy's a good word for Stone's guys. From the description we got of him, Blake's a real heavyweight like you. Someone you might have had a tough time beating when you boxed."

"In those days I was a middleweight."

"Blake's partner in crime, assuming they did it, is this fat Russian immigrant, probably connected with the Red Star, the Russian Mafia."

Marone thoughtfully compressed his thick liver-colored lips before saying, "The Red Star? Hope you're kidding. They're a real tough bunch to deal with. Tougher even than our homegrown brand of Mafiosi, judging from some of the scams we've caught them in so far over in Brooklyn. So you've pinned down two of the guys who might've done it? Are they criminal types?"

"No files. Don't have anything yet on either one of them. Just know that they might have been in the area around the time of the homicide. Couple of possibles to check out."

"Anything else?"

"Let me see." Murphy looked down at his

notepad. "Blake's a Doctor Blake, Doctor Cameron Blake."

"A medical doctor?"

"Nah, a chemist of some sort who works for one of Stone's pet projects, an outfit called the S and P Foundation. He's one of the big honchos of the outfit."

"What does he do there? I've heard of them; don't know what they do. What do they do, this S and P outfit?"

"S stands for shit and P stands for..." The police inspector shook his head. "Hey, too many questions. All we know so far is that this guy Blake is close to Stone. And the other guy, the Russian, he does administrative work for Stone. He was with Blake at the Health Club around the time the body must have been dumped into the pool. As for S and P, someone did mention that it's involved in some kind of population control stuff. Research outfit."

"Looking into the greenhouse effect maybe?"

"More like the outhouse effect since they have people in Africa studying AIDS and the Ebola virus."

"Getting back on track, how much evidence we got so far?"

"Not much. A plastic bag and cadaver whose head appears to be bashed in. Blake and the other guy's being there could just be a big coincidence. They may have a very good alibi. Nordway's a big place. Could have been playing racket ball, as Blake said they were."

"Sounds like you've questioned them already."

"I talked to Blake over the phone. Not the other guy. I'll try and see them both tomorrow."

"What did Blake have to offer?"

"Not much, beyond what I just told you. Ain't

the most sociable type. At least he don't deny that he was there. Getting anything out of him is like pulling teeth."

"Had to play dentist?"

"Yeah, as I said, he ain't the most cooperative, friendly type. Lousy attitude. Tight-lipped, hidden agenda type. Plays his cards close to the vest. Best way I can describe him."

"Hard to talk to."

"Like a stone. And there's an accent there that I can't quite put my finger on, and it ain't Celtic like his name is."

"At least you got an admission that he and this other guy who works for Stone were there. Find their prints, anything connected to them?" Frank Marone stared at a plastic container on Murphy's desk.

"Nothing. Coroner had the plastic bag fumed for prints. It was clean."

"Sounds like we don't have very much. Just some thin, or should I say fat maybe's and a corpse with a bashed in head." Frank Marone rubbed his dark eyes. "You sure he couldn't have done it to himself?"

Murphy appeared skeptical. "How could he do that?"

"Could've put the bag over his head and went in head first, hitting his head on the pool edge before hitting the water?"

Murphy shook his head. "Not according to the M E."

Marone nodded. "He's usually right on target. So we've got very little."

"If those two guys who work for The Nordway Athletic Club didn't identify Blake and the fat Russian guy, and they're not absolutely sure, all we'd have is nothing but a dead man who used to be a very important person around Wall Street and D.C., whose firm did a little bit of work for Byron Stone and his father over the years. And reading between the lines from what Stockton told me, what little work they got from Stone Holdings was mostly due to Stockton's close personal friendship with Byron Stone."

Marone raised his balding head, his puffy face becoming prune-shaped skepticism. "So Blake and this other guy are members of that Nordway Athletic Club. Ain't that one of them real high class, exclusive clubs?"

"It is. Wilson was a regular. According to the pool attendant, he used the pool a lot."

"And you said he was found floating in the pool, stuffed in a heavy duty plastic bag? Did you check out where the bag came from? Had to be special made. Who'd sell such a thing?"

Murphy nodded. "That's something you'll want to check out. Someone said it was foreign made. Maybe made by one of Stone's outfits."

Marone smiled. "That'd be some connection, the deadly Stone bag. Got it?"

Murphy snickered, "I got it."

"Except that your M E says Wilson was killed by a blow to the back of his head before he was stuffed into the plastic bag."

"Morris was pretty sure. There is another connection that I feel needs looking into. I was told that because Wilson's outfit was getting some heat from a Fed probe into influence peddling in Eastern Europe, Wilson tried to weasel out of it by naming and accusing one of Stone's outfits of mining radioactive diamonds in Russia and flooding the U.S. markets with them."

Marone's smile broadened. "Sounds like you think Wilson crossed Stone and Stone wanted to send someone a message."

"Could be, especially if you find that that plastic bag was made by one of his outfits."

"Who knows? Some rich guys get their jollies playing footsies with Mafia types, and Stone Holdings being richer than a lot of countries, it has to be in contact with the Russian Maf."

"There are lots of things to consider in this one, strange friendships, rivalries, international stuff, Russian Mafia."

"So Stone might be connected. His outfit's very international."

"And his administrative assistant is Russian, Boris something or other, who was with our Doctor Blake at Nordway when Wilson was knocked off. What really makes it complicated, though, is the close friendship between Stone and Wilson's partner, Nick Stockton."

"What's the Russian's last name? You got it somewhere?"

Murphy pulled a notebook from his shirt pocket and flipped a few pages. "Boris Kleptokoff."

"That sure is Rooskie. Maybe we've got more than we realize and once the connections are made, the usual ones like motive, intent, we may be okay."

"Except for one thing."

"What's that?"

Murphy grinned. "I've already hinted at it. When a Byron Stone is involved, forget it. He's got friends everywhere in high places, let alone he gets the best lawyers like O.J. Simpson did. It could be real dangerous as well, since it could involve the Red Star. And we both know how vicious the Russian Mafia can be."

Marone nodded. "Much more vicious than their paisano counterpart."

Murphy rubbed his pointed chin. "You should know, since you've already had to deal with them."

"Sounds like I should get started by working on a background check on this Cameron Blake. See where he really comes from." Marone stared at the blank wall in back of Murphy. "Could be a phony name and it might tell us where he might be headed."

Murphy's grin broadened. "You've always had a thing about names. Must be an Eye-talian thing, although it sounds like you suspect a hidden Russian connection?"

"Never know. Certainly doesn't look like an Italian one from what you've been telling me."

5

Sue wedged her novel under the deck chair's pad-
ding. Then she sat up and stretched. The sun had
burned away the morning haze so she could examine the Connecticut coastline, which had been a fuzzy
outline until now. Large shorefront cottages appeared on a sandy beach. She got up unsteadily from
the deck chair. After gaining her sea legs on the gently swaying and rolling deck, she started working her
way with carefully measured steps toward the front
of the yacht. The front deck was deserted, reminding her of her current social status. When she glanced
up at the bridge, the yacht's skipper waved down at
her from his station at the helm. She forced a smile
and waved back. The cool air and tiny spurts of sea
spray were refreshing. When the boat lurched suddenly, she gripped the guard rail firmly with both
hands and continued to edge her way toward the
bow of the large boat, slicing powerfully and gracefully through the shimmering dark green waters of
Long Island Sound.

Sue's eyes swept the distant open water where she saw a variety of sea craft, including several sailboats, which seemed to be competing in a regatta. She cupped her free hand over her eyes to shade them and to keep her hair in place. A lighthouse came into view, looming like a sentinel guarding the mouth of a river. It was then that Sue realized the yacht was heading in a new direction, toward the lighthouse and the mouth of the river.

Sue was focusing on a narrow stone formation resembling dark gray teeth in the broad mouth of the river, when she felt a strong arm reach around her waist. It startled her at first.

"So here's where you've been hanging out."

Byron tilted his head so that his expressive gray-blue eyes were level with hers. It was the first time he'd gotten this close. She felt his breath on her flushed cheeks as he said, "When I took a peek out the window an hour or so ago, you were deeply engrossed in a book. Didn't want to disturb you. Hope you're enjoying the ride. The Zenith is some boat, eh?"

Sue nodded, her heart beating faster. So he hadn't forgotten about her, not completely. She tried to catch her breath as Byron's strong hands slid down to her firmly rounded hips. He steadied the two of them, his muscular body pressing against hers.

"Steady as you go," he said, heading her back toward a heavy metal door which was marked Main Salon. She could smell the liquor on his breath and was amazed that he was having very little trouble keeping his balance on the rocking deck.

Sue finally caught her breath. "It sure is. How large is it?"

Byron pressed her closer to him and smiled playfully. There was no mistaking the hard object she felt on her leg. Yet he said casually, "The Zenith? It's an ocean going vessel. A bit over a hundred fifty feet, I believe, though I'm not absolutely sure." He stood his ground firmly and turned her toward the cabin door. She reached for the doorknob and was about to open the door when he hugged her closer from behind. Sue's heart leaped. She hesitated. She didn't want him to release her.

"I know the Zenith is swift. Are we there already, your place? Is it on a river? Looks like the mouth of a big river." She was breathing hard, the words coming out sporadically.

Byron was enjoying it. He smiled as he moved one hand over her belly button. "It's the Connecticut. Dad and I used to come here with my mom." Sue felt his hand move down her firm belly as his motioning head brushed her hair and acted like electricity. "For lunch, I'm having the Zenith dock for a short while near where Dad used to take me and my mom when I was quite young. Sentimental sort of thing for me now, I guess. Dad would dock our big old boat just a short ways from a place—I've forgotten the name—Terra something or other. Someone told me it was an old Mafia haunt, a hangout for Frank Sinatra and his buddies. Saw him and his boat The Roma there once. We docked next to it. Those were the good old days."

"You make it sound like Sinatra actually was involved with the mob. I thought that was just rumor." Byron's lips brushed her ear. "Oh my." Sue grew limp and craved more.

Byron said, "Rumor or fact, like a lot of people I enjoyed it. Seems so long ago." Byron kissed her on the ear and cheek, making her want much more. "And so much has happened since then. We seem, Dad and I, involved in so many other things. This is one of the few chances I've had to enjoy this boat of ours."

Sue hoped he would go further, much further. Instead the mention of his father had made him relax his hold on her.

He sensed her disappointment. "As much as I hate to let you go, it's time to join the others. Later perhaps."

In the boat's dining room, which was dimly lighted by a fancy brass chandelier, several people were already seated around a thick teak dining table. Byron led Sue by the hand. "Here, we can sit next to Nick and Ruthy, my very closest friends. You'll get a chance to know them better."

She smiled at the Stocktons and the others. They were all strangers to her, even though she had been introduced to them at the yacht club prior to boarding the Zenith. Before she could even begin to get to know any of them, they'd all vanished to their cabins.

Byron pulled a captain's chair away from the table for Sue. "Here, Sue." She sat down and smiled across the table at the friendly appearing couple, which had been introduced to her as Byron's administrative assistant, Boris, and his date, Muriel.

Another couple, the Blakes, merely stared, making her feel very uneasy, especially the husband. His staring eyes roamed to Sue's breasts while he was being reintroduced to Sue as Doctor Cameron Blake. Then as his dark eyes darted to his wife's plunging neckline, it was obvious to Sue that he was making a macho comparison. She was happy Byron was seated between her and the Blakes. She knew there was nothing about them she could like.

As soon as Byron became seated, an attendant began filling the wine glasses near each place setting. Sue was enjoying a glass of Burgundy while talking about her doctoral thesis with the genial Russian, Boris Kleptokoff and his woman friend Muriel when the table was shaken by Byron's fist. His loud voice suddenly commanded everyone's attention even though he was addressing his comment to Nick Stockton.

"C'mon now Nick, that detective wasn't calling me for nothing. I put two and two together, especially after you hinted about John Wilson. I know he made lots of connections when he was Secretary Of Commerce. Some nerve using them to get Stone Holdings accused of mining cheap radioactive diamonds in Russia and flooding our markets; touched off that damned Federal probe. And even though my lawyers told me not to worry about it, I'm sure things are going to get messier now that Wilson's dead."

Nick glanced uncomfortably at Cameron Blake before responding. "Probably, although I'm as much in the dark about the Federal thing as you are."

"C'mon now, Nicky, we both have a good idea of what ticked it off. It's no secret that Wilson and your firm's been doing a lot of work for that clandestine bunch, actually Mafia types from the former Eastern Block, the EEG as they call themselves; we're not the only ones trying to corner the gem and oil markets in Eastern Europe these days." Byron raised his voice even higher. "That rotten bunch most certainly will do anything to make sure that Stone Holdings won't stand in their way." He laughed derisively. "I hope they realize that we're a lot tougher than we look on paper. Too bad they tried to pry Wilson away.

I never though he'd be working for those former Commies."

Nick Stockton's fine, high cheek-boned face forced a smile. He looked across at the Blakes as though seeking their support. "Watch it, Byron. Boris and others around you come from that milieu."

Sue was puzzled by Stockton's remark. She studied his small sensitive eyes and wondered about him as he flashed a feeble smile at Boris Kleptokoff who was obviously embarrassed. Then Nick looked away and laughed nervously before saying flippantly, "Hey, am I surrounded by the enemy here? These guys may all work exclusively for you, remember, kiddo, even though you and I go back a long ways, I work for an old Wall Street firm. It's been engaged in various and independent international transactions involving overseas companies whose ties to our firm go a longer ways back than our personal relationship, almost two centuries. Stone Holdings was still a century away from being founded by your grandfather. And I do realize that my doing some work for Stone Holdings' competitors doesn't make you very happy, but we've discussed that before."

"Individually, you've done a whole lot of work for me through The S&P Foundation, and don't forget my cousin," Byron asserted. "By the way, where in hell is she? I haven't seen her all morning." He looked inquisitively at the Blakes. "Have either one of you seen her?"

An impassive Cameron Blake shrugged his thick shoulders.

"Anyway, Nick, that's a conflict of interest, if I ever saw one. Ain't that so, Doc? Wilson and Nick being members of our board at S&P." Byron looked confidently at Cameron Blake.

Blake's large squarish head nodded ever so slightly. Sue felt that he was being compliant only because Byron had obviously had a lot to drink and Blake knew where his next paycheck was coming from. He reminded Sue of a large bulldog; certainly not anyone she'd ever want to meet on a dark street.

Sue really took notice when Nick Stockton said: "You're the one who had your dad place us on the board at S&P."

Byron shot a furtive glance at Cameron Blake. "I forgot about that. Almost forgot that Wilson was a member of the board. Too many things happening lately to keep a sharp perspective on anything."

After drifting slightly, the large boat lurched and shuddered to a halt.

Byron's face brightened; his contentious mood shifted suddenly into a benign one. "We're anchoring here, Saybrook, while we enjoy some lunch."

There was a lull in talk as a server came around and refilled the empty wine glasses. Then two other servers entered the dining room and placed trays of food on the table.

Muriel's melodious Latin voice broke the silence. "Mister Wilson was definitely the victim of a murder, no? And have they caught yet who done it?"

Silence reigned until Byron said bluntly, "Yeah, good questions, Muriel. When I was questioned about it by some detective, I got the impression that they hadn't a clue yet." Byron turned to Nick. "You have a clue about who, what, or why?"

Nick Stockton shook his head. "Not a clue. The whole thing's bizarre. John had no enemies. As you know, he was a rather laid back–no, that's not the right term—he was a mild mannered type of guy. So I can't imagine who or why anyone would want to do him in. And I don't know about suicide. He liked life. Had a lot to live for. It's all a mystery to me."

Sue studied Nick Stockton's face, its wrinkles and blotched skin already showing signs of serious sun damage. His voice lacked strength and conviction. She looked away and watched while fancy sandwiches were placed on the dining table.

After lunch, with Byron apparently interested only in resuming his conversation with Nick Stockton, Sue decided to follow Boris Kleptokoff and his woman friend out of the yacht's fancy dining room onto the windswept main deck. The yacht had pulled up its anchor and was moving rapidly toward the open waters of Long Island Sound called The Race. Outside on the deck with wind blowing her long dark hair over her expressive eyes, Muriel stopped short so that Boris's protruding belly bumped into her from behind.

The heavyset man with a bull neck let out an Epicure's "Oh dat feel so good."

"Yes, it does."

Sue enjoyed watching the frolicking couple and wished she had that special someone to engage in similar conduct. But that special someone seemed to be more interested in his discussion of politics and business than he was in her. She was about to go back to her novel for the remainder of the trip when she overheard Muriel say, "For good friends they were really arguing heatedly over things and it sounded like serious business to me."

Boris shook his large Baltic head, his mood having changed from light to dark. "They are very close friends, but Mister Stone, who I really respect, doesn't really know the half of it. Sometimes it is difficult to see, what is that expression, what is right under nose.

He may be too close to see what is actually truth, although he wasn't arguing because he is completely blind, cannot see anything." As though wanting to change the subject because he may have said too much, Boris shouted, "Look, the lighthouse in middle of waters, way out from land."

Sue was as intrigued as the others as the yacht slashed its way through the open water no more than a hundred yards from a granite building which seemed to be growing out of the water.

"That is something," Boris enthused. "I believe we are close now to Stonington harbor, our destination. When I was here last time, I remember that we were very close when we reached this point. Beyond New London, Connecticut, I believe. Groton, where the sub base is."

"You Russians were very interested in this area when the cold war was on?"

Though Muriel's question was a rhetorical one, Boris answered solemnly and with a trace of sadness in his voice, "Yes. This where atom subs were, still are made which carried enormous payloads of destruction. There was great interest on the part of Russians in this place, of that I am very certain."

It seemed strange to Sue that the Russian, even with his thick accent, sounded as though he were speaking not as a Russian, but as an outsider.

Sue made a curious face and asked, "Aren't you Russian?"

Boris smiled. "I born in Russia."

"You must know my chief doctoral advisor at the university, Doctor Sobel. He's a Russian too. Does some consulting work for Mister Stone's S and P Foundation. He's been involved in a psycho-social-environments study for some time."

The Russian's smile broadened. "I know him well, a famous man. I work for S&P first, before I get my job for Mister Stone when Doctor Blake tell Mister Stone about my proficiency in Slavic languages and German."

Suddenly Sue was really curious. "So you and Doctor Blake worked together for a while."

The smile on Boris's face disappeared. "Doctor Blake and me worked together for S and P Foundation, yes. He was my boss there. He recruited me from university in Moscow."

"Is he in charge?"

"In charge?"

"The top man."

"Oh yes, I thought you knew. He is top man."

"So Doctor Sobel works for him?"

"Everyone is under him, except for the Stones, of course."

"Of course."

6

Sue Brown held her hair in place with her arm over her eyes, which squinted in the direction of a disappearing sun. The hastening rushes of air were announcing high tide, but she could barely hear the lapping, wind driven waters of the Sound. She looked upward at the darkening sky before shifting her attention back to ground level. She felt an emptiness. Byron had spent more time with everyone else.

And she missed the spectacular, expansive Pacific sunsets north of Point Mugu which she felt couldn't possibly be matched anywhere. Atlantic sunsets even in summer were dull events, she thought. It was peaceful enough, but besides the empty feeling she was experiencing, there was something else nagging at her. For want of something better to do, she started making comparisons. Unless in the throes of a storm, the Atlantic's weakly pulsating waters on the whole seemed insipid. The Pacific waters were more overpowering and vibrant, always commanding one's attention. She remembered how they made her think of the word nirvana, especially at sunset, when those indefinable and elusive ingredients of warm satisfaction and completeness were usually present, especially when she rode her gelding Roy over the sandy beach near her family's small ranch.

Sue shut her eyes and welcomed the gentle strokes of wind brushing her uplifted face. What to do about the boredom? How to escape what was beginning to resemble a social quarantine? These were uppermost in her mind. If she were really assertive, she'd do something dramatic. She tried to imagine the way it felt when Byron had held her before they had entered the main salon of the Zenith at lunchtime. She'd give anything for a chance to relive that special moment. She opened her eyes and reached over to flick at a few specks of sand still clinging to her bare ankles, remnants of her abbreviated walk on the sandy beach earlier. She yawned loudly. Not only did her bones ache, she felt drained.

The festive group of people standing around the bonfire in front of her were having a great time, or so it seemed. Boris Kleptokoff and his girl friend sipping Byron's expensive champagne and listening to some Latin music were closest to her. Though happy, they seemed peculiarly disconnected from the others. Sue both envied and admired them, as she recalled how much Byron's friendly administrative assistant had enjoyed describing the yacht's luxurious suite of rooms where he and his exotic Hispanic girl friend Muriel had spent the morning together.

Sue's eyes roamed over to Byron. She wondered why he'd invited her and not one of his own fancy society types. She'd give anything for some of his attention. At the moment that seemed to be asking the impossible as he seemed completely taken with Ruth Stockton.

Sue shrugged her shoulders and stared. "No use," she muttered to herself. The social gestalt in front of her gave her the feeling that everyone was feeling little or no pain. Byron and Ruth Stockton seemed to be moving in harmony with the waves licking at the beach; they waved their wine glasses precariously as they conversed and gesticulated around the bonfire on the narrow sandy beach.

Although the sun had almost disappeared, Sue could still discern the streamlined smoke stack of the luxurious yacht, which had brought her to Connecticut. From her vantage point, she could make out the outline of the town of Stonington, whose neat quaint houses at this distance appeared like oversized components of a dollhouse community. In the open water, several specks and clusters of boats being lashed by the dark ocean waters bobbed and weaved like free spirits at their moorings, while the boats attached to the docks appeared to be wearing restraints.

Off in the distance to her right, she could see Fishers Island, which someone said belonged to New York State because of some geopolitical quirk. This was a completely different world from the one she'd left behind in the Big Apple with all of its inherent worms. She studied The Zenith. When Byron Stone had invited her to take the weekend off from her grad school research, she had suspected some kind of unusual happening, but not one involving an ocean going luxury yacht. Once it got underway, she'd marveled at its speed and stability. The sleek yacht must have been built in either Germany or Holland for Byron's father at one of his own shipyards. She wondered how anyone could have gained so much wealth. "Richer than the Kings of England," her dad would say. She recalled the first time she met Byron who had come to the Hollywood Park backstretch with his father. She and Byron were both in their early teens. She was so shy. He seemed so sophisticated and confidant, his good looks had hypnotized her. She remembered the day distinctly. It was ten years ago. Byron's dad had sent several horses to her well-known horse trainer father at Hollywood Park.

Sue looked over at Byron again. Along with trying to avoid a sudden explosion of sparking embers flying all around him, he was balancing a glass of white wine in the palm of his hand while using his foot to nudge a fresh log closer to the burning ones. She couldn't make out a word he was saying, yet she listened carefully to catch the sound of his low, well modulated voice and wondered what he'd be like in bed. Although his broad shoulders made him stand out, he appeared to be slightly shorter than the other men standing around the fire. Sue smiled as she thought that what Byron lacked in height he more than made up for with his athletic good looks. She liked the small dimple in the middle of his square jaw and his expressive well-spaced, large gray-blue eyes which made his straight nose seem thinner and smaller. He was smiling. His smile seemed so natural and genuine, especially as his wavy brown hair was being blown wildly about his broad forehead by the wind. It made her shut her eyes for a moment and picture herself doing what the wind was doing, gently running her fingers through his thick hair. The fantasy sent a warm surge of romantic energy through her. It reminded her of the thrill she got on the yacht, when he placed his strong arms around her hips. It was so different from anything she'd experienced that not even the expertise and experience she had acquired as a sex therapist could help her define it. Even the unusual feelings she'd received from using C A T with Jim Morrissey were not the same kind of stimulation. She thought of the word exhilaration. No one else had ever had this effect on her. Sue looked longingly at Byron and then at the seductive appearing woman he called Ruthy.

It seemed that wherever Byron was, Ruth Stockton was, falling all over him, even when her husband Nick was present. Sue felt that no one could blame her for trying, as it somehow fit into the jumbled and somewhat sociopathic New York social scheme of things, a schema which she'd placed on the table when she was searching for subjects and topics for her doctoral thesis. She gaped angrily at Ruth Stockton and wondered how anyone could be so insensitive. Even Byron, no matter how much he'd had to drink. He didn't seem to have a clue of how uncomfortable the situation was for Sue. She had to face up to it. She'd engaged in self-deception. Byron had had no intention of making her his date—right from the get-go. She suddenly felt out of place and knew she had to keep reminding herself: These guys and their wives or dates were from the king's part of the sport of kings fraternity. She and her dad came from the part that supplied services to and for these people.

Sue shifted her attention to the others who were obviously enjoying themselves as much as Byron who seemed so completely oblivious of anything or anyone except Ruth Stockton. Deeply feeling her frustration, Sue returned to watching the man who'd invited her for what she'd originally hoped would be an interesting weekend date. She envied Byron as he played with the logs and continued to have an incessant repartee with a cavorting Ruth Stockton. She wondered what it would take to get someone like Byron interested in her. Racehorses? They both liked thoroughbred horses. What else? What did Ruth Stockton have that she didn't have? She studied the svelte silhouette of the former model for a few minutes. Her thoughts were interrupted when a Germanic sounding voice said loudly, "AIDS? It was not just rumors? How close were you actually?" Sue glanced at the tall thin man, who'd asked the questions. He was talking to Nick Stockton.

Sue studied Nick Stockton's face for his reaction. It had pain written all over it as he responded seriously to the other man's questions. "We were still very close."

The tall thin man said loudly, "Sounds from what you've said that he might be better off dead. So you're certain that even though the state medical examiner's office won't release the body for burial, there is going to be a funeral service for Wilson on Tuesday?"

Sue studied Nick Stockton's face. Close to the fire it didn't appear as pale; nor did he seem at all bothered by his wife's antics. Sue recalled the description of him in the newspaper. At age twenty-nine he was heir apparent of the successful international law firm run by John Wilson. He had a lot to gain from the former Secretary of Commerce's demise. She quickly dismissed the thought, as he was obviously another one of Byron's rich friends who didn't need more wealth. Sue smiled as she surmised how a jealous Jim Morrissey would classify Nick Stockton. He loved to call men like Stockton "soft" and placed "them" on the "left side" of the bell shaped curve. "High-number queers, all of them are definite fives and sixes on the Kinsey scale, definitely queer," he'd say. She knew that Jim was more than a mere borderline homophobic, even though like most homophobes he spent an inordinate amount of time denying it.

She took a long look at the horizon. The summer sun had finally dropped out of sight. She decided that it was time to be assertive and make a move to find out if she were in a self-imposed rut or another person's quarantine, Byron Stone's. She pushed herself up and though assertiveness was on her mind, she took a few tentative steps toward Byron and the bonfire.

As soon as Byron noticed her he said, "Finally decided to join us and get sociable or is the word "social?"

Sue forced a smile. The booze had transformed him a lot, she thought. She had never seen or expected this playful, flamboyant side of Byron Stone.

Trying to sound formal, Byron added, "I've been wondering if and when our resident psychologist in the making were ever going to assert herself and add some of her beauty and grace to this already gorgeous place." Byron's tanned face formed a canvas for the bonfire's flickering flames, which were still shooting embers into the early evening air. "By the way, Susan Brown, how are you doing so far? Isn't this one big wonderland?"

Wonderland for him, she thought. Searching for something to say, Sue tried the timeworn weather approach: "It's getting rather cool."

"Kind of cool for June, but there's nothing like a

nice fire and good booze and friends to warm things up." Byron's eyes ran up and down Sue's body before stopping at her belly button. "Especially young already warm bodies."

Even though she wanted to appear as cool and debonair as Ruth Stockton, Sue smiled compliantly at Byron. The sophistication just isn't there, so don't force it, she thought.

"What would you like to drink, Sue?" Ruth Stockton asked. Her long auburn hair flowed wildly in the breeze. She waved a bottle above her head. "You'll like this stuff, I'm sure." Before coming toward Sue, she reached over and plucked a wine glass from a specially made wood and metal serving cart.

"Yay, Ruthy, you're okay. Maybe it'll get her into the swim. Bulla, bulla." Although it didn't suit him, Byron Stone cheered like a preppy type. "I'll have some more of that stuff too," he said with a wink, his eyes still glued to Sue's belly button.

Sue tugged at her shorts and forced another smile, trying to hide her surprise at Byron's behavior.

Byron studied her face before saying, "I guess you think I've had too much to drink, Susan."

Sue merely held out her glass, which Ruth started filling with an unsteady hand. "Thanks. Just a half glass."

"Fill it up, Ruthy. Got to get her loosened up." Byron laughed raucously. "The night's young and so are we." He held out his glass and after it was filled, tapped Sue's glass. "A toast." He looked skyward. "May the gods see fit to keep our young filly Samsona undefeated for the rest of the Belmont meet, the year actually. Why not? She's got the breeding to be a champion. Too bad your dad isn't training still. I'm sure he'd have made sure it happened if he had her. He was, still is, the best trainer in the U.S. of A. and I could really use him now." His suddenly sober look surprised Sue. She thought he resembled a career counselor as he inquired, "How is it you didn't take up training horses for a living? I've watched you handle them for your father and it appears that some of him rubbed off on you? Funny I always thought that that's what you were going to do and was more than a little surprised when I got a call from your dad to tell me that you were going into psychology and could use a scholarship. What a waste of talent. You were a good assistant trainer from what little I saw and from what your dad said. And I'll never forget the time you saddled one of our horses in place of your dad. You looked real good. As good as your dad, actually." He smiled knowingly. "No, you're much better looking."

Sue loved the sudden outpouring of positive regard, but her voice had a very noticeable nervous quiver in it as she said, "Don't I wish. I believe you have to be born with that kind of talent, as Dad was, not me. I guess I'll have to settle for being a mediocre psychologist, although I'm sure that after a few years of practice I'll probably wish I had become a conditioner of horses rather than of humans."

"You never know how you're going to do at anything until you try."

"True." Sue thought she detected a playful wink from Byron.

Ruth Stockton said, "I guess you weren't there when Byron was telling us about how your dad trained his horses in California. Must have been fun growing up around that kind of environment?"

The comment surprised Sue who said, "It was." Although somewhat on the thin side, Sue thought

Ruth Stockton still had some of the good looks of a former Miss New York and the famous international model that she once was.

When Ruth put her free arm cozily around Byron's broad back, Sue struggled to maintain her friendly smile, especially as she watched Ruth's hand slip slowly down to Byron's waist.

"It was fun much of the time, but it's a hard life working and growing up on the backstretch of a race track. It was only when Dad got a few good clients like Byron's father that things began to improve, that the quality of life changed for our family."

"Quality of life," Byron chortled. "Sound like a psychologist. That's for sure. And when I first met you, all you'd talk about was horses. Quite a change. And you've changed. Into a good looking lady." Byron's eyes brightened as they made their way again from Sue's eyes down to her naked midsection and belly button. "I'm glad you could make it this weekend." He turned toward Ruth. "Do you believe, she's been studying for her doctorate for almost two years now, more even. When did you start grad school?"

"Time flies. Counting summer sessions, I've been in the program almost three years. Be graduating next January."

"I know you'll be getting your Ph.D. in psych, but in what area? Social, educational, clinical, industrial?" Ruth asked flatly.

"Sounds like you know about the many different areas in psych." Sue enjoyed the opportunity to sound like an expert. She wanted to tell Ruth Stockton that her area of specialization was human sexuality, but she felt that in their inebriated states Byron and Ruth might use it as just another forum for having fun at her expense. She said, "Clinical. I hope to get a job as a therapist somewhere."

Byron nodded. "You'll be a shrink and make lots of bucks giving nutty people like us advice, though I still think you'd have more fun conditioning horses, and not people."

"She's got to do what she wants to do, just as we all do." Ruth seemed to be hinting about more than just a job as she nodded her head with a teasing and loving look toward Byron. It made Sue wonder how far Ruth and Byron had gone with their lovemaking.

Before Sue could speculate further, Byron made a surprise move. He released Ruth's hold on him and said bluntly, "Ruthy, could you, please. I'd like a private moment or two with my date. Here take this." Byron handed Ruth his glass, and turned away abruptly, almost rudely, from the pretty former model. After taking Sue's glass from her and dropping it on the ground, Byron took her by the hand and walked her away from the bonfire toward a part of the beach now only lighted by the moon. "Great night for romance, almost anything."

Sue enjoyed it when he gave her hand a sudden squeeze. It hurt, yet felt good. She could feel her heart beat faster and faster. His warm hand pulled her to a wooden bench in a narrow and isolated part of the sandy beach overlooking a stone breakwater and the original concrete quay.

Byron said seriously, "I hope you'll understand and will be receptive of what I'm going to propose, Sue. Dad and I are very fond of your dad, and you and your family. You did a great job for us on the West Coast with our horses. And that's the big reason, though not the only reason for my asking you to come with me this weekend."

Sue became very curious, although her face said she was puzzled and somewhat disappointed.

"My trainer at Belmont Park, Al Carter. You met him. Or was he in Europe when you visited with your dad? No matter. Al fell seriously ill last week. He won't be able to train for a while, if ever, from what I was told by his wife Bev and I even called his doctor to confirm it. So I thought of you, how well you handled our horses as your father's assistant."

Sue's face had the appearance of one who'd suddenly had the wake-up call from a pail of cold water.

Byron released his hold on Sue's hand and stood up. He watched while she rubbed her hand. "Hope I didn't hold it too tight? Some of us don't know our own strength sometimes."

"Or weaknesses, which is worse." Sue tried to appear composed. She forced a smile.

"Sue, what I really was saying, or trying to say, is that I'd love to have you train for me for a while."

The drooping corners of Sue's mouth straightened out. Her eyes brightened as her brain began to process and fully comprehend what Byron had just stated. Her forced smile was replaced with a look that said she didn't know where to turn. Finally composing her self, she said softly, "I'd love to. Boy, I'd sure love to, but I'm not sure I could handle both jobs, train horses and do my research, and do justice to either one, let alone both of them. And lately I've fallen behind in my research work." She shook her head again, reflecting her sudden feeling of insecurity. "Nah, I don't think I could do it justice, training such a potentially great filly like Samsona. I'd be more apt to ruin her than anything else."

"You could and should." Byron smiled. "Not ruin her. I mean, take the time off. You're way too modest. Even Dad once said that he'd have loved to see you train some of his horses after your dad retired and he's a great judge of talent, Dad is. And you probably can use a break about now to do, as you yourself are indicating, something you really want to do. And it would only be my horses in New York. And only until I can get the right trainer, one I'll have confidence in. Hey, who knows, maybe when your dad sees that you're training for me, we'll be able to coax him out of retirement."

"I doubt it. He's had a lot of trouble with his arthritis lately."

"I know, and I must confess that I actually called him, thinking that training a filly like Samsona might work a quick cure on him. But all kidding aside, he politely turned me down and suggested that I talk to you. He really thinks you'd make a good trainer."

"Yeah, Dad never did like the idea of my wanting to be a psychologist."

Byron looked squarely into Sue's eyes as he spoke. "Why not give it a try? You can do it, that I'm certain of. Good pay involved, especially when you throw in the ten percent of the huge purses Samsona and a couple of my seasoned horses may win. Just think of it as a fun summer vacation with great pay."

Sue's face said she was seriously considering his offer. And even though Byron sounded like a salesman trying to close a deal, she was suddenly enjoying the attention. It was making her forget her frustration. She compressed her thick, sensuous lips and smiled whimsically. This was the type of vacation she'd lately been daydreaming about to break the monotony of her doctoral work, with an added bonus, a chance to get closer to Byron.

"What do you say?" Byron prodded.

"I'm sort of overwhelmed by the offer." Sue looked away. She sounded so prissy to herself; she paused and groped for the right words. "I guess what I want to say is that you're a very persuasive salesman, and risk taker. I could ruin a very nice filly or two. Still, I'll have to give it serious thought." Again she realized how stuffy she'd sounded and how stupid it would be to turn down a once in a life-time job offer which would provide her with the best possible way to take a break from a situation she was finding almost unbearable the past week or so. Again she thought of the added bonus of getting closer to Byron, closer than she'd ever imagined she could get. She paused to sort out a more appropriate response and just long enough to give the impression that she wasn't too anxious.

Byron's face said he wouldn't take no for an answer.

Sue looked up and studied Byron's interesting gray-blue eyes as he expectantly examined hers. "I really don't know, Byron. It'd be quite a challenge. Just the thought leaves me breathless, almost speechless."

Byron laughed raucously. "Breathless, I'll accept, maybe even like. Speechless? You're not the type who's ever speechless. Besides, you'd be passing up a big opportunity to see just how good a trainer you really are, although I have all the confidence in the world that you'll be a very good one. You had your dad as your mentor, the very best for my money. So I'm pretty sure you'll be able to meet the challenge. Just think of what you'll be passing up."

Sue thought Byron's voice was more than merely prodding. It was seductive and she knew that he sensed she was weakening and giving his offer serious thought. She tried to compose herself as she cleared her throat. "No, and I know I sound like an impulsive fool, I'm going to take the job, but on one big condition."

"Great. For a moment or two there, I thought you were going to turn me down, my offer that is. That's just great, Sue, condition or no."

"My condition is that as soon as either you or I feel that I'm not doing the filly justice, that I tell you or you tell me immediately and we get someone else to train her."

"You're on." Byron leaned over, grabbed Sue's supple shoulders and upper arms and surprised her with a long gushy kiss on her forehead.

Sue felt her heart leap. She wanted badly to have her lips feel his.

Before straightening up Byron extended his hand to help Sue get up. She grabbed his hand tightly and didn't want to let go even after she was left standing.

After Byron released his grip Sue was still enjoying the thrill of it. Byron said stiffly as though his mind was on something more pressing, "I knew I could count on you or your dad, Sue. I guess I'd better get a move on and see what's cooking for dinner. I had my caretaker's wife order a bunch of lobsters from the locals. Real fresh. Right out of the traps."

"So that's why we first landed near that big docking area across the way, near that Francese place? I'm glad you let us explore the town a bit. Some great little art galleries and gift shops. Quaint place, Stonington. Great history, too."

Byron laughed. "A bit different from Southern Cal.

Wait'll you see Mystic Seaport tomorrow." He

surprised her when he placed his arm around her shoulders and led her back toward the bonfire, which was beginning to diminish in intensity. He said gaily, "Again I apologize for squeezing your hand so tightly before, must have gotten carried away. You've grown into quite a nice looking dish from when I first met you. I can still picture you mucking out stalls that day. Looked more like a young boy, actually. What a change."

Sue said curiously, her heart racing faster, "You remember that day? Funny, now that you mention it, I can even picture it myself. I must have looked like a real farmer or something."

"Or something," Byron teased. "You look a lot better now. Take my word for it. Have to get you into a swimsuit. Never seen you in one." He released her hand when they reached the bonfire whose flames glowed strongly with the sun now completely out of sight. "Here, I'll leave you with Cindy."

The medium sized, slightly puffy faced blond was about ten years older than Sue. When Cindy was first introduced to Sue at the start of the voyage, Sue was aware that this was one of the wealthiest women in America and from a famous family of thoroughbred horsemen. She knew also that Cindy Phillips had never married and that the gossip columns always intimated that she would never be a bride, though she'd had sufficient opportunity.

Byron turned to Sue. "Did you have a chance to talk to her about horses? She's got some of the best in the World." He looked confused for a moment. "Or did I not introduce you two?"

Sue said, "You did, at the yacht club." She knew that Cindy had disappeared like all the others as soon as the voyage up Long Island Sound had gotten under way. Sue flashed a smile at the chunky blond woman whose light blue eyes smiled warmly and genuinely at her.

Cindy said, "Yes at the Stone Henge yacht club. Had no time to talk, and I thought the name sounded familiar." While Byron took the opportunity to slip away, she added, "Did you enjoy the boat trip? I never had a chance to talk with you. I wish I had since I once met your father, the famous trainer in California. But I was ill disposed." Cindy's jolly laugh accompanied her admission. "I got seasick just after we left Stone Henge Harbor and found something for my tummy and a bathroom or head as seamen call it and spent the rest of the trip lying down. My poor date. Have you had a chance to talk with Willi? He stayed by my side all the way here. Poor dear, he's so precious." She motioned toward a tall, slender man with a bony Sherlock Holmes face. "Come join us, Willi."

Willi responded like a trained hound, as though used to answering to her every beck and call.

Sue wondered if this somber and very stiff individual weren't just another hired escort that many wealthy women used for social purposes. She got her answer from Cindy as though the famous heiress had read her mind. "Willi came here all the way from Amsterdam to be with us, me. He is one of Phillips Industries most important executives." She smiled fondly at her escort. "He runs our headquarters almost single handed at times." When Willi was at her side she said, "Sue this is Willi."

Willi Van Woort flashed a polite half interested smile at Sue. He bowed stiffly and took Sue's extended hand and shook it with the formality and abruptness of an army officer.

Sue forced a smile. "I remember meeting you before we boarded the boat."

Willi maintained his mechanical smile "I'm sorry we have waited so long to have conversation with you. I, we, spent the trip to here in one of the stateroom. Cindy was not feeling zo goot. Now she appears zo much better. Yet I was not worry. Many times I have seen these symptoms on boats. Yet Cindy, she is zo very delicate." He looked respectfully, almost obsequiously toward Cindy. "You do seem to have fully recovered, my dear."

Sue studied the Dutchman's impassive face. Even though he was several years younger than his date, Willi reminded Sue of stale bread, of one who wanted to appear older and wiser than his years.

Sue said, "She seems to be doing just fine."

Cindy intervened when she saw that neither Sue nor Willi had any more to say. "Enough said about that minor disaster. I feel so much better. I'll be more fully recovered when we're served some of the great lobsters and the other seafood and stuffing Byron's cook is famous for. Have you ever had a chance to experience her cooking?" She smiled pleasantly at Sue. "Yes, strangely, the Stone's hire only female cooks. But they've always shown a preference for females." She giggled after uttering her observation. "Oh dear, here I am extolling Byron's cook to high heaven. When Byron mentioned that he was taking you on this trip with him, he also mentioned your father. I remember him well, especially since he beat one of my very finest mares. Of course, we were reaching that day, my mare running against some of the best colts and horses in the west, girl against the boys."

"I remember that day too, very well," Sue said.

"That was one of Dad's greatest accomplishments ever. Mister Stone's colt, Ferdulancer, barely beat your great mare. She was something else, even though she lost that day. Wasn't she a champion two years running?"

Cindy nodded and appeared slightly surprised. "You really know your horses. And Byron told me that you helped your father, and that you're going to train Samsona, who incidentally may be as good as my great mare, Rebecca Star."

"He said that? I just found out about it moments ago. He's one very confident kind of a guy."

"That's Byron, always in complete control of things, business, women. You name it." Cindy glanced at Willi to see his reaction. Willi merely smiled faintly and subserviently, causing Sue to think to herself that this woman could have made a great Katherine The Great in a movie about the great monarch.

Cindy continued, "As long as I've known Byron, and we go back to when he was quite small since we're related, he's been a guy who knows what he wants and seems to find ways of getting it no matter what the odds. Can even be ruthless at times. But you'll enjoy working for and with him, I'm sure. You must know from his having used your father for his West Coast stable that Byron will more than likely be giving you a lot of input as to how to run his horses? At least that's how I've always perceived him and I've been watching him a long time, ever since he pulled his first prank on me when we were quite young."

"I'll take all the advice I can get, especially from someone who's spent as much time around horses as Byron has."

Cindy Phillips said, "Ah yes, he does enjoy his horsing around."

Sue was enjoying the double entendre when a loud voice coming from the main house shattered the rapidly cooling night air: "Come and get it."

Everyone around the now weakening bonfire turned toward the shouting captain of Byron's yacht. As he came closer, he announced with the voice and demeanor of one who enjoyed being in charge: "I'll put out the fire, folks. Dinner is ready and waiting to be served."

Boris Kleptokoff almost lifted his girl friend off the ground as he was the first one to respond physically to the chow call. Nick Stockton and his wife took up the rear. They had reached the rear deck of the giant cedar sided contemporary when someone gasped. It was Ruth Stockton. She was leaning over her husband who had collapsed as he started up the steps.

Everyone turned and gathered around him. Ruth asked somberly, "What's the matter Nick?"

Nick shook his head and sat up with his eyes shut tight; he opened them slowly on a face that was pale and worried.

Sue noticed for the first time that the man was actually not just thin but close to anorexic.

Nick said, "You fellas go inside. I'll be okay. Soon as I catch my breath. Get my second wind. Dizzy spell is all. Must have been the wine or something."

Sue watched with great interest as Ruth stood over her husband extremely concerned.

"Ya, too much wine on an empty stomach will have that effect on one," Willi Van Woort declared before he turned sharply and stiffly and led the others through the open sliding glass door.

Sue followed Cindy Phillips into the restaurant-sized dining room in the main wing of the multi-sectioned contemporary. Sue was impressed with the high walls, which reached heights she had seen only in the most fancy of hotels or public buildings. The vaulted ceilings were truly cathedral ceilings. Everything about the place shouted great expense, both as to design and construction. Sue knew that the Stones had homes in a variety of places, but she never thought she'd ever have the chance to experience one of them. She watched as the others began to seat themselves rather nonchalantly around the dining table. They seemed to take the whole place and event for granted, as though they had been involved similarly on numerous other occasions.

Cindy Phillips turned to Sue. "Here Sue. Sit here, next to me and Byron."

"Thanks."

As though on cue, the summer mansion's caretaker and his wife and two servers entered the room. The entryway had a large slab of driftwood over it with the word Galley etched into it. The quartet of servers balanced large trays of steaming lobsters on their shoulders. Going up to each dinner guest, they held out their trays and allowed each individual to select a giant-sized lobster and place it on an oversized dish of gold embossed china.

"Must be three-pounders at least." Sue could feel her saliva accumulate.

Cindy Phillips said, "Glad they're not bigger. It'd be hard to crack them then." She looked away from the table. "There he is. Our host with the most." As soon as Byron sat down, Cindy lifted a glass of expensive Chardonnay and said frivolously, "Long may he reign; no I should say, long may his champion filly Samsona reign, unless of course my own good filly Becky beats her in the Alabama at Saratoga." She sighed. "It's so hard to believe Saratoga Springs is just weeks away."

Byron laughed good-naturedly, "Time flies and I'll even drink to your filly, although I doubt that she'll be close to Samsona. And don't forget the Coaching Club American Oaks, very end of the Belmont meet. I thought you told me you're entered. That's an even more important race."

Sue raised her glass and took a sip before asking Cindy, "Your filly and Samsona are both entered for those races? They're grade one races, I believe."

"That's right. My trainer and I earmarked both races a long time ago. From day one, when we first started her in training, we knew what we had. As did Byron when Samsona started her training. Those two young gals are both well bred and have great conformations. Byron's filly is out of a great mare, a champion at that, as is mine." Cindy laughed heartily. "Of course you know all about that stuff with your having grown up with the darling things. And now that poor Al Carter is seriously ill, you're going to have to saddle Samsona. Won't that be exciting?"

The thought did send a thrill through Sue. "It is and I hate to even think about it. Hope Byron knows what he's doing, letting me take over the training of such a valuable filly."

"Of course if she wins . . ." Cindy let the thought hang.

"And she should," Byron piped in as he turned away from Cameron Blake and picked up on the conversation.

"It'll only be, because she's as talented as she is," Sue said.

"Seriously, though, Sue," Byron said with a wry

smile, "if Cindy's filly beats ours, it won't be a disgrace, you know. She's certainly in the same class as Samsona. Cindy's playing it cool, Sue, as you've already figured, I'm sure. Her filly is a daughter of Rebecca Star, the great mare that used to consistently beat the boys."

Cindy nodded. "I know. Samsona's mom wasn't the only mare that could beat the boys. And it will be graded races like the Coaching Club Oaks that will ultimately decide who will be crowned queen in January and that's what we're all aiming at."

"Hey it's time we dug into our delectable crustaceans," Byron suggested strongly.

Sue grappled with her lobster.

"Notice you don't use the melted lemon butter," Byron remarked after swallowing some food.

"Diet. Can't afford the calories, and for some reason or other, my system won't tolerate butter."

Cindy Phillips daintily removed a morsel of stuffing from the side of her small mouth and placed a small chunk of lobster meat in the dish of lemon butter in front of her. She appeared to be having more fun than a schoolgirl during recess. "Wish I could resist, but lobster just doesn't seem like lobster without the butter."

The wining and dining had been underway for at least ten minutes when the Zenith's captain entered the room from the outside deck. Though the ruddy faced, heavy set man usually had a stereotypically Irish smile and air about him, he appeared somber and business-like as he made his way directly over to Byron and whispered something which sounded to Sue like, "Mister Stockton wanted you to know that he went on board the yacht. After he grabbed a bottle of your expensive Lafitte, I unlocked the door of your, the main stateroom for him, sir. I hope it's okay."

"Of course. I just hope he's okay."

Captain O'Malley smiled. "I'm sure he'll be better off after he sleeps it off."

Ruth Stockton who was sitting opposite Sue picked up on the Captain's last remark and hinted in Byron's direction, "I guess I'll have to sleep alone tonight."

Cindy, shaking her head ever so slightly whispered into Sue's ear, "I'll bet it won't be the first or last time, if I know Nick . . . and Ruth."

Sue smiled even though she was confused.

"I'd better check. Make sure things are okay." Byron stood up. "You'll have to excuse me for a little while. Is there anything anyone wants before I leave?" Without waiting for a response and appearing preoccupied, he followed O'Malley out of the room onto the deck.

As soon as Byron had left the room, Cameron Blake got up from his chair and said in a barely audible voice, which Sue noticed had a hint of unease in it, "Excuse me, folks, I've got to pay a visit, but I'll be back before that creature from the deep can crawl off my plate." He seemed to be beckoning with a small shake of his head toward Boris Kleptokoff.

Just as Blake was about to exit the dining room, Boris Kleptokoff got up and said anxiously, "Sounds like a good idea. Dos drinks, wines, dey are too much to hold, I will be right back, however."

Cindy laughed. "It's funny. Almost as though the boys want to be separated from the girls. Except for you, of course, Willi."

When Byron returned, Sue checked her watch. He'd been gone almost fifteen minutes. But it was another fifteen minutes before Blake and Kleptokoff returned to their places at the table. She wondered why it had taken them so long.

7

Outside someone was shouting. Sue sat up in the king-sized bed and listened. Excited human voices were mixed in with a boat's engine, a dog barking, and seagulls contending for their morning meals. She could feel and smell the fresh sea air wafting into the bedroom through the window she'd left open overnight. She rolled out of bed and rubbed her eyes before getting into her shrunken, worn-thin nightgown.

As Sue made her way to the balcony, she had to cup her hands over her eyes to shield them from the rising sun firing its intrusive rays directly at her room. Down below, she noticed several people scurrying about the yacht including Byron. He was shouting something toward the Zenith's captain and crew who were leaning over the guide rails as though searching for something. Now fully awake, Sue focused on Ruth Stockton wearing an elegant skin tone nightgown who looked ridiculous running in her high-heeled shoes along the stone quay toward the sleek yacht.

Sue slid open the balcony sliders a crack so she could hear Ruth's voice being carried with the help of the sea air: "He would have been in for breakfast by now. He's always been an early riser. Perhaps he decided to take a walk."

"Don't think so, Missus." The crewman who responded sounded Slavic to Sue. It made her wonder how many Russians worked for Byron Stone. "I fishing out here quite early, since before sun has risen and I do not see him."

"He had much drink. Hope he did not decide to take a stroll around deck last night and fall accidental into . . ." The second crewman caught himself before finishing his thought, even though what he was intimating was already on a lot of minds.

Sue listened intently and heard Byron say, "When I checked on him last night, he seemed to be sound asleep. Zonked. But he could have just gone for a walk in the woods real early this morning and got lost. Those woods are pretty thick. Or he may have tried jogging along the beach and then come back through the woods and got lost. I know he used to jog a lot mornings, right Ruth?"

Sue watched and listened intently as Byron turned to face Ruth, who emphasized, "It's hard to believe they haven't found him yet."

"No. Not yet, but I'm sure they will."

One of the crewmen interjected, "He maybe go for early morning walk, which could have been between time we start fishing and time when we take break and go below for coffee. But that only take ten, maybe twenty minutes or so."

Ruth's voice rang out nervously: "We'd better notify the police. Who knows what could have happened."

"Already have, Ma'm," The yacht captain's strong voice asserted. "They should be here any minute now. State troopers. They're bringing along some diving gear just in case." As though suddenly realizing that he may have said the wrong thing, the captain added, "But that was their idea, not mine, and I guess they're just following official standard procedure."

Sue turned away from the frenetic activity outside. She wanted to toilet quickly and get involved in the search for what was now a missing person. She was deeply saddened by the thought. Stripping herself of her nightgown, she tossed it onto the bed before entering the futuristically designed bathroom fully equipped with the very latest gadgets. She was intrigued by the way the rounded door curved into the very wide cavity of a tub that could accommodate a small group. This was luxury she'd only been able to imagine or enjoy vicariously in movies about the rich. As Sue adjusted the shower controls, she couldn't help thinking about Nick Stockton. She liked the man who seemed like a genuine sort, even though she'd had little opportunity to talk with him face to face. Questions that had lurked in her brain surfaced: Why hadn't Nick Stockton joined them for dinner last night? And why had all those men left the table almost simultaneously? Could they have had a private meeting with Stockton?

Was it a business thing? Could it have had something to do with Byron, even, his wanting to iron out something involving Nick's firm? She didn't really know Byron that well and he did seem to be very angry with Nick Stockton's firm. The world since Nicole Simpson's murder was a weird and stranger place for her. She tried to recall the words and hints of discord between the two close friends when they had jousted during lunch. There was definitely an undercurrent of animosity flowing between the two close friends. Could they have fought over Ruth? She quickly rejected the thought.

Sue would have liked to spend more time in the luxurious shower, but after wiping herself dry as quickly as she could with a plush bath towel, she found a fresh pair of panties and slipped into them. Then she pulled on her jeans and donned a loose fitting tee shirt with a logo of Stonington on it. It was her lone purchase in a gift shop in Stonington Village.

Sue hurried out the door and down the stairs. When she arrived at the yacht, she found a state police lieutenant talking to Captain O'Malley and his crew.

Sue waved at Byron Stone who was standing on the forward deck watching the interrogation. Two other troopers and two individuals equipped with diving gear were getting into a Boston Whaler to begin a search of the murky water around the yacht.

"Hi Sue."

"What are they doing there?" Sue shouted to Byron.

"Divers."

"Could use all the professional help we can get," The state police lieutenant said as he walked away from Captain O'Malley and his crew. "With all this help, we should be able to find Stockton soon, or at least rule out his falling into the water around here."

Byron motioned toward Sue. "Lieutenant, this is Sue Brown. Sue's another of my guests. Actually she'll be working for me, training horses." Byron smiled toward Sue and gave her a confident wink.

"You've got horses? In Connecticut?"

"In New York. Race them there."

"You must have known Mister Wimfenimer. Raced in New York. I pass by his place a lot, even been over there a few times. He had some great horses from what I hear. Me and my daughters love horses. Ride them as much as we can."

"I knew Jack. Great guy. Raced against him, quite a bit, actually." Byron turned abruptly toward Sue. "Have you had breakfast yet?" Without waiting for her answer, he suggested, "Be a good idea to have breakfast."

Sue said, "I'd like to help in the search."

"That kind of work's best left to the experts to do, kiddo."

Sue's squinting eyes said she disagreed and resented something. Though barely two years older than she, Byron always treated her as though he were much older and more mature than she. "I'd just like to help."

The head state trooper intervened. "I'm sure we'll be able to handle the search without you folks for a while."

Sue forced a smile at the police lieutenant who had a romantic twinkle in his eye.

Shooting a look of disdain at the trooper, Byron said, "Oh hell, c'mon, Sue, I'll buy us some breakfast. Maybe later on we can both go out and look together."

Sue looked up and saw Ruth Stockton whose face was very pale without make-up. Nowhere near as attractive without make-up, Sue thought. Here's where she had an edge on the former model.

Byron extended his hand to a very confused appearing Ruth Stockton. "C'mon Ruthy, we'll let the experts do their jobs; besides, we'll all be better off if we get some food in us." Ruth walked limply by his side with Sue following close behind.

When they arrived at the house, they were met by Willi Van Woort. He looked bewildered. "What has happened?"

"Where's Cindy?" Byron asked.

"She has been still sound asleep when I last looked. The wing where we and some of the others sleep is on other side of house. We heard nothing. I just noticed when I come outside. Then I ask myself if something is wrong? What is going on, Byron?"

"Nick's missing."

Willi's broad brow became wrinkled with concern. "On, no. What can we do?"

"The state police have been conducting a pretty extensive search."

"Many strange things have been happening in the U.S. of late, no?" the Dutchman countered. "Every day the newspapers are telling about the killings in school houses and post offices, drive-bys, terrorist bombings, even kidnappings of executives, especially internationally involved ones, oftentimes for a large ransom. I even worry about it for mine self. And certainly one in your position must be very careful, no?"

"Mister Stone, Mister Stone." The caretaker's wife was shouting and waving to Byron from the deck of the smallest hexagonal component of the giant contemporary.

"Sarah. What's up?" Byron Stone shouted. Under his breath, he added an angry, "Now what?"

"A woman from Channel Three called, the television station, heard from the cops that something's happened here. Wanted directions."

Byron appeared indignant. "You didn't provide them with any?"

"Not a chance," Sarah said, catching her breath.

"We know, Thomas and me, how important your privacy is to you, sir."

"Thank you, Sarah. You did good." Byron's voice was more subdued. "We're all pretty hungry, better get the cook mobilized, you and Tommy, breakfast. Maybe we'll be able to get out of here before the television people arrive. I'm sure they're in constant touch with the state police now."

"Breakfast's ready to be served, sir."

Byron shook his head. "May as well eat then." He turned and faced the small group of guests who had congregated on the back deck and stood staring at the activities of the search party now fully underway around the Zenith. "Looks like our party's over for a while, until Nick shows up."

"I've always enjoyed your optimism, Cuz," Cindy Phillips said while straining to appear upbeat. She added with a hint of skepticism in her voice, "Hope he's okay. He should have shown up by now." Then she shifted gears: "Still, It's breakfast time."

As though taking her advice, almost in unison all of the guests turned and began to file into the dining room.

While everyone was being seated, Byron said, "I've heard some of you say you want to join in the search of the woods out back; they're pretty thick. We might lose you in them. I have a feeling we'd better stay out of harms way."

Several large trays full of bacon, sausages, scrambled eggs and an assortment of breads and buns were brought in and placed on the table. They were attacked immediately.

"When will we be able to leave for home, do you think, Byron?" Willi Van Woort asked.

"Hopefully before noon."

Cindy Phillips asked, "What if they don't find Nick by then? And what about Ruth?"

"They should. Or their dogs will. If they don't find Nick by then, Ruth can remain here until they do and I'll have a limo take her home later."

After another bite of her pancake, Sue asked, "Has Nick ever done this before? Gone for long treks in the woods?"

Byron grimaced. "Not in those woods."

Willi said, "Sounds like they are not a good place to be. They are thick woods. Though the officer in charge seems like a capable sort of man, I will have more confidence in him after he succeeds."

Byron acknowledged the Dutchman's attempt at humor with a snicker.

"Does the lieutenant or anyone have any idea what happened to Nick?" Cindy Phillips asked.

"Not yet." Byron tried to sound optimistic: "They've called in more than enough troops to help get the job done quickly. And the dogs should help."

Cindy made a sad face. "Sounds like a serious situation."

Sue placed her fork next to the remaining pancake on her plate. "I'm so full I could burst." Then she heard dogs barking. "Byron, you were right, they've brought in some dogs. Hounds?"

"Either Hounds or Shepherds," Ingrid Blake said with her thick accent. "I saw a program recently about some special German Shepherd dog, who could sense the presence not only of drugs, but who can sense, too, the presence of persons even under water. And I believe it's right here in Connecticut that such a dog exists."

Cameron Blake got up and motioned toward his wife with his square bulldog's head. "It's time to move,

Ingrid. Like Byron's told us, Nick merely took a morning hike and got lost. Those woods are pretty thick. Knowing Nick as well as I do, I'm sure he show up sooner or later."

Sue noticed Cameron Blake's foreign accent for the first time. She said, "He should have shown up by now."

Cindy nodded. "You're right. Doesn't look very promising. Still I'm all set to go home." She stood up and left the table, followed by Sue who went upstairs to pack her bag for the journey home. Before returning downstairs Sue went to the balcony to take one last look at the search activities. Two divers were making their plunges into the murky waters around the Zenith. They seemed to be enjoying their work even though it was connected with the work of the grim reaper. Sue shuddered at the thought. She had never been this close to such a situation before, even though death and disappearing people were everyday occurrences all around her neighborhood in NYC. She felt sad. Even though she'd just met Nick Stockton, she sensed something special about him; he seemed a sensitive kind of person who was much deeper and more feeling about his fellow humans than most. She'd immediately felt that she'd known him a long time when he was introduced to her. She rarely cried, yet couldn't hold back the persistent tears. Turning away from the scene below, she went into the bathroom and was splashing some water on her face when she thought she heard a voice.

"Sue." Byron's call preceded his sharp knock on the bedroom door.

"Just a minute. Oh heck, come on in." She hurriedly wiped her face before leaving the bathroom.

Byron said, "I just talked to the head trooper on the phone and he assured me that with all the help he's getting they should find Nick soon. Regardless, we can leave soon."

"How soon?"

"Soon as they're satisfied that they've searched the entire area around the boat." He checked his watch. "Sorry this turned out to be such a messy weekend. I had hoped that you would enjoy your very first weekend with me." He paused and took a gentle hold of her shoulders before kissing her on her forehead. "But there'll be others." Then he stepped back and held her at arms length. Although his expensive cologne was strong, she enjoyed it, though not as much as the contagious smile his handsome face produced. It made her think of Clark Gable in Gone With The Wind. She had always looked forward to seeing it, whenever he came to Santa Anita or Hollywood Park to see about Old Stone Stable's horses. It usually made her blush then, but now something new was added, a funny fuzzy feeling, more like an urge to take hold of him and hug and squeeze his muscular body.

Sue wanted him to hold her tight, even grab her bottom and pull her toward and into him. She tried to move forward but his strong arms held her firmly in place, as though he sensed her feelings and wasn't sure of what he wanted to do. She couldn't contain the sudden flash of heat rushing through her and up into her cheeks. She tried to cover it up with a smile and even though he smiled back, she felt embarrassed until he bailed her out with, "As soon as we get back home, The Island, that is, when you come over to live with us, I'll make it up to you." He paused. "That is, I hope you'll come live at our place while

you're training Samsona. We've got a great
guesthouse. Remember?"

Sue shook her head, trying to recall.

"When you came from California with your parents to check out the university, you and they stayed
in it for a few days."

Byron released her. She caught her breath. Again
she had the urge to step forward into his arms. Instead she did the expected and stepped back. She
said, "Yeah, it was great."

"And this trip started out so great. Nevertheless,
I will make it up to you."

Sue smiled. Even though the trip didn't start out
so great, she was getting closer to this mysterious man.
She turned abruptly and picked up her bag, which
was next to her feet. She said, "It would have been
good if—I feel so bad about Nick."

"Hey, he may still turn up safe and sound."

"Hope so, even though I've got this awful feeling.
Doesn't look good. Anyway, Byron, since we're going
to leave shortly and I have nothing else to do, to kill
some time I was wondering if I couldn't put my bag
on the boat and help a little with the search. I'm
part native-American you know. My dad's
grandmother was the daughter of a Pierce Nez
chief."

"No sense." He gave her a funny look and glanced
at his watch. "Lots of Indians at the casinos up the
road from here if we need one. Try to be optimistic.
We should be heading out of here soon. Besides, I
don't think the guys in uniform down there'd appreciate it. We should be getting the final word and
all be putting our stuff on board then." He turned
and walked toward the stairway saying, "On second
thought you could break the ice and go put your

bag on board now. I'll see you on the Zenith after I mobilize the others, my cook, et cetera."

Sue was halfway along the concrete quay when a storm of activity erupted at the rear of the yacht. She heard someone shout, "She spotted the thing in some shallow water. Must have sensed it like she was trained to do. She's a marvel."

Sue watched as the entire search team converged around the area where two divers were struggling to raise something out of the water. She moved quickly along the quay and onto a floating dock to get a closer look. Two other divers joined in the struggle to pull the rather unwieldy and bulky object onto a motorboat.

Sue's heart leaped. It was a scantily clad body with a plastic covering of some kind over its head. She stood frozen for a moment, then limp, nearly dropping her overnight bag. It had to be Nick, a whole lot worse off than he'd been not very many hours ago. She shuddered as she turned and saw Byron and several of his guests approach.

"What's going on, Sue?" She could barely hear Byron's voice among the sounds of men shouting and dogs barking.

"I believe they've found someone, something," Sue shouted back toward the house. She couldn't make herself say Nick's name.

When Byron and some of his other guests reached her, Sue led them quickly along the bouncing floating dock and up the boarding ramp. On the deck of the Zenith she was met by one of the state troopers who put his hand up stiffly, as though she and the others were traffic to be halted. He said sternly, "Hold it right there, folks."

"Is it Nick Stockton?" Byron's voice rang out from in back of Sue as he boarded the yacht.

The trooper said, "Must be."

Now at Sue's side, yet oblivious of her, Byron asked the trooper, "What happened to him?

A voice from an area beyond the trooper responded, "It's him. We won't know what happened to him until a complete autopsy is done." The state police lieutenant emerged from a doorway nearby.

"Did he drown? Are you sure it's him?"

"It's gotta be him. That's all I can say right now. We're getting ready to take the body to our lab for a complete examination."

"Damned shame." Byron Stone's tanned face had suddenly become blanched.

"They have found him?" Willi Van Woort pushed his way to the front of the group and stood at attention next to Sue. He turned to Sue. "He is dead?"

Sue nodded.

"The World has gone crazy. They were very good persons who had no enemies," Van Woort said. He turned to Byron. "Did they."

"You're assuming they were murdered," Byron said. He addressed the state trooper, "Couldn't it have been a suicide, Lieutenant?"

The state police lieutenant said, "Don't know anything yet. I'd appreciate it if you folks would report, turn in, any note or info you might come up with. If it's a suicide there's usually a note or some indication."

Sue nodded; she recalled her short course on depression and suicide.

A body bag lugged by two troopers crossed the deck in front of Sue. Quiet prevailed while they proceeded down the ramp to the dock.

Byron finally broke the silence: "How long before we can go back to New York, sail out of here, Lieutenant?"

"Probably around noon or soon thereafter. We should have everything that we want from you folks by then."

"That's a couple of hours from now," Byron said.

The state police lieutenant merely shrugged and returned to his main job of putting the finishing touches on the search operation. Before Byron and Sue were off the boat, the lieutenant's voice could be heard shouting orders to his men.

Byron said, "I'd better find Ruth and tell her. We'd better assemble on the back deck of the house."

Sue was surprised by his sudden cool.

"What a disaster. I can't believe it," Willi said stiffly.

As they walked along the quay, Sue heard Ingrid Blake behind her say, "Perhaps, he did a suicide. I hear rumor at club, Nick is very ill, something like his partner John Wilson. I paid no attention, as no one, Ruthy nor him, never say anything about it to me."

When they reached the main house's redwood deck, they all sat down around portable tables. Sue asked, "Where did these tables come from? Things happen like magic around here."

Cindy, who had emerged from the house at that moment, said angrily, "Byron ordered them. Wish he'd ordered Nick to stay with Ruth last night. I just heard the bad news. Poor, poor Nick, he was just telling me about how much he hated to have to go to Jack Wilson's funeral." Tears escaped from Cindy's reddened eyes.

Sue asked, "How well did you know Wilson?"

"I hardly knew him," Cindy said. "Knew him mainly through Nick." Cindy looked around her with a puzzled expression, as though noticing for the first time that someone was missing. "Where is Ruth? And Byron, where is he, Sue? No, what am I saying, I talked with her just before all the commotion started. She's probably in her room being comforted by Byron."

"They were real close, all three," Sue said.

"Yes they were. All three of them. Like three peas in a pod. Grew up together. Even though she was married to Nick, who is two or three years older than Byron, she and Byron and Nick, that was a triumvirate you might say."

"Certainly Wilson's death was not a suicide from what I have heard and read." Willi shook his head in disbelief. "Yet it is possible, of course, that Nick was a suicide. He had zo many health problems."

Cindy said begrudgingly, "Health or no, Nick had too much to live for. Although, if it were murder, who could have done such a horrible thing?"

Willi said, "Who knows? Today the world is crazy. There are so many socio-paths, so many serial type killings. Crazy people everywhere."

Cindy said, "Don't you think there is some connection between this death and Wilson's?" She looked at Willi and Sue as though expecting a response.

Sue said, "I wish I knew." She looked around before adding, "Hope Ruth and Byron'll be okay."

Willi responded, "Byron, he will be okay. He is not like Ruth. He is very strong."

Cindy Phillips said sharply, "You sound so cold blooded, Willi. Have a heart. This is a close friend of ours we're talking about. Oh dear, let's please change the subject. Nick was such a dear man. They were both good men, Nick and John."

Ingrid Blake piped in, "Look there, the wagon.

They take him away. Hope they don't take long with
their investigation. Now that this has happened, I
can't wait to get out of here."

"Nor I," piped in her husband who was standing
in back of her passively watching the proceedings."

"What a shame," Cindy Philips said. "Too young
to die and like this. I've known and done business
with Nick off and on, especially since he became a
member of our board at S and P Foundation. He was
a rising star. He was involved with a lot of our powerful overseas interests and contacts. Wasn't he
Cameron?"

Cameron Blake surprised Sue with his frank response: "Yes, Nick had made some good contacts with
the new entrepreneurs in the former Soviet Union
and Eastern Block countries with whom we are negotiating." Suddenly Cameron Blake appeared agitated as he gazed in the direction of the Zenith. "Now
what?"

Everyone turned to look toward the docking area.
The state police lieutenant approached them. He
shouted, "Folks, I've got some good news for ya. You'll
be able to leave as soon as I complete my task of taking all your names and addresses. Routine stuff. Just
so we know where and how to get in touch with you.
And oh, yes, we'll also need a short statement about
what each of you was doing and where each of you
was last night."

"So it does look like foul play, murder to you,
Lieutenant?" Sue asked bluntly.

The head trooper shrugged his shoulders and
adjusted his Stetson, hiding his eyes. Before walking
away he tugged at his pants belt and said, "Can't really
say, Ma'm. We've just started our investigation."

When the lieutenant was out of earshot, Willi Van

Woort stated, "I am not certain he is very capable as I do not know him. But police have zo many helps these days. The dogs and such."

"Yes, those animals are wonderful," Cindy said. "Of course, the ones used by the troopers are extensively trained."

Obviously relieved that the conversation was being led onto a more pleasant plane Ingrid Blake said, "Mine parents had a shepherd dog when I was a child. Ivan was his name. He was more intelligent in some ways than some humans I know." She turned towards Cindy. "You have many horse, Cindy. And I'm sure you have been ask before; which is more intelligent, the horse or the dog?"

"I don't really know for sure. I've heard the dog, but Sue might know which one. She's both a psychologist and horseperson."

Sue gave her a stock answer used by some psychologists: "Probably dogs according to work I saw done by Doctor Hebb up in Canada, who found in his studies that the more intelligent the animal the more complex its emotional makeup. So we can extrapolate from this finding that dogs appear to be more intelligent, in as much as they seem to exhibit more emotion than horses. But it's really hard to say with a great deal of accuracy, because after all is said and done we have to admit that all animals have their own unique intelligences. And even within any species or group that is so. A human who may not seem very intelligent in one area or field of endeavor may be quite intelligent in another. One may have an intelligence for doing mechanical operations, or things, whereas he may not be able to read very fast, while his friend who reads very quickly may not be able to do the mechanical stuff."

"Spoken like a true scientist," Willi said admiringly, apparently appreciative of things intellectual. "You will be a good psychiatrist, I'm certain"

"Psychologist," Sue corrected. "I'm getting my Ph.D. not MD."

"Oh yes, how foolish of me. I really do know the difference."

Cindy, who had wiped away some of the wetness from around her eyes, smiled prettily. "Willi really does, you know. He got his advanced degree from the London School of Economics."

Sue smiled. Even though an airhead, this rich woman had to at least know the distinction between economics and psychology.

8

The highway traffic was bumper to bumper. "Two more exits and we'll be there." Byron eased the fancy convertible into the inner lane.

"I sort of knew that the S and P Foundation provided me with my scholarship. Sent me my monthly checks and now I know why Sobel was assigned my doctorate advisor. He works for S and P. What does S and P stand for and do?"

Byron smiled. "What does S and P stand for and do? Good question. What is man's greatest problem?"

"Man's inhumanity to man, i.e., aggression like we have in the Middle East, or the Balkans, et cetera?"

Byron laughed. "Population, pollution, et cetera. Like the Mayan civilization, overpopulation and overbuilding will eventually lead to pollution and annihilation."

"S and P is working on pollution control?"

"You got it. Pollution control, which starts with and includes population control."

"How is the entire project going? Any real

progress? India's population is approaching China's. Over a billion mouths to feed. And I know the earth is only able to sustain three billion of us and we now have over six."

"We're making some progress," Byron scoffed. "It's tough dealing with religious fanatics and centuries of accumulated ignorance."

"And still accumulating. Sounds like it's hopeless and only going to lead to another power struggle."

"Power is right. What we're dealing with involves power. Water for example. It's one of S and P's big concerns. Bad water could be disastrous. Water is more essential to life than oil or gas. Wars may eventually be fought over water. Already have been. Places which we thought would never be involved in water pollution are currently experiencing lots of it. Even in places such as the Saint John River in Canada according to our people there."

"What if it gets into the wrong hands? This kind of power I mean. Say, some outfit like S and P gained control of the World's potable water, wouldn't they be as dangerous as the fanatics? To be able to say who will have clean water or no is tantamount to saying who will live or die, I should think. That's mind boggling to me."

Byron laughed again. "You're right. Certainly don't have to worry about S and P. As long as my cousin and I are in control, there's no need to worry." He steered the car onto a ramp off the highway. "Hey let's talk about more important stuff. Us and your new job."

Even though Sue wondered how much of the earth's water supply S and P was looking to own, she asked, "Have you heard anything new concerning Nick?"

"Nothing yet." Obviously wanting to avoid any discussion of Nick Stockton's death, Byron said bluntly, "Ordinarily, I get into the track through the backstretch entrance. You'll probably want to use that gate when you get the hang of things around here. Since today's a race day, this entrance is open and I've got to stop at the clubhouse. Other than the smaller crowds, nothing's changed much since you were here with your dad to see our horses when you came with him and your mom to check out Columbia and the other schools, and you've probably been to the track several times since coming to New York."

Byron came to a halt at the red light across from the main gate of Belmont Park. There was scarcely any traffic on Hempstead Turnpike, it being too early for the race fans to arrive. He turned and glanced at her. "Sue, hey, you seem mesmerized."

Sue snapped to attention as though out of a trance. She scanned the many football fields of parking space outside the imposing ivy covered brick structure built by August Belmont and other business tycoons at the turn of the century. "I still can't get my mind off of Nick Stockton. He and Wilson were both members of the S and P board of directors. Do you think that may have had something to do with their murders?"

"To tell you the truth, I haven't given it much thought."

Sue persisted, "And if there is some connection, since both you and Doctor Blake are key members, wouldn't you both be in danger?"

Byron didn't respond.

"I guess I'm probing in an area where I shouldn't be."

Byron nodded, his lips compressed. Then he smiled and said,

"That reminds me. You can use one of my dad's clunkers, an old Buick. He had it specially done over, equipped with a new engine. When he wasn't chauffeured, he used it around The Big Apple, where, as you know, cars get ripped off within minutes of your leaving them to go somewhere. It's got a lot of dents as well as character. I'll give you the keys as soon as we get back to your new home."

Sue enthused, "This is like a dream come true. I've always wanted to train, but at Belmont and under these circumstances?" She appeared overwhelmed. "And I still can't get over the fact that they're letting me take out a new license here even though my California trainer's license expired a long time ago.

The light changed to green. "I don't see why not." Byron waved at an attendant in a white cap and navy uniform who recognized him.

Sue could already smell the uniquely sweet mixture of horse manure, freshly mowed lawn, and a vast variety of plants and shrubs commingling with the crisp early morning summer air. The shrubs and variegated trees of the well-maintained grounds of the premier racetrack were in full bloom. She asked him a question that had been on her mind for some time: "What happened to Ruth Stockton? She seemed to have disappeared right after Nick's body was found."

Byron's mind seemed elsewhere as he steered the Mercedes sports car into the "owners" parking lot of the Belmont Park clubhouse and parked. "I'll be right out. Got to stop here for a minute."

While Sue waited, she enjoyed the architecture

and horticulture of the magnificent and famous race-track. She studied the clubhouse's ivy covered brick walls, which had the largest Palladian windows she'd ever seen and could feel a crescendo of excitement about the place where she could pursue things which she could only have imagined before in some wild daydream. She would be training outstanding horses and be close to the man she admired the most. She shuddered with excitement at the very thought. Perhaps she was reaching for the impossible. And only a few days before, it seemed certain that she was going to be doomed to spend most of her summer in the confines of the dank, musty and often foul smelling ambiances of a rotting apartment and aging university library building, with an occasional foray into Central Park providing the only respite.

Sue watched as Byron approached the car. She sensed from the expression on Byron's face that he was enjoying something. "That didn't take long. How'd it go?"

"Great. Had to go to the men's room, actually. Sorry to keep you waiting."

She thought it strange that so mundane a thing as relieving oneself could produce such satisfaction in someone like Byron Stone. Little things still meant a lot.

Byron started up the car and drove it into the main road again. "How've you been doing so far?"

Sue wanted to tell him about all the jealousy and anger she'd been experiencing on account of him. Instead, she contained herself and said, "It's been like a maelstrom." Fidgeting slightly after pronouncing the last word, while Byron slowed down to turn into another road, she added, "No that's the wrong word, as it's been mostly exciting and wonderful except for what happened to Nick of course."

Byron turned on his winning smile and said, "Glad you're enjoying it." Then turning the winning smile off, he commented, "We'll have to turn the last page on Nick Stockton, close the book on what happened to him. I'm sure he had his reasons for his suicide."

"Suicide?" Sue studied Byron's handsome profile. "You're not serious? The way he looked when I saw him, I just can't see how he could have done it to himself."

"Could have been aided. As a matter of fact, knowing him as well as I did, he certainly had a good reason to." Byron flashed his winning smile back on. "Let's change the subject to something more pleasant, eh?"

"Okay."

"How'd you sleep in your new place? I wish now I'd had it freshened up more, or at least freshly painted, before you moved in. But I couldn't wait for you to be closer to the track, and I have to confess, to me."

Sue turned a pained look toward him. "C'mon Byron. Be serious. I hate it when you or anyone toys around with me."

"I'm not toying around. I'm not the toying around type." He kept his eyes focused on the road while Sue recalled how he had played around with Ruth Stockton on the beach in Connecticut.

Sue still wasn't convinced. "We all toy around at one time or another."

"Glad you decided to stay at Stone Henge. That trip you'd have had to make from the City to the track is brutal."

Sue remained silent; her heart pounded so hard she could feel it in her throat. Perhaps he genuinely did want her to be closer to him. He was so hard to figure out.

Sue said, "Glad you got me to move, although it wasn't a priority."

"Training at Belmont Park has to be a top priority of yours right now and anything that will help you do your job better should be considered seriously."

Sue nodded, her heart beating faster. As if training a potential champion wasn't enough, she had also been handed the opportunity to be close to the man she wanted more than anything in the world.

The car slowed down, interrupting her thoughts.

Byron said, "We're there, Sue. Your new adventure begins." The Mercedes sports car came to a crawl and stopped in front of one of the large horse barns lining the narrow road.

Sue got out of the roadster and looked around. Steam was rising from two concrete manure bins across the way. She took a deep breath. "So this is my new place of work?"

Byron nodded. His sterile expression reminded her that she had to get her mind off him and onto the business at hand. Byron watched stoically while two horses were being led across the road in front of him.

Sue tried to sound upbeat. "From a university grad student to Belmont Park, one not so easy leap for mankind ordinarily; so far you've helped me make the transition rather smoothly. Hope I don't disappoint you, though."

When the road was completely clear of horses and horsemen, Byron stepped ahead of Sue. He grinned and said confidently, "Don't worry keed, you won't. Not with your talent. Just try not to sound too collegiate around here. You'll make a good trainer. Both me and Dad discussed it once, as I said before, and my dad seldom made a mistake when it comes to hiring talented help, and I've been doing a fairly good job of it myself, although I shouldn't be beating my own drum." He slid open a large barn door. "Sue, from here on in, we're going to have to act like owner and trainer. Yuck. That almost sounds like me Tarzan, you Jane. Sorry. I do hope you don't mind." His sudden shift to a more lighthearted mood caused Sue to decide that she liked him most when he was like this.

Sue wondered if there were some side of him that she'd hate, one she hadn't seen yet; there had been hints of a darker side of him on their trip to Connecticut. "Not one bit," she laughed. "I understand fully, boss, sir."

Byron said, "Let's not get carried away. Byron is still preferable to boss or sir."

Byron led Sue down a broad corridor of the cavernous barn. Here and there a curious horse stuck its head out over the closed bottom half of the Dutch door, which kept the animal safely sequestered in its stall. One lunged and tried to bite Sue as she came close to its stall opening, but she merely flicked her hand toward the animal and it jumped like a scared rabbit back into the safety of its habitation.

"Only cowards do things like that," Sue kidded toward the handsome gray animal.

"Guess most of them have some of that in them," Byron remarked.

"Humans too."

"Incidentally, that gray is Nickelo, one of our new charges. Should be a good one."

"Named after Nick Stockton?"

Byron's head dropped a notch. "Not even close. Although that would have been nice."

"How'd he get his name? Stud?"

"Yep. He's by Northern Nickel, one of the leaders at stud last year." Byron halted at next stall where a wooden box full of liniments and wrapping material lay just below some webbing stretching across the entrance. "Hey Jose, que pasa? Could you stop uno momento, to meet your new boss, Sue Brown. My new trainer, from California."

A medium-sized man with an unkempt beard stopped rubbing down a dark bay horse and came out of the stall. He said in broken English, "I happy to meet you."

Sue shook Jose's hand after he wiped it on his blue workpants. Sue turned toward Byron. "I believe I met a couple of your help when Dad and I came here three years or so ago. I don't remember Jose. Your trainer, Al Carter, hired a whole new cast of people since then?"

Byron stated, "No, he's been with Old Stone Stable a long, long time." He winked a smile at Jose. "The Browns, Sue and her dad trained for me and my father at Santa Anita and Hollywood Park, so she is familiar with the big time tracks and how to run horses there. I'm sure you've already been clued in, the way news travels around the backstretch of any race track." Byron appeared confident as he added, "Yep, she's going to be in charge from now on. Where's Joe?" He turned toward Sue. "Joe is an exercise rider Al Carter hired recently. Joe was trying to become an assistant trainer under Al." He turned to confront Jose. "Is Joe at the track kitchen? I thought he was supposed to work Samsona this morning."

"Joe, he work her already." Jose looked toward

an open door on the other side of the corridor across from the stalls. "I just see heem a minute ago. He must be in thee tack room. He was hold up by police detective just after the workout."

"I'll be right there, sir," a serious brown face said as it appeared from behind the open door. "I'm getting some salve for the filly. She scratched herself this morning during her work."

"Nothing serious, I hope," Byron shouted toward the door.

"Just a scratch, believe me sir. Nothing to worry about." The exercise rider, his riding helmet still on his head, emerged from the tack room and came toward Byron.

"It nice to meet you. Be lookin' forward to work with you," Jose said as he slipped back into the horse stall to complete his work.

Byron said, "Sue, this is Joe King."

Sue offered her hand and smiled broadly. "Joking? That's a good name. Hi Joe, you've probably had enough of that pun?"

"Too much." Joe King shook Sue's hand while displaying a genuine smile. After the handshake, Sue stepped back and studied the new assistant trainer. She tried to estimate how much weight his horses had to carry. He was about her height of five six or a little under, and weighed a bit more than she, since he appeared to be quite muscular.

Byron appeared pleased. "Al was right when he suggested Joe. He'll be your right hand man. He really knows his stuff, is an outstanding exercise rider, and he'll, therefore, probably make a great trainer one of these days."

Sue made a funny face. "Perhaps he's the one you should have named as Al's replacement."

Byron said abruptly, "No way. I've picked the right person for now."

Joe's toothy smile revealed some chipped front teeth, which he'd gotten in a bad spill off a horse he was working out of the gate. "Welcome aboard, Ma'm. I'll do everything I can to help." Joe's face became serious as he turned to Byron and said, "Mister Stone, a police detective man was here a short while ago. He asked me some questions and said he was going to try and find you. After I told him you might drop by this morning, he left this with me. Told me he'd appreciate a call from you if you did come by the barn this morning." Joe produced a small card from his shirt pocket and handed it to Byron.

Byron took the business card from the new assistant trainer. "Marone." Byron turned toward Sue and said, "After I have Joe show you Sammy, I'll go give this guy a quick call. Also have to stop by the Racing Secretary's office. Almost forgot to deposit the money for the stakes race."

Joe King led Sue to a stall further up the shed row. The stall was distinguished from the others by a large specially engraved bronze plate. Etched on it was the name Samsona with her sire and dam's names in smaller letters on either side underneath her name. Joe's face had the look of a proud father as he stopped before the stall, which had been very recently immaculately cleaned and bedded with fresh straw. "Here's our champion. Really something special. She was second high weighted as a two year old and just missed being recognized for what she really is, a champ. Even though she just missed, she's still our champ and will more than likely make it as a three year old this year."

The big chestnut filly looked wide-eyed at Sue

and Joe as though sizing them up as much as Sue was sizing her up. Sue examined Samsona's powerful chest and sloping shoulder. Then she stepped close enough to place her fisted hand under the filly's head. "She's got a great throatlatch."

Joe King said, "Yep. She won't ever have trouble breathing."

Sue unlatched the stall door and passed her hand over the strapping filly's withers and broad back. Then she tried lifting her tail. Sue's father used to remark that one could always tell that a filly was strong if she had a stubborn tail. "She's strong and I love her withers and hind quarters."

"Yep. She's got a big engine. And she worked good this morning, real good, half mile in forty seven and change, bullet work, I believe."

"She'll be ready for the race, Sunday," Byron said as he rubbed the filly's neck before walking away. "You're in good hands, Samsona, and you are too, Sue."

Sue nodded. She liked the way Byron rubbed the filly's neck. He had to know that horses liked to be rubbed and not patted.

"Should be ready." Joe went into the stall and gently turned the filly around a couple of times. "Isn't she something?" He handed the lead line to Sue. The precocious appearing filly's big eyes were expressing question and interest with respect to this new human. Joe spoke softly to the filly, "Sammy. This is your new trainer, Sue Brown." He continued to talk to her as though the filly were a small child. Like any knowledgeable and professional horseperson, he instinctively knew that even mature horses were like five-year-old humans and had to be treated accordingly. "Here Sammy, I'm gonna let Sue take you out for a good look and feel." Joe placed a halter over the filly's head.

"So you call her Sammy. Love the name." Sue gently petted the filly on the side of her neck, before leading her out of the stall and down the corridor. "She sure feels strong on this line. She feels like her name." At the end of the wide corridor, Sue turned and walked Samsona back to Joe. "Could you hold her, Joe, while I check out her ankles. I thought I noticed a slight swelling in her left ankle."

Joe, appeared slightly apprehensive but not surprised. "I know. Already applied a wound wash of povidone iodine saline solution." The assistant trainer took hold of the line and steadied the filly.

"Let me take a closer look." Sue started her examination from Samsona's forearm way up above the knee and gently slid her hand down to her cannon bone and finally to her ankle, which Sue held firmly for a moment. Then she flexed the ankle of the cooperative filly, which seemed to be very familiar with the procedure. "She's been well handled."

"How's it look?"

Sue shook her head and straightened up. "No heat in it, though I felt a little softness."

"She could have taken a bad step in her work this morning. I'll watch it, though."

Sue said, "Maybe some super-antiphlogistine, our own mixture of "gunk" as my dad calls it, would help. Works quick and is a lot better than most treatments."

"Anything you need, you'll get, although I'm not too sure our medicine cabinet'll contain exactly what you want. If it don't, I'll go to the tack shop and get whatever you need. They've got everything."

"I'll check see what you've got in your medicine arsenal. Even if we come close. My dad's gunk is especially good for ankle problems. It's stuff he developed on his own. He hated injecting joints, or blistering even. He claims blistering hurts and only takes the place of waiting on them while they heal."

"Seems I read that recently, though I haven't met a trainer who don't believe in blistering."

"Some day I may even can his formula and sell it."

"Could be lucrative."

Sue looked at Joe. His vocabulary surprised her. "It won't take much to treat her, I'm pretty certain. She was walking real strong and sound. Pretty certain she'll be okay."

"She's not walking gimpy. Certainly don't need to get the vet."

Sue smiled reassuringly. "Nope. I've been around these critters long enough to know when they're lame and when they're not. Although they sure are fragile and have a lot of our weaknesses and infirmities."

Joe looked like he was waiting for her next move.

Sue reluctantly gave her first orders as boss woman. "We'll take Sammy back into her stall and get started on her treatment before we look at the other guys. Also get her some feed. What has she been getting?"

"I'll show you, Ma'm," Joe said politely, as he led her into the small storeroom, which served as an office and tack room.

Sue stopped before a desk, slightly larger than a child's, whose warped top needed refinishing. "Not a bad little place. Real neat. Even got an electric heater and cot. Ever stay overnight, Joe?"

"Whenever a horse gets to feelin' sick, I do."

Sue smiled approvingly as she surveyed the entire room. Her eyes stopped at a shelf just below eye level. "I see you've got plenty of MSO." When Joe opened a cabinet above the MSO, she said, "Just need some reducine, or antiphlogistine, as my dad calls that other stuff in the can you've got there. And I see the other stuff I'll need. If Dad ran out of the canned stuff, he used a substitute consisting of clay, glycerine, vinegar and Epsom salts."

"Good old fashioned stuff. I've used it way back when."

"Yep, after we apply this stuff to her ankle, we'll get her back to normal in a jiffy. Need a pail."

Joe handed her a white pail.

"Perfect. I'll mix this stuff while you get her feed."

While Sue began to mix some "gunk" in the white plastic baker's pail, Joe pulled open the top of a galvanized metal bin and began to fill a feed bucket with grain. While he did so, he said, "With her morning feed, Ma'm, she gets a couple flakes of good Canadian hay that has alfalfa in it. Keeps her busy after she finishes her oats, four quarts of oats mixed with a little sweet feed, vitamins, some corn oil, maybe wheat germ, dependin' on the time of year. As you know, corn oil is good for energy, but we cut back a little in the summer as it's heatenin' and add a little wheat germ and or soy."

"She's well fed."

After he finished filling the feed bucket with dry feed, Joe knelt down and reached into a wooden cabinet for a five-gallon plastic jug. He poured some corn oil into a measuring cup, dumped it over the other ingredients in the pail and then mixed the contents with his hands.

When Joe stood up, he gestured toward a cot, which had a couple of newspapers on it. "Too bad about Mister Stockton. He was a very good man."

Sue stopped mixing the ingredients of her special poultice, stood up and went over to read the
headline of the New York newspaper whose headline was about Nick Stockton: Wall Streeter, Dead
Like His Partner. Sue looked at Joe. "How well did
you know Nick Stockton? He come here with Byron?
I know he must have liked horses from his having
gone to Ireland to watch Mister Stone's horse run in
the Irish Derby and also from the way he talked about
them on the boat the other day."

Joe's intelligent dark eyes blinked nervously and
grew darker. "He came here quite often, especially
when a good horse was running. He and Al, Mister
Carter, were real good friends, close."

"He and Mister Carter?" Sue noticed that Joe
looked down at his shoes as he said the trainer's
name. Hidden agenda was written all over his face.
It made her wonder about Byron's relationship with
his help. "How close are Mister Carter and Mister
Stone?"

"Real close friends."

Sue made a shuddering movement. "So they'll
both miss Mister Stockton? I can still picture him
being taken from the water. Hard to erase."

Joe, his wrinkled face totally dominated by sadness, nodded in full agreement. "He's gonna be
missed, especially by . . . Sure is crazy, the way he died.
I could hardly believe it when I read about it. And
you were there? Must have been a god-awful sight to
see. If it was a murder like some say it was, I hope
they get the guys or guy what did it."

"Hope I never have to look at something so grotesque ever again. Sounds like you knew a little about
him. Have any idea who might have wanted to do
such a thing to him?

Joe shook his head sadly. Then his brown face brightened up unexpectedly as though a light had been turned onto it. "Funny though that this thing happened aboard Mister Stone's boat. The whole thing, from what I read about it, was like something out of an Edgar Allen Poe novel, plastic bag and all. Although the newspaper, and even you, seem so sure it was a murder, I still got this funny feeling it could've been a suicide."

Sue studied Joe's face before saying, "Funny, Mister Stone gave me the impression that he, too, thought that it might be a suicide." She nodded. "I sort of can see how Nick Stockton might have done it, placing the bag over his head and jumping overboard. But then again, from what little I know about Mister Stockton, he seemed to have no reason to commit suicide."

"I shouldn't tell you this, Sue, but in my mind, Mister Stockton may have had a very good reason to commit suicide." Joe shook his head and paused. "Heck, I guess I better not read too much into things." He shook his head again. "No, I can't imagine anyone wantin' to kill him. Such a nice guy."

"You say Stockton had a good reason to commit suicide? What makes you say that?"

Joe looked away. Then he said, "When I first read about Mister Stockton it reminded me of a novel I read this past winter."

Sue was surprised. "You read novels?"

"Yup and the hero of the story I read owned a couple of horses and he liked them and had a good friend who had good horses."

Sue listened intently.

Joe continued. "It was similar to Mister Stockton's situation, only in Mister Stockton's situation, he's got a friend who owns real good horses and another friend he really likes a lot who trains them horses."

Sue said, "I assume you're referring to Mister Stone and Al Carter? You said they had a close relationship too. Like Mister Stockton?"

"Not quite. No, not at all the same."

Sue became suspicious. "You never read such a novel, did you?"

Joe's smile said no.

"I think I'm beginning to get the picture. Enough said for now, I guess. We'd better fix up the filly and feed her." Sue waved toward the feed bucket Joe had rested at his feet. He followed her out the door.

Joe placed the feed bucket outside of Samsona's stall and held Samsona steady with a lead line while Sue applied the special treatment. "May as well do them both."

"Can't hurt."

When Sue was finished and standing, she was startled slightly by the presence of a man just outside of Samsona's stall.

The man called out in a weak raspy voice, "Joey."

Sue examined the hunched-over individual whose misshapen face was marked by blotches and sores. He seemed to be struggling to stand and steady himself even as he supported himself by grasping the wood frame of the stall's doorway. He was beaming a sickly smile at Sue and Joe when a woman trailing him appeared.

Joe King finished dumping Samsona's feed into her feed tub and said, "Al, how ya been? Never expected to see you today. And your wife. Hi Bev. Come on in. Introduce you folks to the new trainer, Miz . . ."

"Sue Brown." Sue smiled and offered her hand to the emaciated, almost shriveled replica of a man, the one she was replacing. He didn't look at all like the yahoo or crusty hard-boot she'd pictured when Byron described him to her. His sports jacket had four buttons and looked expensive.

"Al Carter. This is my wife Bev." The Hall Of Fame trainer smiled faintly and after turning slightly toward his wife, feebly shook Sue's hand. "We thought we'd come by and see the new trainer Mister Stone told us about last Thursday."

Sue's smile dimmed. "Last Thursday? That guy sure is a confident super salesman type. I didn't know about it myself until about four days ago. Saturday night to be exact."

"He's a clever man, Mister Stone, as was his dad." Carter coughed hard several times before continuing: "Too bad about him, his stroke." The middle-aged man appeared very sad while shaking his head. "When I was at the hospital getting my treatments yesterday, we tried to get to see Mister Stone, but he was so badly off we couldn't. He really is badly off."

Sue thought it curious that this man, who was more than likely as sick or sicker than he looked, was talking about someone else's illness as though he himself had none. She couldn't suppress the sudden urge to ask her predecessor about his own ailment. "How are you doing? Any improvement?" She felt foolish after asking her question. On her visits to the various health clinics and hospitals around NYC, she had noticed several people with his taut, blanched look and hacking cough, the latter stages of HIV. From the way the trainer looked, he had to have full blown AIDS.

Bev Carter forced a smile, which remained as though etched into her pasty skin. She got closer to Sue and answered for her husband with her deep

drawl: "He's feelin' a little bit better today. But even
if he wasn't, he'd have to be half dead before anyone could stop him from a comin' here to see you
and check on Samsona before Sunday's big race."

Sue felt as sorry for the woman as she did for the
man. She too must be HIV although she didn't look
half as bad as her husband. Sue tried hard to maintain her smile. With Al on one side of her and his
wife on the other, Sue clucked to Samsona and tried
to get her to leave her feed tub.

"She a real doer," Al Carter said. "There's only
one way she's going to leave her feed."

"He's right," Bev said. Samsona raised her head
ever so slightly while chewing a mouthful of her food.
Before sending a curious look Bev's way, the precocious filly seemed to be saying what are you bother-
ing me about now. "Here girl." As though suddenly
recognizing the woman who had given her treats of
sugar from the first day she'd arrived at the track,
Samsona came over to Bev. Patting the chestnut filly
gently on her dished face, Bev said, "I know I ain't
supposed to pat you on the head. The filly looked as
though she understood as she raised her head and
took the tiny cube of sugar Bev had been hiding in
her hand.

"There's a nice girl," the trainer's wife said softly.
"I ain't forgot ya. One a day won't do her no harm."
She rubbed her hand gently along Samsona's long
neck and behind her ears. The filly's big eyes showed
her appreciation. "She's my, our little girl, and she's
gonna win big fer us, Sunday."

"By the way, Sue, I understand that you was with
Nick Stockton on that trip he died on." Al Carter's
voice trembled as he spoke. "Would you have any
idea about when he's gonna be waked? I, and Bev,

would like to go." He lowered his head and gazed sadly at the floor. "He was a very good friend."

"I know, Joe was telling me, just before you fellas arrived. It'll probably be as soon as the state medical examiner's office in Connecticut is done with its examination." Sue glanced sideways at Bev whose inquisitive eyes were squinting at Sue. "Byron might have heard more by now. He's been in contact with the detectives handling the investigation." She checked her watch. "He should be back in a little while. He ran over to the track office for a few minutes to deposit money and call a police detective who's investigating Nick Stockton's death."

"I still can't believe it," Al Carter said.

Sue said, "No one can."

"Getting back to Sammy here. Is there anything I can do to help you prepare her for her race?"

Sue looked squarely at Al Carter. "I'm sure you've gotten her ready, although you can tell me about Sammy's running style or anything that will help me handle her better. And will you be able to make the race Sunday?"

"He . . ." Bev started answering for her husband.

Al Carter put up his hand feebly. Yet he sounded determined as he said, "I'll certainly try to be here for Sunday no matter how I feel. As fer the way she runs, besides her past charts, you ought to take a look at her past races. They'll be glad to show you in the viewing room. Have you been there yet?"

"Not yet. I was going to do it tomorrow."

"Joey will take you there. Samsona, she likes to front run it like a lot of horses with classic speed. But I've been getting her to relax more lately and rate and she's been winning much easier by running from just off the pace. She's becoming a push button kind

a horse. That's why everyone connected with her,
just loves her. The jocks all want to ride her of course,
but I been usin' Angel and even though he's been
havin' trouble makin' the weight, I still use him. I'd
rather sacrifice a little weight, pound or two don't
matter anyhow, than sacrifice the experience."

"That sounds like my dad," Sue interjected. "He
always prefers an experienced rider unless the apprentice is a potential Arcaro or Cauthen type. He
says experience always knows how to work its way out
of tough situations in a race, whereas inexperience
doesn't and can even create dangerous situations for
the other jocks and their mounts. Sounds like you
feel the same way about it."

"Right on," Al Carter said enthusiastically. "I'm
sure you're gonna do okay with Old Stone Stable's
horses, but I may as well tell you about the others,
besides Samsona. Just happens that among the older
horses we don't have any grade one stakes horses
right now 'cept the one who ran in Ireland. They'll
win still, mostly money allowance and cheap stakes.
As for the two year olds, them two colts are real special. They're both just about ready to start. Royally
Sure? To me he seems the better of the two right
now. Maybe 'cause he's come to hand and developed
quicker and shows a bit more stamina as well as speed.
Although Nickster as I call the other colt, he's bred
to go farther. He had us worried for a while, though."

"Worried?"

"Yeah. When he come here off the training farm,
vet said he had cardiac arrhythmias first time he examined him. So Mister Stone had someone from
Cornell who was doing a study on arrhythmias come
down and check. Did an EKG and found that he was
normal. Also said his abnormal heartbeat or arrhyth-

mia could have been induced by a drug they were giving him on the training farm."

"Has it ever occurred again?"

"Nope and we've been training him hard lately. Next year maybe, he'll be the one we'll like for the classics. Right now though, Sure, as I calls the other fella just as you folks must, he's ready for a race, baby one at least. Five and half, maybe five furlongs to start with."

Sue could see that Al Carter was growing tired. "I appreciate your help, Al, and I'm looking forward to training Samsona and the younger guys as well. Just hope I can continue your good work with them as well as with the older horses in the barn."

"From where I stand and from what Mister Stone told me about you and I know about your daddy. You'll do okay, maybe better than me."

"I doubt it, but I hope, really hope you'll be here Sunday. It'll be like an insurance policy." Sue plucked some hay out of the hay net while watching Samsona, who had gone back to her feed tub and hadn't taken her head out of it. "She looks like a real doer. But then most of the good ones are." Sue sniffed at the hay in her hand and asked, "How much alfalfa is she getting?"

Joe, who was standing in back of the group, volunteered, "As I mentioned to you earlier, Ma'm, I order the hay and I try to get a good mix of hay, and as I mentioned before, mostly Canadian hay. And the hay I prefer is a bit courser with some timothy mixed in and not too much alfalfa, but it's a good mix and the horses seem to love it."

"I guess I taught him that. Couldn't have summed it up better myself." Al Carter chuckled feebly. "And I know, even though Joe didn't say it, too much al-

falfa might make a horse sick. Don't get me wrong; I
like alfalfa. It's plenty rich and can give a horse a
boost, but I prefer a good mix. The hay and even the
grain we use may cost a little more, but it's well worth
it when you consider the results. Trouble with too
many trainers as you know, Ma'm, is that they try to
cut corners, skimp, and end up with poor results almost every time. And I don't believe in quick fixes
like a lot of guys out there. Like injections of vitamins and glucose just before a race. Only ones them
quick fixes helps is the vets. Don't do no good at all
for the horse, only makes the vets richer."

"That's exactly what my dad says." Sue tossed her
fist full of hay into Samsona's stall. "It makes much
more sense to feed them vitamins like selenium and
vitamins B and C over a period of time; otherwise
the quick fix cocktail of vitamins and minerals just
go in and out of the animal's body real fast and produce no benefit at all, do nothing for the horse, just
like with humans.

"Hey folks," Byron's voice boomed. When he
spotted Bev and Al, he said, "Well, what have we here.
Glad to see you guys. Have you gotten Sue
straightened out yet?"

"She's got us all straightened out," Al said. "I
heard a lot about her dad, and if she learned from
him, she's gonna be A okay." His face suddenly
seemed to become more gray and drawn as he
looked down at the floor in front of him. "Sir, Mister
Stone, I'd like to talk to you privately for a minute or
two."

"Sure, Al. Let's go outside." Byron's handsome
face forced a look of chiseled stone. He tried hard
to keep his feelings from showing as he headed for
the side entryway. When he noticed that Al was lag-

ging behind, he slowed down to allow Al to catch up
to him.

Sue watched sadly until Byron and his former
trainer had disappeared out the wide doorway. "He
looks like he's in a lot of pain."

Bev shook her head and made what sounded like
a sobbing sound. "He's really in pain. He's been takin'
a lot of stuff for his illness, even stuff smuggled in
from France that's illegal. Mister Stone got it for him.
Took a chance. And it ain't helped much. Hospital
may have to be the next step even though he's really
fightin' it." She forced a faint smile onto her pale
face. "He's still determined to lick it, though, and
he'll probably be here for Samsona's race Sunday.
But that may be it. Even though he talks about goin'
up to Saratoga." She held her head high and shook
her head again, more vigorously this time.

Sue admired the frail woman's struggle to appear dignified. A torrent of tears was being held in
check by the mere force of pride and courage. She
said, "Hope he does. I could use all the help I can
get."

"I am so happy you responded quickly to my call,
Sue."

Doctor Sobel stroked his goatee before pointing
to a plain wooden chair fronting his desk.

Sue folded herself into the chair, stared at the
octogenarian and waited for him to speak. The top
of Sobel's desk was so loaded with piles of papers
and note books, she could see only the top of his
dark suit and shirt. Sobel's square wrinkled face
showed its years today. When Sobel was assigned as
one of her advisors, Sue thought him to be her

father's age. And although she was surprised at first to discover that he was eighty, she recalled from an economic geography course in high school that many people like Sobel who came from some parts of Georgia in the old Soviet Union lived well beyond one hundred.

Doctor Sobel said bluntly, "When Doctor Blake told me about your new position, I was somewhat alarmed."

"Doctor Blake called you?"

"Yes, I am doing a project for the foundation he heads, S and P, who provides you with your scholarship, as he reminded me. And that is why I called you."

Sue squirmed in the rickety chair.

Sobel studied her face. "I want to make sure we know where we stand. First of all you are not going to be able to serve two masters. When Doctor Blake told me that you were working at the racetrack, he did not sound too happy, and I could not believe it. You are already way behind in your research. I have not received anything from you in months."

"That's because I haven't pulled all my research together yet."

Sobel nodded; his probing dark eyes made Sue squirm again. He said, "Ah yes, one has to pull things together. I am in that very predicament myself for the project I am doing currently for Doctor Blake and S and P."

"What is the project about specifically, Doctor? Something I could use in my research? I know it takes you to Russia a lot." Sue studied the Georgian's dark eyes. Sue sensed distrust in them.

Sobel's suspicious face cracked a dim smile. "It is about sexual behavior of Russian people, Russian woman in particular." He pushed aside some papers and craned his neck, his dark eyes all over Sue's breasts, making her very uncomfortable.

"Did you know that Russian women are much less inhibited than American women? And that is the problem. That is why HIV and drugs have become endemic, such an enormous problem among women and children in Moscow and other cities in Russia."

"How is it you came to work for S and P in the first place, Doctor, I'm curious?"

"Doctor Blake. He hired me. He came from same place in the old USSR. His parents take him here when he is quite young. His name is really Blakoviev."

Sue tried to maintain a passive look on her face even though Sobel's information made her speculate about Blake. "How did Doctor Blake get his job at S and P?"

Sobel shrugged. He adjusted his wrinkled suit jacket before replying. "Who knows? He must have applied after university. He has worked long time for S and P."

"Do you and he go to Georgia to visit family and friends? You must."

"I do. Blake has gone, I'm sure, even though turmoil and civil war exist there now. But I have only seen him in Moscow. He has many friends there, as his father was once high official in government. This has been useful for our research there; open many doors which would otherwise be closed."

"He goes to Moscow often?"

"Often enough." Sobel's ruddy face cracked a suspicious smile. "You are asking so many questions. Why?"

"Professional curiosity is all. I was wondering if he got out into the field very often. How close he got to the research material. So many heads of projects don't, especially when they're as high up as he is."

Before Sue had completed her response, Sobel was saying, "Again I must advise you, Sue Brown, you cannot work at track and neglect your work at university. One cannot serve two masters. I have not received reports in allotted time." Sobel cleared his throat. "However, I give you extension, but you must do the work or…" He left the dire consequences hanging.

Sue stood up and turned toward the door. "I'll have to think about it." Over her shoulder, she asked, "You must have talked to Doctor Blake about me? Sounds like you talk to him often."

Since there was no response, Sue felt she knew the answer. She was about to slam the door shut, then caught herself and said calmly over her shoulder, "Incidentally, Doctor Sobel, perhaps you need reminding, some people around here take time off on summer break, no?"

"Glad you could make it, Jimbo. Come on in and make yourself homely." Sue waved toward a cream-colored leather sofa and matching chairs, which formed a cozy grouping in front of an elaborate stone and white Roman brick fireplace.

Jim Morrissey looked at her in amazement. "Is this place some kind of fortress or something?"

"Why?"

"Glad you left my name with the guards at the main gate."

Jim Morrissey hesitated before taking a couple more steps. Even though over six feet tall, Jim appeared small as he raised his head to study the high walls and ceilings of his surroundings. His ruddy face had become reddened almost to the same shade of his rusty hair. "Man alive, or should I say woman alive. What's going on? When you told me you were moving to a new place, you never said anything about a Taj Mahal complex. I suspected your dad must've made some good connections through the horse business, but this." He started waving his hands in different directions. "How'd you wangle all this?"

"Wangle? Where'd you dig up that word?" Sue's smile said she was enjoying his surprise as much as he. "Fell into it this time."

"I called and called, Saturday, Sunday. Finally got your message on your new answering machine Monday. Glad you went and got one of those things."

"Just got it Monday. Knew I'd be getting calls there."

"Smart. You sure didn't take long to vacate."

"Didn't have anything to move. How's your latest research project been going?"

"To hell with the research. I'd like to know more about this. You said something about training horses, not about this." Jim extended both of his arms as far as they could reach. "Rich relatives of yours that you've never mentioned?"

"You're not going to believe me when I tell you all about it, or most of it. I'll save some of it for dinner at this great seafood place that Byron Stone took me to near Oyster Bay yesterday for lunch. And I'm treating now that I've got me a good paying job."

Jim blinked foolishly. "Oyster Bay? That's quite a ways from here. Ay-ooga. Did you say job? So this horse training thing is for real?"

"It sure is."

"What about your doctoral thesis? And you said

something about Sobel." Jim almost tripped as he stepped across the slated area in front of the fireplace onto the plush wall to wall carpet. After righting himself, he took several steps over the thick carpeting and sat down on a soft Italian leather couch.

"Sobel? He's like most guys with doctorates, doesn't do a damn thing; certainly can't teach. And of course he doesn't like it one bit, my working for the Stones. He called me in to tell me. And it's so dumb, it being school break for most normal humans. And the irony of it all is that the guy does some work for Byron Stone himself, consulting work for his S and P Foundation. Spends more time with that than his regular job."

"When you said you were going to work for Byron Stone, training, I couldn't believe it. How'd you get this job?" Jim's reddened face became a puzzled mosaic.

"He and his dad were clients of my old man's in California. Great clients, I should add."

"Extremely wealthy ones is what I immediately thought when I found this place. I've seen a lot of rich people's places around Greenwich, Stamford, my neck of the woods, nothing like this place. An army could swim in the pool of water in front of the main house. Couldn't believe the waterfall of water gushing out of what looked like giant dolphins. Must've cost a fortune. And there's a private landing field and other buildings. It's more like a small town than someone's estate. After I was allowed through that enormous front gate, the road alone I used must cost a fortune to maintain let alone build. Stone's main building must be a copy of a palazzo from the Italian Renaissance period, the plush grounds and trees and all."

"So welcome to my new home, Jimbo, Stone Henge and the other part of the real world."

"Stone Henge?" Jim studied a horse sculpture on a pedestal in one corner of the room. "You mean to tell me this is where you're going to be living from now on? Stone Henge?" He looked up at the fifteen-foot high ceilings and all around the very large living room at the stark white walls covered with what appeared to be authentic paintings. "No wonder the guy's got a lot of security; just those paintings alone must be worth a king's ransom. What a haul for someone."

"I'll only be living here a short while, probably just for the summer."

"So tell me about this training job."

"Not much to tell. I'll be working full time as a trainer at Belmont Park."

"For this Stone Guy?" Jim shut his eyes and shook his head. "That's crazy. And as a trainer at Belmont Park. It's mind-boggling."

Sue nodded, a whimsical expression stretching across her pretty face. "Yep, little old me, your occasional nocturnal date and schoolmate. Of course there's always a fly in the ointment. Sobel wants me to stick to my thesis research and not work at the track. I guess he doesn't know me very well."

"You're full of surprises, that's for sure. I knew you were talented, but not like this talented, enough to be the big time trainer of horses. Wow, I still don't believe this."

"You've got no choice. You're going to have to believe. And we'll have a drink here before we leave. There's plenty of it in the bar over there." Sue nodded toward a small bar with a marble slab. "We may as well take advantage unless you want a guided tour around this place first."

"I'll take the guided tour first."

"C'mon, the fresh air'll do us both some good and there's a terrific view of the ocean.

Jim got up and laughed derisively, "Yeah, I'm game if it's okay with the lord of the manor."

They walked side by side down a long asphalt drive, which was lined with mature shade trees, mostly red maples and lush shrubs in full bloom. As they approached the imposing Italian Renaissance inspired main house, Sue spotted a plain black Ford with a Connecticut license plate. "Wonder who that could be?" They both stopped to examine the two cars parked in front of a broad stone stairway.

"Troopers' cars. One from Connecticut," Jim said curiously. "What would they be doing here?"

"State police investigators, investigating Nick Stockton's death. Close friend of Byron Stone's. You probably read about it."

Jim's eyes lighted up. "Now I know where I heard the name, Byron Stone. Ah ha."

"Sue, hey Sue," a voice called out.

Sue looked up. Byron Stone was shouting at her from a first floor window of the huge brick Italianate structure.

"I'd like to see you for a minute or two. Our visitors do, at least." Byron's voice sounded demanding and tired. "I'll meet you at the front door."

Jim accompanied Sue up the broad granite stairs to the ornate metal and oak front door that went with the Renaissance design of the large structure.

"C'mon in, Sue." Byron eyed Jim suspiciously, while holding the door open.

Sue said, "Byron, this is Jim Morrissey, a fellow grad school student and a close friend."

Byron cracked a smile with a look that said I wonder how close a friend. "Hi, c'mon in." He held the door open until Sue and Jim were both inside the building. Byron led them into a sitting room just off the wide vestibule where Byron turned to Jim and said, "Jim, if you don't mind, Sue and I will be talking to a couple of investigators, New York and Connecticut State Policemen. Shouldn't take too long. Please have a seat and make yourself comfortable. There's a TV, some magazines." Byron motioned toward a long table against a mahogany paneled, ornately wainscoted wall. "Sue and I'll be right back."

Byron escorted Sue out of the room and across an extra wide hallway. They entered a large room that had the appearance of both library and law office. Two men in dark suits stood up alertly.

"Sue Brown," Byron said formally, "this is Billie Williams, Connecticut State Police and Frank Marone, New York State Police. They're investigating Nick Stockton's death. They want to ask you a few questions." He turned and addressed Williams. "Do you want me to leave while you interrogate Sue?"

Billie's high cheek boned, African American face smiled accommodatingly. "We may have a question or two which both of you might be able to answer. Better if you're both here. As I explained to you, Mister Stone, all the evidence we've come up with thus far points toward homicide, even though you don't seem entirely convinced that Nick Stockton didn't commit suicide. We don't have a complete report from the Medical Examiner on Stockton and there wasn't a suicide note. Unless you folks can help us with that, we're staying with the M E's preliminary report. A note isn't all that's missing, however. If it's homicide, we need to come up with a motive yet for both Wilson and Stockton. You and Stockton being close friends, maybe you can throw some light on why their deaths happened so close and with the same MO."

Byron sounded adamant: "I only said I think Nick's could be a suicide."

Marone piped in, "In Wilson's case the M E says Wilson was definitely bashed from behind and suggested that people with Mister Stockton's or John Wilson's backgrounds don't commit suicide without leaving a note or something."

Byron shrugged. "Sounds like you have your answers then. Don't really see how we can help in any way whatsoever."

Marone said, "We only thought that maybe you, Stockton's friends, being at the scene could throw some light, more light, on things." Frank Marone reminded Sue of a heavier version of the old movie actor, George Raft, even though the detective's face was rounder as was his body. Marone spoke with the tough guy's confident air, and with an attitude and voice contrasting sharply with the Connecticut State trooper's. Billie was less intense, almost casual and more polished. It seemed to her that Frank Marone was not unlike the many New Yorkers who seemed to go out of their way to sound aggressive and macho.

"Unlike Byron, I hardly knew him," Sue offered.

The New York trooper ignored her comment even as he seemed to be sizing her up with his squinting eyes. "Mister Stone said that Nick Stockton had been rather despondent of late and that you were talking to him also that day before he was found dead.

And if I might ask you, Miz Brown, when you talked to Nick Stockton the day before he died, did he indicate in any way at all that he might be in danger or even assuming it was suicide in his case that he might do something to himself?"

"I didn't have much chance to talk to him. Certainly can't recall anything he said to me that might be important to your investigation."

"He didn't say anything that hinted or showed he felt insecure, in danger?"

Sue reflected deeply before saying, "As far as I could tell from what little I saw of him, he sure didn't give the impression of feeling at all insecure. But he did seem rather worn out, sick, appeared like he was out of breath and close to collapsing."

Marone said sharply, "He was?" He turned to Byron. "You never said anything like that about him."

Byron shrugged his shoulders. "I didn't feel it was significant. He was just a bit tired as far as I was concerned."

Marone asked Sue, "Can you elaborate further?"

Sue shut her eyes as though trying to recall more clearly Nick's condition, as she perceived it to be the night before he died. She opened her eyes and said, "I'm afraid that's all I can recall right now. He looked gaunt and worn out. From what, I couldn't tell. Someone at the track said something that made me think he might have been HIV."

Billie Williams appeared very interested. "That could be significant, Miz." He turned and smiled confidently at his sidekick. "Wilson had AIDS."

The other detective tweaked the long crooked nose on his puffy, well-tanned face. After passing his stubby outstretched hand over his head as though checking to see if the hair he had left were still covering a bald spot, Frank Marone said to Byron Stone, "You never mentioned that about your close friend, Stockton. You must've known. Is that why you thought he committed suicide?"

Byron frowned and looked down at the toes of his polished loafers.

Marone turned to Sue as though he wanted to be one on one. He said, "Did anybody else say or do something unusual on that Connecticut trip that you think might be connected with Stockton's death? Any strange or unusual behavior on the part of anyone?" He glanced at Byron Stone. Then he flipped a page of the small notebook he held in his hand and checked what was on the next page. "There was a Doctor Blake and his wife. You get to talk with them?"

"Very little."

Marone looked down at the page again. "A Miz Phillips and her boyfriend, Willi. Can't quite make out his last name, and a Boris Kleptokoff and his lady friend. What could you tell us about them that could help in our investigation?"

"I didn't know any of them, never even saw any of them before the trip." Sue paused and eyed Byron whose handsome face was contorted into a look of total disdain. "Only knew Mister Stone. He invited me to go on the trip and other than that, I really have no other information for you." She would have liked to mention Ruth Stockton's behavior, but was able to control the jealous impulse.

"Weren't you at all surprised and shocked at what happened?" The stocky detective asked before shooting a glance at Byron.

Sue stared at Byron who looked bored as he stared out the window. She said, "Of course. We all were." And she wondered what might really be on

Byron's mind and how he might be involved with Nick's death. He didn't seem to be taking his best friend's death too hard.

Marone stared suspiciously at Sue as though trying to fathom what was on her mind while she was studying Byron's face. Then Marone turned his attention to Byron. "Backfire. We found the word on a piece of notepaper in his wallet, Nick Stockton's. Does that word mean anything to either one of you?"

Sue looked puzzled.

Although appearing interested for the first time, Byron shook his head and answered, "Backfire? You did say backfire? Not a clue."

Marone nodded his big head slowly, unbelievingly. "You're sure now?" He carefully examined Byron's face before switching his attention to Sue's. "There's nothing else you can tell us," the balding investigator persisted, glancing again inquisitively at Byron and then back to Sue before turning to his fellow investigator to see if he had any further questions for Sue or Byron.

The Connecticut investigator prodded, "You're sure now that there isn't something more you can or would like to reveal about the whole thing before we wrap this up? Anything at all."

Both Sue and Byron shook their heads decisively.

"Thanks a bunch folks. We'll be in touch." Billie Williams glanced at Marone and nodded toward the doorway. "Guess we'll have to head out, Frank. The well's about run dry here for now."

"I guess." Marone sent a leer toward Byron.

The Connecticut investigator said, "This thing is far from over. There are a lot of unanswered questions still, and we may have more questions for you to answer, especially after the autopsies are com-

pleted on both victims. Sometimes it takes a great
deal of time and effort to get to the bottom of things."

"Yeah," Marone grumbled.

Byron showed the two detectives to the door and
returned. "Sue, sorry you had to go through all this
stuff. As far as I'm concerned, I still think it might
have been a suicide in Nick's case and it'll all be over
as soon as they have the autopsy results." His face
shifted from serious to pleasantly interested. "How
did Samsona look today? Better I hope."

"Much improved," Sue enthused. "Not a pimple
on her now. It wasn't even a slight sprain. And as you
must know, you mostly can't tell how serious something is until the next day after a work, usually. Not
even the slightest bit of swelling, though. Her ankles
are clean now. Dad's gunk may have helped. And
she finished her feed this morning like she was a
vacuum cleaner. I've never seen anything quite like
it, her, I mean."

"You're too modest. That gunk had to help and no
doubt was what she needed to keep her ankle from
getting worse. She should be ready for Sunday then?"

"Most certainly. I hope the track isn't too cuppy,
although I don't know if Al ever told you this, she's
sort of flat footed. She's done so well so far and with
her rather large flat feet and her action, she should
be even better on the grass. Could even be a champion there, as well as dirt. Of course, we'll run her in
her three-year old races first. Coaching Club and
Alabama first." Sue got up slowly from her chair and
started toward the doorway. "I hope you don't mind,
but I thought I'd show Jim the great view of the Atlantic you've got here at Stone Henge. By the way
who picked that name for this place?"

"My Great Grand Daddy Marcus, and I hope I

won't have to keep reminding you, Sue, that you must just make yourself at home. While you're living here, just pretend, no that's the wrong word, just treat it like it's your own home. See ya later." He turned and walked down the long center corridor toward the back of the house.

When Sue and Jim stepped outside, they found the New York state police detective waiting for them. Marone said, "Sue Brown, may I have another word with you?" He looked at Jim. "It'll just take a minute or two."

Jim got the hint and walked down the granite steps.

Marone's eyes locked onto Sue's. "I know you said you didn't know Doctor Cameron Blake very well when I talked to you inside Stone's mansion with Stone around. Being he ain't around here now to hear, there must be something you've heard or seen about Blake that could help me form a better picture of who and where he comes from."

"I just started working for the Stones. All I know is that he works for Mister Stone and heads up the S and P Foundation. And oh yes, I discovered yesterday by talking to my doctoral advisor at the university that Doctor Blake was born in the old Soviet Union and that his real name is Blakoviev."

"Your advisor?"

"Doctor Sobel. He's one of my advisors at the university where I'm studying for my doctorate."

"How did your advisor know all this?"

"He comes from the same area in the old USSR as Blake, Georgia, and does some consulting for S and P."

Marone made a curious face. "What'd you say this advisor's full name is?"

"Doctor Vladimir Sobel."

"Doctor Vladimir Sobel." Marone wrote on his notepad. "I'll have to pay him a visit. What else did Sobel say about Blake?"

"He did say something about Blake's father. Important NKVD official in the old USSR."

"Aha. The old internal security outfit. Figures." Again Marone made a notation in his notebook. "Thanks. You've been a big help." He started down the stairs. "I'll probably be seeing you again. Thanks."

When Marone was out of sight, Jim asked, "What did that bird want?" When Sue didn't respond, he said, "Funny that the guy who owns this universe is a little guy."

"He's not that little. He's slightly shorter than you but quite a bit more muscular," Sue said glibly. Adding with a defiant look, "And what does size have to do with anything?"

Jim knew that she was referring to one of their biggest bones of contention: the over-emphasis on bigness in the U.S., big boobs, big penises, big everything. "I hope we don't lapse into a confrontation before dinner."

"You know that I don't have confrontations unless I'm going to learn something. Going over old ground, I'm definitely not interested in that today." She checked her watch. "Or even tonight. We'd better get a move on if we're going to eat before midnight, and we're going to have to pass on looking at the ocean tonight. We'll have just enough time for dinner at the Captain's Table, and maybe a little fun after that. Hope you don't mind, I have to get up before five o'clock, so that I can be at the track on time."

"Guess trainers don't have bankers' hours."

"That's for sure." Sue pushed him playfully as they walked along the wide estate road.

"By the way," Jim said, regaining his composure after her playful nudge. "As you know, my doctoral work ties sex into economics and vice versa."

Sue became playfully attentive: "Screwing economically?"

"By the way, wasn't your meeting with those two guys and your friend Byron all about Nick Stockton's death."

"Yeah, the trip I went on with Byron Stone over the weekend."

"The newspaper didn't have much of a story on it. You must know much more. I know that I do."

"I'll tell you about it later. Why? What do you know about it?"

"When I was reading some financial tabloids for one of my research projects, I recall reading about some of Wilson's contacts when he was Secretary of Commerce. Seems that those contacts helped him and Stockton unload a lot of stock for a client. Stock of an international department store chain expanding into Eastern Europe, called Baxters. That client had also invested in another chain in Europe called Marins. Marins had sold all of its bad stores to Baxters and Marins keeps its good stuff, the moneymaking components, the inter-net catalog and warehouse business. Wilson's outfit, which includes Stockton, of course, was instrumental in getting Baxters to buy the stores, which were operating mostly in the red. A year after the sale, Baxters is forced into bankruptcy."

"Chapter eleven?"

"Yeah, reorganization. There's more. Much more. Because Marins was able to divest itself of the red ink stores by selling its bad stuff to Baxters, Marins becomes a stronger company with solid earnings and voila, like magic, its stock not only doubles but triples in price. And guess what? Your friend Nick Stockton, who is now a dead friend unfortunately, was behind the whole scheme, and it is discovered that he sold all of his bad Baxters stock through and maybe to one of Byron Stone's Holding Companies and buys a whole mess of stock in Marins before the buyout takes place. But that's only the half of it. It was discovered, or at least there's some evidence, though never proven, at least not yet, that Stockton and his partner John Wilson bought the good Marins stock on behalf of a bunch of guys in Eastern Europe, an outfit referred to as the EEG; some of those EEG guys came from the old guard in the Communist party in Moscow, former Kremlin big wigs."

Sue appeared worried. "So Byron had good reason to be angry at his buddy?"

"I'd say yes except that Byron's outfit also owned a big chunk of Marins stock. And it really gets messy as it looks like those guys who belonged to the good old boys network in the former Soviet Union are now playing footsies with some of the same types of guys who belong to the good old boys network here in the U S of A. And there's even a link to the Sicilian Mafia as well as the Russian Mafia called The Red Star. Fed discovered the whole thing when they found out that the EEG guys were dumping gold to help make the purchases. Sure didn't help the precious metals market."

Sue appeared stunned. "If you know about this, lots of other guys must, especially Byron Stone. They were very close, Nick and he, very close."

"Of course. And Stone might even have been

involved in the whole transaction. One way or another, through one or more of his companies who do business in and with the Eastern block.." Jim suddenly appeared concerned. "Hey, you don't think your friend could have had something to do with Wilson's murder, or even Stockton's, do you? How well do you know Byron Stone?"

"Well enough to know he wouldn't murder his best friend."

"Never know about those big exploiter types. And it seems now that we're on the subject, I read in the Times just last week that Stone Holdings was being investigated for dumping a lot of cheap radioactively contaminated diamonds onto the gem markets."

Sue looked angry. "You really don't like Byron Stone. C'mon now."

"Byron's father was mentioned mostly, Stone Holdings."

"I'm sure you don't know the whole story, even though you read that stuff about Nick Stockton. There are a lot of investigations talked about in the newspapers; how many times do we read that they're fruitless and just a newspaper reporter's attempt to sell more newspapers? Reporters are just like politicians. They may not be lying to us, but they sure as hell are bullmanuring us."

"True, but hey, I just mentioned it to you for whatever it's worth. And oh yes, I remember now. The Stones and their S and P Foundation, they're the ones who provided you with your scholarship. That's why you're so protective of the Byron. And now he's got you living in one of his fancy homes like a kept woman."

"More gibberish. Enough garbage for one day, Jim.

No. One more thing. Do you recall ever having read about Backfire, an organization or some such thing?"

Jim appeared puzzled. "Backfire? Like in stopping forest fires?"

"That's the word."

"Nope." Jim shook his head. "Can't say that it rings a bell, anything. Sorry. Why? Is it of any value to you to know what it is?"

Sue laughed. "Value? Hey, let's go get something that is worth something right now into my empty stomach." She ignored Jim's devious look and added complacently, "I'm sure those cops'll dig into his background and find out as much, if not more than the reporter who concocted that story you read. And from the facts you told me, what Nick did might amount to just another successful business maneuver or venture of a clever Wall Street lawyer-banker. Most likely all legal."

Jim said, "Except that the Russian Mafia was mentioned as well as Byron Stone's outfit."

"As the guys in Brooklyn would say, forget about it. Next thing you'll be telling me is that Byron and his father had someone kill Stockton and his partner because of their involvement in the Marins, Baxters deal, or that radioactive diamonds stuff. I don't think so and I don't want to deal with it. Right now I'd rather deal with filling my empty stomach."

"Yeah, I hear you loud and clear. I'll enjoy filling your stomach, and mine," Jim snickered. "Almost as much as I'll enjoy leaving this American Taj Mahal." He looked all around him and over at some rolling very green terrain. "This place even has its own golf course. Look at that flag over there. Got a number on it." He pointed in the direction of a flag fluttering in the sea breeze.

"It has. It's got just about everything, I guess."

"Yeah," Jim grumbled and looked around. "This place most likely was bought with the billions of bucks they launder in their international laundry. Hey, looks like another state trooper's car."

A sedan resembling the standard state trooper's car drove away from in front of the guesthouse. They watched with puzzled looks on their faces. There appeared to be only one driver who was too far away for them to identify. "Wonder what he was doing there."

"Planting a bug while the other two guys were diverting our attention?" Jim shrugged his shoulders with an air of the fully informed. "You sure this Stone guy isn't connected?"

Sue smirked, "Mafia? C'mon now, be realistic; paranoia may be next. Why would anyone want to bug me? Except maybe you?" She made a clownish face.

Trying to duplicate her funny face, Jim said smugly, "Who knows what evil lurks, especially in the hearts and minds of the obscene rich? Look at the Kennedy's." Trying to appear the arrogant authority, Jim added, "The psyche of the rich guy is a strange one. Just read some of my research material, or the whole thing after I'm finished. You'll especially enjoy the sleaze, mostly concerning the very rich and infamous."

"Sounds like you're doing your research for some cheap tabloid."

Jim stopped to study the imposing flat-roofed contemporary, which could have been designed by a Frank Lloyd Wright or one of his disciples. "Why do you suppose they built this new place with all the rooms they have in the old one? That's really bloated conspicuous consumption, if you ask me."

Sue snapped, "Good no one's asking you," she

said. "Come to think of it, Dad told me once when he stayed here that Byron's mother was an invalid in her last years and they probably wanted a place mostly on ground level, so that she'd have easy access to it. As well as to the beautiful gardens surrounding it. There is a picture of her in my bedroom, one of the larger bedrooms on the ground level."

"Sounds logical, for the filthy rich, that is." Jim slowed down so that he could check out Sue's swaying hips. His eyes focusing on her shapely buns, he said brightly, "You know something, I'm looking forward to using one of those giant plush beds in one of those luxury bedrooms in that new pad of yours. We've never done that CAT thing of yours except on that moth eaten dwarf bed of yours. Should be a real treat."

Enjoying the thought of his using the Tantric Coital Alignment Technique to satisfy her, Sue picked up the pace. Swinging her hips more vigorously so as to tease him. A barely audible squeal of delight slipped from her sensuous lips as she turned her head and glanced down at the crotch of Jim's tight blue jeans. The bulge was unmistakable, even bordering on the obscene where the zipper area appeared more faded.

She slowed down as they approached the front door. Flashing a knowing smile and nodding as she took his hot hand into hers, she opened the front door and led him into the house. "Yeah, let's do it. It's been a while. After some food," she teased. She knew that he couldn't wait and suddenly even her empty stomach would have to wait until they were both satisfied sexually, especially if he used the coital alignment technique.

10

Sue surveyed the saddling area in front of her. Her eyes came to rest on the statue of the great horse Secretariat. A jazz band was playing in the background and a carnival spirit prevailed. Several horses of the seven-horse field had already arrived. Sue watched a couple of them being led around the walking ring. Both were on their toes. She gazed up at the large tote board nearby and whispered, "Two to one," to Byron, who appeared tense and fidgety all of a sudden.

"Be lower than that," Byron said. He took a long hard look in the direction of a tunnel under the road, which led up to a fenced-in alleyway through which the grooms brought their horses into the saddling enclosure from the backstretch. "Jose's taking his time today. Hope everything is okay."

"Don't worry," Sue said, even though she could feel the increasing tension. "There she is. No mistaking that crooked Northern Dancer blaze."

The beautiful chestnut with the identical white

markings of her grandsire, though he was a bay, was moving along gracefully beside her groom. Jose appeared to have a tight hold on the long striding filly. He led her toward Sue so that she could remove the filly's green blanket with the initials OSS printed in large black letters on it. The blanket was designed to match the famous green cross on solid black racing silks of Old Stone Stable. "She's as mellow and relaxed as an old pro," Sue bragged. "She's hardly sweating, even though it's got to be close to ninety out in the sun. As soon as they see her in the walking ring, the odds are going to be even lower."

After a track official checked Samsona's tattoo inside her upper lip, Sue helped a valet place the saddle over Samsona's saddle clothe just below her high withers. After giving an extra cautionary tug on the girth strap to insure that the saddle had been put on snugly and safely, Sue patted Samsona gently on her muscular neck. "She's all yours, Jose. Take her around the circle a few times. Gotta keep her limber."

Even though he didn't have a clue as to the meaning of the word limber, Jose's pleasant face broke out into a big smile toward Sue. He tugged at Samsona's lead line and led the fully compliant filly to the walking ring area. As soon as Samsona stepped onto the oval surface where other horses were already being walked, there seemed to be more spring in her legs. She appeared to be on her toes and ready to lunge past what she instinctively knew was some of her competition.

Sue and Byron were joined by Bev Carter who had entered the walking ring from the tunnel area under the clubhouse.

Bev spoke first. "Left Al in the Turf Room. He'll

watch the race up there with some owner friends he's made over the years."

Sue smiled. "And he's made a bunch of them I'm sure.

Bev's bloodshot eyes blinked nervously and expressively in their deep-seated sockets. It was obvious to Sue that Bev had made an all out effort to look and dress appropriately for the occasion. The designer dress must have cost a small fortune. Her husband's top trainer's pay had made Bev and her husband wealthy over the years so they could easily afford the best, Sue thought. The Stones had taken good care of them. Even the medical costs must have been covered fully by the Stones. And they had to have the same retirement and insurance plans the Stones had given her father. She'd picked up on what Bev had said the other day about Byron's going as far as obtaining not yet accepted and patently illegal drugs from France to help Al fight his malady.

"We're down to four to five," Byron announced as he glanced up at the tote board, which had just blinked on a new set of numbers.

Sue scanned the board. "And Cindy Phillips' filly is three to two. By the way, where is she? I half expected to see her for lunch today."

"Don't worry she'll show up," Byron assured. "What am I saying? Hey, I'm too young to be getting senile. I saw her and her friend Willi in their box seats about a half hour ago. They arrived at the track late today. She doesn't always come down to the saddling area. Rarely does."

They watched Jose lead Samsona around the walking ring under a tight hold. After several minutes, Sue's eyes shifted right. She scanned the fenced off terraced area where spectators of all sizes,

color and dress were assembled. Some were dressed
in suits and fancy dresses, while most were casually
dressed on this warm, muggy day with the hot sun
glaring down at them. Many watched the fillies being
paraded around the walking area. Some of the fans
glanced at their programs, matching up horse and
post-position, while others seemed to be studying the
Racing Form as well as checking out how the fillies
appeared physically. Sue had learned from her father
how to judge a horse's fitness for a race by looking
for certain signs: the way the animal walked; was the
horse on its toes or was it two timing it, noticeably
bobbing its head to one side as though favoring a
gimpy leg? Was it sweating too much, giving the
animal a washed out appearance? Was there a white
foam coating between its hind legs called kidney
sweat? An indication that the animal might be
hurting could be found in the condition of its coat.
Was it shiny and healthy or ratty looking? Was the
horse behaving calmly and positively or did it appear
too rank? This often indicated that the horse didn't
want to compete that day. Even the way a horse
reacted in the saddling procedure or an equipment
change such as blinkers on or off or a shadow roll
could provide a clue.

Sue examined one of the fillies, which she noticed had its tongue tied. In addition, the filly had a
shadow roll. Sue glanced at Samsona whose shiny coat
glistened as it reflected the sunlight. She needed
no extra equipment whatsoever.

The diminutive jockeys started emerging from
the tunnel under the clubhouse building. The moment of truth was at hand. When Sue spotted
Samsona's jockey, she joined Byron and Bev just inside the walking ring where there were the usual

handshakes. Samsona's regular jockey, Angel Santos, was the leading jockey at the meet. He appeared serious and confident and listened carefully to Sue's instructions. "Al Carter told me that he's been running her successfully just off the pace and saving her great speed for last."

Angel smiled.

Sue continued: "Guess I don't have to remind you there's only one other horse with her speed; we don't want to get into a speed duel, so just take her back a little and let her loose close to the top of the stretch." Sue capped her instructions with the caveat, "You've ridden her enough times, Angel, if she gets caught in traffic, just don't get checked. She's so good you can take her to the outside if you get blocked. I don't have to tell you, Angel, that a push button horse like her'll run anywhere."

Angel nodded and smiled confidently.

An official's voice shouted, "Riders up."

Jose held the filly steady as Sue helped give Angel a leg up onto Samsona's broad, short-coupled back.

Byron grunted an obligatory "Good luck," which the diminutive athlete acknowledged with a wave of his whip as he steered the filly next to a lead pony, which would escort Samsona around the track as she warmed up for the race. Byron watched her disappear into the tunnel under the clubhouse; then he said, "She looks ready."

Sue said, "Only thing that'll stop her is bad racing luck."

"Or a bad ride by our jock. That's why they're called pinheads." Byron looked as though he'd tasted something bitter. "Don't even want to think about that and I can't think of anything that'll stop her, not even my cousin's filly."

"We're in the number one post-position. That could be a problem if she doesn't break well."

"Hasn't happened yet," Bev said. "And she's been gate broke real good."

The trio followed the last horse and jockey into the wide tunnel under the clubhouse. Byron preceded Sue up some metal stairs to the reserved boxes. After a quick look around, he said, "You'd think this was the first day of the meet. This race sure drew them here today. Almost like the good old days. I guess the true racing fans'll come when they feel some real good horses are going to compete against each other. Here we are," Byron stopped before a box marked Old Stone Stable, a permanently reserved box directly across from the finish line.

Sue spotted Cindy Phillips seated in her own reserved box nearby. When the friendly owner of Samsona's chief competition, Becky's Girl, spotted Sue and Byron approaching, she frivolously blew them a kiss and shouted, "Glad to see you guys." To Sue she said, "You must be doubly excited, what with your being the trainer of Sammy as well as her being the heavy favorite in this race."

Byron scoffed, "Hardly the favorite, Cuz. You're like the coach who is glad her team's not favored and is just waiting for the opportunity to demolish the over confident opposition."

Cindy's eyes rolled upward as she turned to Sue. "He loves playing games, toying around with people. Samsona beat us last year as a two year old."

Byron scoffed. "The race was a photo finish. We beat her by a short head and her filly has done as well as ours since then. As far as I can tell from her workout times in The Racing Form, she's training well for this race."

"Should be a close race," Sue said. "I watched the tapes of their past two races. We'll know who's best in a few minutes or so; from the way I analyzed this race in The Racing Form, our filly seems faster and classier off her form than any horse in the race including Becky's Girl, although she could make it very exciting." Sue glanced at Byron and wondered if he ever realized just how powerful and lucky he was. And how it would feel to have such power and control over things.

A conservatively dressed man wearing a navy sports jacket and red tie tapped Byron on the shoulder. His thin face producing a smile from ear to ear, he said respectfully, "I really like your filly's chances."

Byron turned and shook the man's extended hand. "Thanks Claude. Sorry your horse didn't win earlier today. I bet him. Thought he had it won coming down the lane for home."

"I did too, but he just ran out of gas today, pure and simple."

"Next time." Byron turned to Sue and then back to the elderly man, "This is my new trainer, Sue Brown from Santa Anita, replaced Al this week. This is Claude Harding. He's been running horses a long time around these parts." Byron turned to Claude and said, "I'm sure you've heard of her dad who trained for us on the West coast."

"Of course." The octogenarian's wrinkled face flashed a surprised smile. "When I saw her name on the program, I never expected someone so young and so beautiful." He forced himself up from his bent over position and politely extended his hand.

Sue wouldn't have been more flattered if the compliment had come from a much younger man. She stood up and adjusted her plain denim skirt before shaking hands. "Happy to meet you, sir." She had learned from her dad that a lot of owners liked to be addressed as sir. Goes back to the time when horseracing was truly the sport of kings, he'd remind her.

"Good luck, Sue," Harding said before turning to Byron again. "Too bad about Nick and his partner, John Wilson. Read about it in the newspapers. That was some strange happening. Hope they find who did it. Newspaper I read didn't make it clear about Nick. Did he commit suicide?"

"I'm not sure. Could have done it to himself. He has had a lot of problems lately." Byron didn't sound very convincing to Sue. "Serious health problems."

Claude Harding shook his head. "I did hear that at the club." Claude sat down when he saw that Byron was no longer paying attention to him.

Byron turned to Sue and said, "Ill be right back. I'm going to place my bets before it's too late. I'll bet a few bucks on Samsona for you also." Before she could respond, he scooted up the many tiers of broad cement steps and disappeared into the second floor betting area.

Sue used the binoculars, which Byron had placed in a small steel basket attached to the guardrail in front of her. She watched as the fillies warmed up on the other side of the mile and a quarter oval main track. When Sue spotted Angel in Old Stone Stable's black and green silks, he was urging Samsona to move a little faster at the trot. She seemed to glide as she picked up the pace. After watching her for a couple of minutes, Sue turned her attention to Cindy Phillips' filly. Becky's Girl was a little farther back. Soon all the fillies were done with their warm-up exercises and were slowing down to a walk, forming a slow moving parade behind the official track post rider dressed in bright red. He led the single file of horses toward the starting gate. When the post rider arrived at the metal starting gate which resembled a giant erector set laid across the track, the track announcer's voice came over the track's loudspeaker: "The horses for the fifteenth running of the Martha Wilson Stakes are approaching the starting gate. It is now one minute to post time."

Sue placed the binoculars into the metal receptacle in front of her and glanced at the giant tote board in the infield. "Four to five and two to one." She liked the odds on both fillies, Byron's and Cindy's. She looked all around her. People were returning to their seats from their trips to the betting windows. Out of the corner of her eye she spotted Byron taking giant strides down the cascading floor of the grandstand.

"Here you go, Sue," Byron said, handing her ten tickets. "It's now crunch time, fer sure."

"It is now post time," the track announcer shouted sharply. "They're all in line. They're off." His voice was crisp announcing the running order as soon as the horses sprang from the gate: "My Girl Trudy came out first and quickly went to the lead, followed by Jackie O. Becky's Girl is half a length back with Sarah's Slipper and Money's Dear. Then it's Junie and Dinky side-by-side two lengths back. Samsona, the favorite, in this race has had a bad start and is far back, her rider almost got thrown coming out of the starting gate."

Byron groaned, "Almost got thrown coming out of the starting gate? Damn."

Sue watched with a painful expression. "Real bad start for her."

The track announcer's voice continued: "Looks like it's going to be hard for Samsona to make up the lost ground."

The cadence of the announcer's voice matched the rapid movement of the racehorses down the backstretch toward the far turn in the six-furlong event.

As the uneven array of horses approached the three eighth's pole around the turn, Sue got to her feet and started urging, "C'mon Angel get her back in the race." Byron, who had risen as soon as the starting gate was sprung open, stood frozen in place, his facial expression changing from disbelief to disappointment and finally to disgust.

"They ran the quarter in a fast twenty one and two, and the half in forty five. A very fast pace," the announcer's voice said emphatically, just before it became distorted and almost drowned out as the horses started their run for home. The noisy crescendo of an extremely excited crowd was building. He repeated the running order as the fillies approached the eighth pole, his murmuring voice seemingly rising above the crescendo of the crowd's noisy urgings. "Trudy's faded to third and now it looks like a two horse race with Becky's Girl beginning to put her head out in front." He paused for a moment. "Dinky's gonna come back. No. It looks like it's . . . it is, Becky's Girl's gonna win it by at least a length, then Dinky and . . . Yes, Junie, by a nose or two over My Girl Trudy, but there'll be a photo there for third."

Sue and Byron watched helplessly as Samsona passed the finish line last and continued on at an ever-slowing gallop. A short distance past the finish line the jockey started pulling her up. "What the hell's the matter with her?" Byron appeared livid and

confused. "Hope we don't have another broodmare.
Hope she's not lame or badly hurt. Ligament or
something." He seemed to have completely lost his
cool.

Sue never thought she'd see Byron like this. For
her, he represented the assertive individual who was
always in complete control of self and all situations.

Sue said, "I'm not absolutely sure. It sure did look
like the filly broke poorly and I do remember Al
Carter mentioning that the filly needed more training out of the gate." After the filly had gone a few
hundred feet beyond the finish line, she was pulled
up. A post rider rode quickly in her direction and
grabbed her reins while the jockey got off her.
"Something's wrong with Angel. He's gritting his
teeth and favoring his leg."

The jockey staggered; then he sat down clumsily
before he lay back onto his side.

"What now?" Byron was having a difficulty
controlling his temper.

"I should have known," Sue said. "When they
broke, she appeared to be slanted sideways in the
gate; too far to see clearly with the naked eye. I'd
better go down and find out what happened."

Sue walked hurriedly toward the stairs, followed
closely by Byron. When they reached the ground
floor they brushed past a couple of sad-faced, white-
capped attendants who knew Byron. "Too bad, too
bad," one of the guards said. After allowing an anxious Byron to precede her, Sue followed him through
the gate leading onto the main track.

"The ambulance is here." Sue pointed as she
jogged past Byron. "Looks like they're getting ready
to put the jock onto a stretcher."

An ambulance attendant was trying to comfort

the closed-eyed jockey. "What happened?" Sue asked.

"He says he hurt his knee coming out of the gate," the ambulance attendant said seriously. "Caught it on the gate post coming out. Might've broken it. We'll find out at the hospital."

"Damn it all," Byron said with an additional curse thrown in under his breath.

The jockey, responding to Byron's angry voice, opened his eyes and said through tightly clenched teeth, "Sorry. Hit the darned metal bar in the gate just as it opened; almost got my knee tore off. I blame the starter. Held her tail just before we broke and must have pulled too hard to one side. Sorry again folks. Freak accident." He shut his eyes again and made a distorted face, indicating great pain.

Sue said with a discouraged look, "I'd better check Sammy, although she seems okay."

The post rider was walking the sweating and bewildered looking filly around in circles to keep her under control until her groom arrived. The intelligent chestnut filly had never had anything close to this happen to her before and she seemed to be showing it with her large expressive eyes.

Byron, trying hard now to appear stoical, said consolingly, "Welcome to the world of training as your dad, I'm sure, would say. Hard enough to win a race with good luck. No one can beat bad luck. I'm sure she'd have won. Just one of those quirks of fate."

Bev Carter and Joe King, who had been watching the race with some track cronies, arrived before Samsona's groom. Joe King took hold of Samsona's reins just before Jose appeared and handed Samsona over to the groom who attached a lead line onto her halter. While the groom held Samsona in place, Sue and Byron walked around the filly to see if they could detect a tear or cut of any kind. Sue stopped in front of the filly and said softly, "Easy girl, I'm going to examine those legs of yours." Sue crouched and started running her hand up and down each leg.

After fully examining the filly's legs, Sue smiled up at Byron from her kneeling position. "As Jose would say, not a pimple on her. We'll have to wait for the next big one to celebrate."

Jose's solemn expression gradually disappeared. "Look like she not even race. Too bad. Too bad. I no can believe."

"I really can't believe it, either," Byron repeated. "Though I have to admit, I've seen much worse situations here at the Belmont over the past ten years. At least she didn't break down. Track surfaces have too much sand on them these days. In the old days the footing was much better."

Sue nodded. "Could have been a lot worse; Sammy could have been hurt as well. As for the jock, I'm glad he's not hurt that seriously. Too many jocks getting hurt of late. And Sammy, she'll be able to make up for this race next time around. Have to do more gate training."

"She'll do better in the Coaching Club," Byron said with a shrug.

"I feel bad for Angel," Sue said. "He may be out quite a while."

Joe King piped in, "He'll probably have to miss the Saratoga meet where he usually is the leading rider. He's a big drawing card there and the fans, some of which never go to any other track but Saratoga, will miss him, his personality and winning smile as well as his great riding style and ability. He may be very demanding and hard on a horse at times, but no one can boot a horse home better than him."

Noticing the impatient expression on Byron's agitated face, Sue interrupted, "I'd better follow Sammy back to the stable area, watch her groom cool her out and wash her down."

"Good idea," Byron grumbled. Then changing to a more conciliatory mood, he said, "I'll see you later. I promised Bev that I'd take her and Al to Stone Henge tonight. They've been board members of S and P since it began and there's some business I want to discuss with them. Maybe you'll want to join us later on for dinner, say around eight?"

"I'd love to."

"See you there, then."

11

Frank Marone watched slant-eyed while the heavy-duty crane lifted the sports car out of the water. The small car resembled a metal fish dangling from the end of a heavy line as it was swung through the air. When it came to rest on its four tires, the water streaming out of the vehicle while it was swinging through the air became a mere trickle. Marone and a couple of other men, dressed in state troopers uniforms, quickly forced the door open, causing more of the dark salty water to flow from the car. When the car was almost clear of all seawater, Marone and his men, along with the medical examiner, started removing the two dead bodies from the front seat.

"Man I can't believe it," Marone said. His voice could barely be heard above the loud crackling noise of the crane's diesel engine. "Same MO as the others. Same heavy duty plastic bags et cetera."

"Hope there is an et cetera here," the medical examiner said. He started undoing the bag ties.

"Whoops, spoke too soon. From the looks of them, they may have been strangled first." He got closer to the victims, examining first one, then the other. After a few minutes of concentrating on the necks, Doctor Melli nodded, and said confidently, "Sure looks like it. Strangled first. We'll know for sure when I get a chance to do a full autopsy."

"Poor jokers. They didn't have a chance. Them bags again, and yet they're strangled. Someone's lousy joke? Doesn't add up." Marone appeared frustrated. "What kind of nut are we dealing with, Doc?"

"I don't know. Lots of serials out there these days, Frank."

"Tons of psychopaths. And one of them is some dumb jerk who thinks we'll buy suicide."

The medical examiner's eyebrows became raised. "Only possible if they could drive with them bags over their heads. Nope. I'm sure they were strangled. Looks like the Wilson and Stockton theme, definitely not suicides." He turned toward an assistant. May as well put them into our own bags and have them delivered to the lab." He started removing his rubber gloves. "Have you fellas been able to do anything with the info you've gotten so far?"

Marone shook his head. "Nothing from your stuff so far, plastic bags, dead bodies. Have you been able to come up with any new stuff?"

The medical examiner shrugged his broad shoulders. "Besides alcohol, found traces of sedative and another drug in Stockton. As soon as I identify the stuff, I'll pass the information along to you."

"I'd appreciate any help you can give me, Doc."

"I should have a full report to you by next week some time."

"Sooner the better, Doc."

"Yeah, sooner the better," a voice said behind Marone.

Marone turned around. "Hi Murph. Glad you got my message."

"Two more members of the plastic bag club I see."

"Yep."

"Discover anything else?"

"Not here. Making some headway elsewhere. Interviewed this Professor Sobel at Columbia."

"How'd you connect to him?"

Marone didn't want to tell him about Sue Brown. It would only diminish his mystique. "I got my sources. And it sure looks now that Wilson's and Stockton's murders definitely had a Russian flavor and all roads lead to the S and P Foundation."

"S and P Foundation? They another front for the Red Star?"

"Who knows? All I know is that it's a big outfit, supposedly non-profit, owned and run by the Stone family."

"A front?"

"Could be. So far my research says its part of a holding company and does a lot of research projects in third world countries and Eastern Europe, mostly former USSR ones. Probably why it hires a lot of Rooskies. The real catch here is that the foundation doesn't just fund projects from endowment money. It owns some mines, chemical plants. You name it. Gets a lot of its backing and funds from them."

Murphy grinned knowingly. "Connected to the EEG or The Red Star guys?"

"Maybe both."

"So where does all this take us?"

"For me, all roads lead to Byron Stone and company."

"Just like I suspected when I recommended you to Albany."

"And probably the real why behind the Feds investigating Stone's outfit."

12

Sue drove her borrowed ten-year old Buick past the multi-storied building used by the S and P Foundation as headquarters. She noted that the first floor lights were on. People working late to save the world? She sighed and turned into the driveway of the estate's main garage and parked next to two Mercedes and a shiny Rolls Royce housed in the cavernous red brick structure whose Italianate design matched the main house. When Sue got out of the car and started walking toward the road, her legs felt like lumps of iron, reminding her of the long day's work and the night before. She had gone to bed way beyond her usual bedtime, Byron having wined and dined her and the Carters almost until midnight. In spite of that, she'd arisen religiously at the usual time before sun up and had spent the entire day at Belmont, training in the morning and even watching the races in the afternoon to check out a highly touted potential rival for Samsona.

Unfortunately, the filly was in the eighth and feature race. After checking all of her charges before heading for home, Sue had noticed that one of her horses, the two-year old gray colt that Byron was very high on, wasn't eating and seemed to have a fever. Of course she had to call the vet, who responded immediately, drawing some blood samples from the apparently sick animal. Before she could finally call it a day, she went to the vet's animal hospital in Elmont to check on the blood tests.

She marched up the incline toward the guesthouse, her new home while she trained for Byron. She hesitated when she spotted someone waving at her from a maroon car parked in front of the modern mansion.

"Miz Brown, may I have a word with you."

Sue recognized the paunchy state police detective. She said sharply, "What's up?"

"You mean what's going down. We've had a couple of new homicides." Although the detective made a concerted effort to soften his usually tough sounding voice, it didn't work.

Sue appeared puzzled. "Connected with Nick Stockton's?"

"Yeah, him and his partner Wilson. We found two new bodies, woman and man, husband, wife. Found by some kids fishing from a pier when the tide went out. They see the car. Town not far from here."

"Did someone identify them? How did they die? Not like the others?"

Marone smiled at the barrage of questions. "Similar. Clear heavy duty plastic bag and all."

"Made to look like a weird suicide." Suddenly Sue forgot about her aches and pains. Her eyes said she didn't understand what was going on. "Who was it? Sounds like people I know or you wouldn't be asking me about them."

"Hate to make you stand out there in the middle of the road." The detective motioned toward the guesthouse. "Would you mind if we went to your place and sat down? I may have to take a statement from you."

"Let's make it brief. I've had a long tiring day." Sue led the way toward the guesthouse.

"That was tough luck yesterday. Too bad about Stone's horse."

"That's horse racing, as they say in the business. Luck plays a big role in any race." Sue really didn't want to discuss Samsona's race again. That was all she seemed to be doing that day whenever she saw anyone who knew she was connected with the filly.

"And in life," the detective said philosophically. "Luck, timing is everything, more important than anything else certainly. Location, location, location. Never know when you're going to be at the right place with the right person."

"Or wrong place with the wrong person," Sue snapped back, not wanting to get involved in a low-grade philosophical discussion. Sue found her keys and unlocked the front door.

A swaggering Frank Marone followed her into the house and stopped in the middle of the living room. He looked all about him with a devouring expression on his face. He had scar tissue above the eyes close to each temple, which Sue noticed. She had seen it on a groom who'd worked for her father and remembered it as the kind of scar tissue usually acquired from being battered about the face in the boxing ring.

"This is some nice place. I realize that you and Mister Stone are good friends and that you train for

him. He told me all about your relationship. You sure
are lucky to have a friend like him."

Sue didn't like the implication in Marone's voice
nor his sucking on his front teeth. "If you don't mind,
I've had a long hard day. Let's get your business over
with as soon as possible, okay?"

"Okay." The detective's eyes seemed to be all over
her, starting with her breasts and working their way
down the front of her body, making Sue very
uncomfortable. "Mind if I sit?"

"Please do." Sue plopped her own tired body into
one of the comfortable soft leather chairs.

Marone picked the couch across from her. Reaching into his soiled navy blazer, he fished out a small
notebook and a gold plated pen. "How long you
known or done things for Mister Stone?"

"Several years." Sue stared inquisitively at Marone.
"Would you mind telling me who the murder victims
are?"

The detective quickly wrote something in his
notebook before looking up and saying, "Sue, Miz
Brown. May I call you Sue?"

"You may. The murdered duo, were they people
I know?"

"I can say a definite yes."

Sue waited while Marone adjusted his pen.

"It was the guy you replaced as trainer for Byron
Stone, Al Carter, and his wife."

Sue's jaw dropped. She didn't know what to say
at first. Then with what little energy remained in
her, she said, "Al Carter and his wife, plastic bags over
their heads?"

"Same as the others."

"Why them? Doesn't make any sense, does it?"

"What does? In my eight years with homicide I've
seen a lot of things that don't jive."

"I just had dinner with him and his wife and Byron Stone. Do you have any suspects yet?"

"Hold on a sec. You had dinner with them and Stone? When?"

"Last night."

The detective wrote into his notebook. Then he looked up and said flippantly, "They must've been nabbed and iced right after." With brows raised, the detective looked over at one of the seascapes on the stark white walls. "Boy that must be worth a few bucks. Ever wonder what kind of money bought them? I'd have a tough time not being tempted with all the goodies in this place. Lately the market for stolen masterpieces has been growing. In the old days you could never get rid of the stuff, not today."

"Are we done, Mister Marone?"

Marone looked surprised. "Done? Far from it." He placed his notebook and pen into his blazer's inside pocket. "I guess I can dispense with this for now, although I'd like to see more of you soon. For now we could just discuss things informally." He raised an arrogant brow and reached into his shirt pocket. With a flourish he pulled out a fat cigar. "Mind if I light up? Don't smell no smoke in this room so I take it you don't smoke." He made a circular motion in the air with the hand holding the cigar, but made no attempt at lighting up as he studied Sue's face carefully for a reaction. "My former wife hated me smoking these things. You ain't been married yet?"

Sue's face said that she very much minded. Although he was supposed to represent the law and safety, she felt neither secure nor comfortable with Marone. She stood up, hoping the confident smiling detective would get the hint. Instead he sat back and asked, "Since you're single, you must date a lot?" It sounded like a request.

Sue stared coldly until Marone erased his arrogant smile and stuck the cigar back into his shirt pocket.

With forced sincerity Marone said, "Sue, you must get lonely up here. Long way from your real home in Southern Cal. That's where Mister Stone says you're from."

Sue just stared.

"You're a good looking girl. There must be a million guys at the university who'd give anything to date you."

Sue stated bluntly, "I don't mind answering a few questions that might help you in your investigation, but let's leave out the personal, Mister."

"Marone. Frank to my friends."

"Mister Marone, if you don't mind I've had a real long and hard day today. If you don't have any more questions, I'd appreciate your leaving so I can get myself some food and sleep."

"Food?" The detective stood up. "I'd be glad to take you somewhere for a bite. We could continue my interrogation there."

"Some other time maybe, Frank. For now, tonight, I'll have to pass."

"I get the message, Sue; although, when a lady says maybe, she usually means yes. Nah, I understand fully how tired you must be. I'm a bit tired myself." The detective suddenly tried to appear formal and professional. "I don't have any more questions for now, but this thing is far from over. Being solved. So I'll be keepin' in touch." He arose and started for the door. Grabbing the doorknob on the fixed side of the double entry doors, he said, "Whoops. I do it every time. Sort of doing and grabbing the wrong thing. Even saying the wrong thing sometimes."

"We all make mistakes."

"Sorry to keep you." Marone turned and smiled sheepishly after opening the front door. "You live here alone, I take it?"

"All alone, why?"

"You don't feel insecure?"

"There's plenty of security, including the guards at the front gate."

Marone smiled. "That's maybe like saying the guards are watching the chicken coop while the fox is inside."

"Byron Stone?" Sue sagged. "C'mon, you don't suspect him?"

"Not him, not yet at least."

"Who Then?"

"Don't want to say, yet. But I'd be careful of who I'd let into this place."

Before the detective stepped out the door, Sue asked curiously and assertively, "Where did you say the bodies were found?"

"Not too far from here, near a fishing pier. Kids fishing off the pier spotted their car, low tide."

Sue shut her eyes. When she reopened them she said, "Poor Al, Bev. It had to be someone they knew, no? What with all the bodies having been found in plastic bags and the way all the victims are somehow related to Stone Holdings' S and P Foundation, you must be able now to make some connections? Both Al and his wife were directors."

Marone scratched his considerable belly. "They were? Now why would they be members of that board? Do you know?"

"When I was having dinner with them and Byron

Stone last night, I was curious about that too, so I asked. Byron explained that his father made them directors so that they would have the extra income that goes with being a director."

"Hell, Sue, you should be the investigator on this case. Seems everything's beginning to point toward Stone Holdings. Now all we're lacking is the motive. That's got us a little baffled. Still, we'll solve this one. I can guarantee it, and it's not just a gut feeling I've got and I'd appreciate you keeping your eyes and ears open, especially since you're working so close to the S and P Foundation."

Sue said smugly, "Hope you come up with something soon. It's a scary kind of homicide, to say the least. If they're all really homicides."

"Funny you should say that. Mister Stone kept saying the exact same thing; makes me wonder why, since I've already assured him it is homicide, according to the autopsy reports." The detective hesitated just outside the doorway and looked like a serious parent admonishing a child. "Keep your doors and windows locked at all times and don't hesitate to use the 911 number. You must have a cordless?"

Sue patted her hip pocket. "I do."

Marone reached into his blazer and after fumbling around in his wallet pulled out a soiled business card. "Here keep this handy. This number'll beep me. Hold on a sec." He took out his pen and wrote something on the back of the card. "And my home phone is on the back as well. If you have any information that might help us in our investigation, don't hesitate to call me. Remember, there's a cold-blooded killer out there, several, so be careful. And believe me when I say that all I'm here for is to serve and help."

"Of course." Sue went to the door, took his card and forced it into the front pocket of her jeans.

"Them's sure are tight fitting jeans you wear, padnuh," Marone said trying to imitate a cowboy. Sue gave Marone a dirty look and shut the door in his face. After checking through the peephole to see if Marone had gone to his car, she turned and headed into a long corridor, which ran the length of the house to a kitchen. After switching on the ceiling lights, she pulled open several closet doors and found a teapot.

So far she'd never prepared a meal in her new kitchen. Even though she'd had a bite at the track kitchen just before afternoon feed time, she suddenly craved some tea that would help wash down the giant cranberry nut muffins which Byron's cook had sent over to her the day before.

Sue was about to turn away from the cabinet when her elbow caused something to fall off the shelf. When she looked down, there they were, a tightly packed bundle of plastic bags. Her heart leaped. She placed the teapot next to her feet and pulled a couple of bags from the bundle. She examined one of them, her heart racing faster and faster. She wondered what these were doing here. The bags were heavier and quite unlike any other type she had ever used or seen before, other than the one that encased Nick Stockton when they found his partially submerged body.

Sue shuddered at the thought. She'd never be able to erase that horrifying image totally from her mind. The detective's words of caution came to mind. She froze and looked around the kitchen. "What in hell are these doing here, in this closet?" They certainly weren't the types of plastic bag one found in a kitchen closet. She thought about the deaths and the location of the bags. As much as she disliked the man, she suddenly felt compelled to run after Marone.

Sue dropped the bag she was holding and rushed down the corridor. Once outside she realized that Marone was long gone. It would be a better idea to try to get him on his car phone. She felt foolish. No reason to panic. No one would have any reason to do anything to her.

Suddenly she felt a chill even though the night was warm. Could there be a psychopathic killer nearby? On the way back to the kitchen other questions entered her mind: How does Byron fit into the puzzle? Wilson, Nick, the Carters, they could all be HIV. Could all of the killings have been mercy killings? Byron didn't just know the victims; he was close to them. She shut her eyes. Except for John Wilson. "Have to show Marone the bag." She felt into her pocket for her phone. "Nah. Had enough of him for one day." She stooped and picked up the plastic bag where she'd dropped it and rolled it up before stuffing it into the back pocket of her jeans. She spotted the small teakettle she'd dropped on the floor and filled it with water.

While waiting for the water to boil, Sue pondered how the plastic bags might have been placed in the kitchen cabinet. The cleaning staff would know.

She barely heard the knock, knock at the front door. Then the doorbell rang. She listened hard before yelling, "Just a minute." She lowered her voice and said, "Maybe that dumb cop again."

She hurried down the corridor and opened the front door.

Facing her with a sad look on his face was the one person she didn't expect to see.

"Byron."

"Yeah, me. Thought I'd come down and give you the bad news about the Carters."

"I heard. That detective Marone stopped by."

Byron nodded. "The jerk wasted a lot of my time trying to get information from me about the Carters, especially Al, and how he was connected to Nick Stockton."

"C'mon in." Sue backed away after placing her hand into her back pocket to check on the plastic bag she'd found in the kitchen closet.

"I'll take a rain check. I promised the Blakes I'd be having dinner with them this evening. The Blakes and Carters had become friends."

Sue nodded. "They served on the S and P board with Blake."

"Even before my dad appointed the Carters to the board of S and P."

13

The track kitchen was filled with the odor of fried eggs and bacon as well as cigar and cigarette smoke and noise. Sue scanned the crowded, backstretch, dining Mecca. Marone hadn't arrived yet. She checked her watch.

After getting herself a bagel and a cup of the strong coffee, Sue located a corner table where she placed her tray and then planted her tired body onto a plain metal folding chair. Before she could look up, a jockey's agent had sat down on the other side of the table.

"Hi, Miz Brown. I was hoping You'd give my boy a chance on that promising two year old you'll be running soon."

"Hi Ben. We aren't ready to run yet. When it's time I'll consider him."

The little man with circles around his dark eyes looked like a sad owl. "Someone in the know told me that Al and his wife Bev was found murdered."

"I never cease to be amazed. News always travels

faster on the backstretch than anywhere else in the world."

The jockey's agent shook his head solemnly. "Someone said it was in the newspapers. Who'd do such a crazy thing? Too bad; too, too bad. Them was good folks. I ain't seen this morning's paper yet; heard it was grim stuff. Some crazy guy out there's doing strange things."

"Lots of crazies out there."

Sensing that Sue wasn't in the mood to kick things around with him, the jockey's agent placed his cigar into his mouth and moved on, hoping to find a more talkative companion.

After a sip of coffee and another bite of her bagel, Sue checked her watch again. Out of the corner of her eye she caught the detective's stocky body waddling toward her.

"Sue Brown. We meet again." Frank Marone acted as though he owned the place. "How's the coffee in this joint?"

"Rather good." They resembled a duo on a seesaw, as he sat down and she stood up. "Would you like a cup?"

He glanced at her mug of coffee. "Sounds great. Black, like yours. Gotta watch the calories these days."

After she returned with his cup, Marone sipped some coffee and asked, "So what's this important information or item you mentioned on the phone this morning?" Marone leaned forward and bounced his chair closer to the table.

"After talking to you last night, I found something that might interest you."

Marone suddenly appeared pleased and greatly interested, welcoming the unexpected opportunity of getting new information as well as being able to sit so close to Sue.

She looked all around her before whispering cautiously, "It's in my car. Hope it's worth the bother of your coming here.

Marone shrugged. "Never a bother to see you." He took a sip and nodded. "Good stuff. I've actually had no coffee this morning." He took another sip of coffee as though it were a top priority. "I gotta say this to ya, that if I've learned anything from doing this job of mine over the years, I've learned that you never know when an important clue or item might show up. You can't discount or overlook anything."

"May as well finish your coffee. This thing can wait."

Marone placed his coffee cup on the table. "Had enough." He followed Sue to the door.

Outside, Sue said, "I found some large plastic bags in the kitchen of the guest house. Right after you left me. I'm sure they're like the one someone placed over Nick Stockton's head."

Marone appeared skeptical. "That's right too. You were there when he was pulled out of the water."

Sue nodded. "I've never seen that kind anywhere else."

Bemused, Marone said, "Hey, you may have found something big. Who knows?" He shook his big head. "We've already done some research on them. They're actually manufactured by one of Stone's overseas companies. Let's go take a look."

Marone escorted Sue to his faded maroon Ford and drove it slowly up the road toward Sue's barn area. "You must be having a good time living in that fancy place, eh? Strange, though, that you and Byron Stone don't have a thing going between you."

Marone sounded as though he were probing. "He's supposed to be quite the ladies' man from what I been learning about him. Bet like one of our Presidents, he doesn't ever pass up a good one. And I've been learning other things about him as well."

Sue asked seriously, "You don't actually suspect him? Why would he want to do such a thing?"

"Or have done by someone else, you mean."

"Do you have anyone in mind yet?"

Deep in thought, Marone steered the car around a sharp turn in the road. "Right now we suspect a few people, but we still don't have all the pieces of the puzzle, evidence, motive, the usual things yet."

"I have a theory of my own."

Marone slowed the car almost to a halt. "I'm listening."

"It appears that all the victims were HIV or had AIDS. Isn't it possible that someone like Byron Stone could have had them killed out of compassion."

"A mercy killing-like?"

Sue nodded.

"Not very likely. Although, I myself have been toying with that angle, especially with a guy like Stone. He probably feels like he owns the world and can do anything he likes."

Sue shook her head. "If so, why the large plastic bags like the ones I found?"

"Who knows? Sending a message? Still, I'm glad you stumbled onto them. Whoever used the bags could have been using your place to store them."

"Byron Stone?"

"Maybe. All I really know right now is that they appear on these people's bodies that are killed and that they're heavy duty bags used only in some manufacturing programs."

"Certainly not by some of the wealthy on their estates?"

"Don't think so." Marone smiled and looked like the friendly cop on the beat as he added good-naturedly, "I ain't ever seen those bags before."

Marone parked his car across from Old Stone Stable's barn. He got out of the car and said, "Let's see what you got."

Fully satisfied that the area was clear of other humans, Sue unlocked the trunk of her borrowed Buick and handed a shopping bag containing the plastic bag to Marone.

The detective looked inside and liked what he saw. "You'll be hearing from me soon. This might be another nail in the killer's coffin. And I do like your theory about the victims being put out of their misery since they all had AIDS; thanks again for the coffee. Sure wish we could have more than coffee sometime."

Sue wanted to say: Don't count on it. Instead she just turned away quickly.

14

Royally Sure was all charged up. The powerful colt knew this wasn't his regular rider and Sue could feel it as the colt put his head down and took hold of the bit with his neck arched. Even though she had exercised a lot of horses for her father, suddenly she wasn't certain this was such a good idea. But she was stuck with it, even though the embarrassment of falling off the colt was uppermost in her mind.

Sue could feel the explosive energy radiate into the reins and up her arms. Not unlike a firecracker about to go off. As she looked back of her, she realized she had let up a little more on the reins than she should have. An older and more experienced horse was barreling up along the guardrail, a faster than usual morning workout. She knew that Royally Sure like all truly competitive thoroughbreds would want to go after the fast breezing horse. Sue stood up and tugged on the reins as the powerful colt reacted instinctively to the challenge of the horse going by him.

Barely regaining her composure while attempting to hold the colt in check, Sue pulled him further from the white plastic rail, finally allowing him to go freely at a gallop. As soon as the colt sensed her confident command, she could feel the sudden surge of power and prepared herself to go flying over the sandy soil of the deep track. Suddenly, the long striding colt's acceleration made a gentle morning breeze feel like a stormy wind. As good a rider as she was, Sue barely managed to control the huge bodied animal.

"Whoa, you're going too fast, boy," she said. Of course, it was talking to the wind. The pace was way too fast for a gallop. There was nothing else she could do but hold on and go for the ride of her life. The young colt was merely feeling good and had to release some of the explosive energy built up over time and stored inside his massive body in the confines of his stall. He seemed to be enjoying every second of his released time. Now Sue finally and actually could understand why Joe King was so high on the colt. This was truly a superior racing machine. She was happy to feel the two-year old change leads automatically as he came out of the turn and started down the home stretch toward the finish line. Out of the corner of her eye, Sue was able to see some of the spectators who had already gathered in the expansive grandstand to the right of her. It sent a thrill through her and reminded her of her younger days, when she used to bug her father about becoming a jockey; then she grew to her present size, certainly too heavy to be a jockey.

Rider and horse had rapidly reached the clubhouse turn where Sue again began to get the feeling that she had better restrain Royally Sure. He was gaining momentum and seemed to want to get away from her strong hold. She stood up in her saddle again, pulling harder on the reins with her feet pushing forward and against the irons. It was hardly enough to restrain the colt even though Joe King had said that his training had been complete, and that he was a push button horse. Just as she began to wonder about it, she was surprised when he responded positively. Horse and rider glided rapidly as one past the clockers' area where a small crowd of spectators, comprised mostly of trainers, owners, and grooms gaped.

It was obvious that most of the spectators had switched their focus to her and Royally Sure. Just beyond the clockers' stand, Sue spotted Byron standing next to Joe King. Byron waved as she went by. She would have waved back except that the colt was still giving her as much as she could handle. They were reaching the end of the gallop and though her arms and shoulders ached, she had to show the strong colt that she was still in control; yet she knew that she couldn't win in a tug of war with this particular animal, so she sat up and gently pulled on the rein as she eased back and rocked ever so slightly. Then like magic the colt started pulling up to a halt; again verifying what Joe King said: "Hard to believe, but this colt's a push-button horse."

Colt and rider had reached the area from which they'd started, so Sue trotted the colt back to an opening in the rail of the training track and pulled the colt up. She dismounted as soon as the colt's groom came over, placed a halter over Royally Sure's head and quickly snapped a lead line onto the halter.

Sue removed her sweaty riding helmet and

turned to look around for Byron, who was almost on top of her.

"Not bad." Byron put his hand on her shoulder.

Sue blushed. The adrenaline was still flowing and her lungs burned, and though she was trying to catch her breath, she said, "The ride you mean."

"What else."

"Adequate."

"You're being modest, kiddo. Especially loved your seat and the way you seemed to blend in and bounce so gracefully in harmony with the moves of your mount. Wish I could ride like that. I'd have made All-American on the polo team in college."

Although Sue resented being called kiddo, she managed a smile. "Polo? Didn't know you rode that much. Matter of fact, didn't know you rode at all. Maybe we can go riding together someday."

"Soon, I hope." Byron watched while the colt was being led away by Jose and another groom, who was apparently still learning the ropes of grooming from Jose.

"How does the colt seem?" Byron asked.

"Sure? He sure is ready. That's why I wanted to ride him today. To find out for myself." Sue smiled, swiping away some perspiration with the back of her hand to keep it from going into her eyes.

"How ready? Break his maiden first timeout?"

"He was really anchoring. Could hardly hold him. Actually gallops faster than most colts breeze, just as Joe says." She nodded decisively. "I'd say, we should be looking for him to be in the very next Maiden Allowance race in the condition book. Shouldn't wait any longer, actually. He's right there now, peaking. He needs a race and as Dad says, you can over train a young horse, any horse for that matter."

"You're the trainer." Byron stopped in his tracks. "How about you and me having dinner tonight to talk about it? Over at my place. I've been meaning to get together again for dinner, but I got all tied up by some important business."

"Connected with S and P? That seems to be a pretty active outfit lately."

He ignored her question. "We can discuss Sammy's next race as well as all the others."

"Sounds like fun."

"I came by purposely to watch you gallop the colt this morning; got to get back to my office in Manhattan." Byron checked his Piaget. "Really running late. I'll see you at the house around six."

15

Sue stood in front of the authentic renaissance door
and waited. One of the certified English butlers who
had served the Stones since the completion of his
butlers' school training opened the door and
enunciated a very British "Good evening."

"I'm here to see Mister Stone. Sue Brown."

"For dinner. He's been expecting you." The
butler showed Sue into the dining room where he
pulled one of the tufted chairs out from the long
dark mahogany dining table.

The butler announced stiffly and formally, "Mister Stone told me to tell you, Miz Brown, that he
would be running a little late. Please do make yourself comfortable. Would you like a cool drink or a
glass of wine while you wait?"

Sue shook her head and sat down. "No thank
you. I'll just wait until Mister Stone arrives."

The man's ruddy face remained impassive as he
backed away with a superior air, faint smile and a
slight nod. Sue looked all about her at the rococo

decorations of the dining hall whose darkly papered walls were vaguely lighted by a massive crystal chandelier hanging over a dining table, which could accommodate a battalion. Tall Palladian windows were partially covered by yards of faded red satin drapes, perhaps the original window dressing, only adding to the room's drab appearance.

Sue was staring at the drapes and wondering why people with so much money had neglected such a basic thing as changing them when a door at one end of the dining room swung open.

"Sorry I'm a bit late, Sue. It's been one long hard day. Haven't even had a chance to freshen up."

Sue was surprised at how tired Byron appeared. His groomed look was totally missing. Even his expensive suit jacket, looking more like clothing in the category of a Salvation Army hand me down, could have used a good pressing. She wanted to say: You do look like you've had what you just said you've had, but didn't dare.

"Did you see that investigator guy, Frank something or other? He was here when I came home. The guy can really be a nuisance, although it goes with the territory, his job, I suppose."

Sue nodded. "He can be a nuisance. What did he want this time?"

"Found a plastic bag like the one Nick Stockton was covered by."

"Did he say where he'd found it?"

Byron shrugged and sat down at the end of the table. "He wanted to know where we got the plastic bags we use around here since he knows they're not available in our local supermarkets." Byron studied Sue's face while he spoke. "Of course I gave him what he wanted to know. Those bags are produced by one

of our companies in Europe. Manufactures them
mostly for the European industrial market. The bags
are used for packaging, canvass mostly, I believe. Dad
must have started using them around Stone Henge
several years ago. You'll find them handy for garbage
disposal and such."

"Did he say he wanted to see me?"

Byron gave Sue a penetrating look. "Come to
think of it, he didn't say anything about wanting to
see you. Just asked if you were around."

"I never saw him. By the way, did you know that
both Nick and John Wilson had the AIDS virus? Also
Al and Bev Carter?"

"I had an inkling," Byron said, displaying no
emotion.

"As you know, except for Wilson, we became the
closest of friends, all three of us."

Sue made a face. "Closest?"

Byron gave her a dirty look. Then smiled broadly.
"You don't have to worry about me. I'm totally hetero,
straight arrow. Nick was like a brother to me. And
his wife Ruth was . . . She wasn't like a sister, though
we were very close, very close." He suddenly appeared
very sad.

"I know it's a bit forward of me, but were you
and Ruth ever in love with one another?"

Byron replied bluntly, "I love Ruthy a lot as a
friend; we were never what you'd call in love, though
we were lovers once. And Nick even knew about it.
He didn't mind, or at least never showed it." Byron
paused and his face and demeanor changed radi-
cally as he shouted over his shoulder, "Hey, where's
the beef? Jerry."

Two male servants, who had to be waiting just
outside the dining room doors, burst into the room

through the swinging double doors, pushing before them fancy plated carts containing large trays of filet mignon, bowls filled with endive salad, fancy rice, baked potatoes, and vegetables, including grilled asparagus.

"Help yourself, keed," Byron encouraged.

Sue didn't like the "keed" stuff, though she immediately attacked the filet mignon, which was as good as she'd ever had. "This is the very best. My fight against cholesterol hasn't allowed me to eat much of this lately. Mostly oatmeal, mush and such, it seems. Couldn't afford this, anyway, as a student."

While cutting up his filet mignon, Byron asked, "What're you going to do after you complete your studies? Probably hang out a shingle; maybe even meet a guy and before your biological clock strikes, you'll have a couple or so young ones like everyone else out there. Motherhood and apple pie stuff?"

"I don't know. Applehood and Mother pie? They're getting over-hyped lately by the media."

Byron laughed. "You mean to tell me you don't want your baby plaything and all the great stuff that goes with mothering and smotherhood? Although, I must admit that you don't seem like the nurturing type."

"There are probably too many hoods around already. I think there may be too many people on the planet. Twice as many as it can support. And a moratorium is needed on human reproduction for a while. Too many sick people out there. Even the music reflects it. All that Rap stuff. Any psychologist worth his salt will tell you that it's merely a form of clang association, schizophrenic stuff, reflecting a sick planet."

"You sound like a non-conformist."

"I guess I want to be different from most people

who seem to just do things by the numbers, a bunch of blah, number painting sequentials. And maybe I'm too idealistic, but I often think it foolish to bring anyone into a very tough and imperfect world, even with a diminished nuclear threat. Although I do fear a lurking nuclear threat from some lesser power, maybe even China, as well as a population which is gradually killing itself off with things like HIV and horrible viruses like Ebola, unless we quickly start doing something drastic about it."

"Love it, love it, really love it. Something drastic has to be done and can be done about AIDS, and Ebola; that's for sure. We think alike, you and me," Byron proclaimed happily. "Then why even bother with your doctorate, especially when you can train and work for me for the rest of your life. S and P Foundation started a new program recently that's trying to address the AIDS crisis; according to Cameron Blake it's firing on all cylinders."

"Cameron Blake?" The name tasted bitter.

"You remember him, don't you?"

"How can I forget. Met him on your boat. CEO of S and P, I discovered. You've given him an awful lot of power. Why him?"

"Dad got to know his father well and did a lot of business with his help in the Eastern block countries when no one else was doing any business there."

"Like Doctor Armand Hammer?"

"Sort of."

"I didn't know that."

Byron smiled mysteriously. "There's a lot you don't know about us. The latest program they're working on at S and P is designed to help eliminate AIDS. I'd really love to do something about the AIDS problem. Fast. A real cure's needed."

Sue's eyes lighted up. "I knew that S and P did a lot of environmental stuff. Didn't know any of the specifics."

"And that Jim guy, are you serious about him? He appears to be a nice guy. What's his specialty?"

"His research is connected with demographics, also the environment and economics."

"Stuff S and P's involved with. Think he'd be interested in a job? Love to see you end up with a decent guy."

"He's really just a friend. Someone to date. Nothing serious."

Byron sensed Sue's disappointment. "Sort of like me and Ruth." Byron shook his head and said sadly in a complete emotional about face, "I really feel bad about her and the others. AIDS has been totally devastating to my friends."

"Is Ruth HIV?"

"I've never asked her. Crazy world isn't it? Enough to drive one to drink and usually does." Byron noticed the worried look on Sue's face. Again he sounded like he had to reassure her. "I've had myself tested a couple of times. I don't have it. It's ironic, though, that my very best friends have it. That's probably why I got S and P involved."

"Damned shame."

"And you want to know something, it wasn't until after Nick married Ruthy, that I found out he's gay".

"You must have always had an inkling?"

Byron shut his eyes and shook his head. "Not a clue. He never gave a hint. And I knew the guy most of my life. Maybe I didn't want to know. By the way, why haven't you and Jim gotten serious?"

Sue shrugged. "No real spark, I guess. Chemistry?"

"Or psychology? You're both heading in the same direction, psychology. What area of psych for you? Have you decided yet?"

Sue hesitated before answering. "Oh hell. I may as well tell you. Human sexuality and sex therapy is my area of concentration."

Byron grinned. "Aha. Or should I say ah so? And you must then understand and be able to explain to someone like me, why some of us are gay and most of us aren't?"

"I wish I could. Lots of research points to its being something we're born with, the tendency that is."

"It's physiological?"

"According to one study I saw recently."

Byron smiled. "Glad I was born hetero."

"Why?"

"Less problems."

"I'm not so certain about that as you seem to be."

Byron laughed. "What about a bi?"

"What about them?"

I suppose a bi person must have the best of all possible worlds."

"Who knows? Sex can be a problem for everyone or anyone, depending on the circumstance. Even a president of the United States. Look at Clinton." She thought about her current status. "Even though I'm doing my doctoral dissertation in the area of human sexuality, I can only tell you it's a very complex subject. Take the area I'm doing my research on. I've discovered that a much larger segment of the general population are bisexual than people realize, may enjoy sex with either sex, and many of them, whom I've interviewed lately for my research project, even feel that they enjoy normal sex, whatever that is, with either sex."

"I thought you said you saw research which says we're born with our sexual tendency."

"I did."

Byron, shaking his head, said solemnly, "Hard for me to understand. Sure wish I could."

"Understand those guys you knew?"

"Yeah. Seems though, that with all this HIV stuff going around, they were doomed from the start."

Although she didn't agree with him, Sue sensed his compassion and wondered if and how someone who appeared so empathetic might be able to commit an act of homicide. Would someone like him be able to justify a mercy killing? While she and Byron ate some of their filet, she reflected on her hypothesis. With his resources, he could have had someone else do it. Someone employed by him? Was AIDS enough motivation for killing someone? Her thoughts flashed back to the night that Nick Stockton was murdered. Could it have been Cameron Blake or the fat Russian, or even Willi? Or all three? Or the yacht captain and his crew who worked for the Stones? No one really seemed to be the type, but then a lot of murderers don't seem the type. Even psychopaths and serial killers may go for years without being identified as such. Son Of Sam had a gun permit.

The questions were buzzing around inside her head when she looked up and saw that Byron was chewing on more than some of his filet mignon; his mind had to be chewing on a deep thought. After she washed down some food with a long sip of red wine, she broke the brief silence by asking, "How do you manage to stay so slim and trim with all this rich food that you eat? It is delicious and you've got one great cook."

Byron came out of his deep trance and flashed a pleased smile. "Elaine? Yeah, she is that. Dad found her many moons ago when he was on a fishing trip up in Canada. New Brunswick. He hired both Elaine and her husband on the spot and brought them back here. She can really cook Cajun style food, stuff Dad really enjoys. I should say enjoyed." He shook his head sadly. "He's taken a turn for the worse. Could be any day now."

"I wish I could see him."

"Wouldn't do any good, even if you could. He's been in a deep coma now for weeks. I'm at the point now of having to make a decision about the life support thing." Byron's strained face produced a feeble smile, as he consciously made an effort to switch topics. "To change the subject to a more pleasant one for both of us, how does our big filly, Sammy, look for next Saturday's big race?"

"She's ready, for sure. Been ready actually for weeks. We can throw out that last race, of course. She was as sharp as a tack for that one, and she hasn't lost her edge one bit from what I can tell." Sue laughed. "And you should have seen her yesterday. At the end of her gallop, from out of the blue, she jumped up in the air and almost threw me. She's really feeling good."

"You have no idea how happy I am to have you training for us, me. From what I've observed so far, and from what the other help at the track has told me, you're missing your calling by becoming a psycho." Byron paused and grinned devilishly. "A psychologist, I mean."

She moved her head sideways and said, "Not really." Then she resumed her attack on the filet for a few minutes.

Byron sounded apologetic: "You asked me about keeping fit. I do it in the gym, daily exercise program. Talking about exercise, that colt of ours, Royally Sure, was real great in his work the other day and looked even better today when you galloped him. I guess you're looking for a race for him soon, and from all the things everyone has said about him, he's going to win at first asking. Or is he? Will he be as good as Samsona?"

Sue's face brightened. "Could be. As I mentioned this morning, I've been looking for a race for him. Found one in the new condition book; Friday, this week."

"I'll be there. What race on the card and who will ride now that our contract rider is still hurt? Oh heck, you won't know for sure until you enter him. Let me know, though." Byron looked at her inquisitively. "Maybe I'm insecure. I have to ask my question again. Could Royally Sure be as good as his half sister, Samsona, or maybe even better? Maybe even compete in the big races?"

Sue waited until she swallowed her food before saying, "He shows all the signs of being a good horse. Too soon to talk about the Triple Crown or Breeders Cup. And we'd better take one thing at a time. He's got to break his maiden first. Though, I'm certain, that won't be any problem, not from the way he's been training. When we worked him out of the gate last time at five eighths, he manhandled the other two horses that worked with him. I believe one of those horses has been around a while. Running cheap now, but he was strictly allowance and handicap at one time."

"Sounds good."

"So far so good, knock wood." She knocked at

her head; then she wiped her mouth with her pink linen napkin. "This was great." She stood up. "A real treat."

Byron looked disappointed. "What? No dessert? You didn't eat that much. Like a bird. Our cook's pastries are the world's greatest, by far."

Sue placed a hand over her slightly rounded belly and patted it gently. "That food was dessert, especially the steak. And I'm tired, all fagged out. Getting up real early these days as you know."

Byron's eyes remained glued to her belly and seemed to say I'd love to rub it for you. He said, "I know and I'm responsible to a large extent. Still, you could stay a little longer, no, lots longer. You sure you won't have a coffee and an after dinner liqueur?"

Sue looked at him squarely and sighed. She wondered if this would be an opportunity missed. She said, "No room for anything else, and coffee this time of day will just keep me from getting the sleep I need to tend to your horses in the morning. It's a hands on job."

Byron winked. "I know, keed. Some other time perhaps. Keep up the good work at your hands on job. Kind I'd like to do if I had your expertise."

She would have liked having his hands on her and felt his eyes on her butt as she exited, still wondering if she was losing an opportunity that would never present itself again. But she ached and she could barely keep her eyes open.

Outside it was semi-darkness. The cool sea breeze felt good in the clear summer night illuminated by a near full moon, the centerpiece for a supporting cast of sparkling stars. With a burdened look distorting her face, Sue picked up the pace as she headed toward the guesthouse. She occasionally swatted at some of the imagined, as well as real, mosquitoes and bugs attacking her. Just beyond the lighted area of the imposing main building of the S and P Foundation, she glanced left and right, as though expecting someone or something to dart out at her. She stumbled over a speed bump and caught herself before going down. She adjusted her slacks while continuing along gingerly. Some of the smaller trees, whose branches reached out, resembled people with long arms stretching toward her. It seemed peculiar to her that what had appeared friendly by day could resemble a threatening enemy at night.

She had reached the estate garage and was happy that it was all lighted up, its lights flooding a large portion of road ahead of her. She continued at a brisk pace until she saw the car in front of the guesthouse and someone standing next to the car.

"Hey Sue. Thought you'd never get here." It was Frank Marone. Though she couldn't make out his face, there was no mistaking the coarse New Yorker voice.

She hesitated; then speeded up.

"Thought you'd never get done with whatever you and he was doing in the main house." In the detective's harsh sounding voice there was the suggestion that some kind of clandestine, perhaps even perverse, activity could have taken place.

"Dinner," Sue explained dryly. "Dinner with the boss, that was all."

"I'll bet."

The detective's contemptuous smirk was all Sue needed to make her wish that Marone would disappear. She asked angrily, "What's up, Mister Marone?"

"That plastic bag you gave me. Talked to Stone

and he admitted where it came from." Marone paused. "I seen him before I ran over to a small village restaurant a short ways from here to get a bite while I was waitin' for you, good little place, The Sea Farer. Really ain't too far from here." His knobby face grew a smile. "Me and you should try it together some time. Incidentally, I've done a little research on Stone Holdings and discovered that your boss ain't just a millionaire; he's maybe richer than the Microsoft guy, Gates, a bigger billionaire than him. Imagine. Though that don't mean he can't do murder. That's really why I'm here. You gotta be careful. Can't trust nobody these days. Nobody. Seems half the world is nuts. So you'll have plenty of work when you finish school."

"Sounds like you're convinced they were all murdered. And by the same perpetrators."

"I know they were." Marone's face assumed a confidential look. "I realize you've known this guy Stone for some time, but we found a large quantity of a strong illegal drug in the body of that Carter guy you replaced and his wife, even though they were strangled as well. And even some traces in that Stockton guy and his working buddy, Wilson. With him, at first we wasn't sure what it was, as it didn't seem to be anything lethal. It's weird. This whole thing is weird. The coroner's chief chemist and his counterpart up in Connecticut, who really keep up with the latest, traced its origins and it turns out to be a drug produced by another of Stone's outfits, in France. A big pharmaceutical outfit. Drug is used to combat AIDS. This Stone family is into everything, and Billie, my Connecticut state trooper friend, thinks he's on the trail now of some kind of conspiracy, that there's a possible link." He nodded toward the S and P Foundation building. "That big private foundation of Stone's, S and P. You know what the S and P stands for?"

Sue said wryly, "I should. I've received money from the outfit for my graduate schoolwork, a nice scholarship covering all my expenses and tuition. It was the Stone family and his cousins, the Phillips, who put it together. They even paid for my undergraduate degree. It's rather well known in academic circles and society derives great benefit from some of its research projects."

"Yeah, it's like the Ford Foundation, only bigger and more international in scope. And that prof, Doctor Sobel, who you told me is your advisor, he's in charge of some big project connected with HIV, which I found out just recently is being funded by S and P."

"You don't think that he's involved in a conspiracy under the control of Stone Holdings, do you?"

Marone's eyes lighted up. "Could be. Stone Holdings and Phillips Holdings, the big Dutch outfit. As you know, the P stands for Phillips as in Cynthia Phillips, Stone's cousin. And they do provide a lot of money for medical research as well as things like your scholarship. Various kinds of medicine related projects. Do a lot of good. And that particular drug we found in the victims was produced in one of them companies overseas that both the Stones and Phillips family owns. And it's definitely illegal in the U.S." He shook his head in disbelief. "Anyways, until we can come up with more evidence and the real motive, we can't charge anyone; still I'd be very careful if I was you. And, before I forget it, I'd appreciate if you could find out anything else that might throw some more light on this foundation, S and P. Sounds like the stock market, Standard and Poors, don't it?"

"I'll keep my eyes peeled." Sue yawned.

Marone grunted, "Don't take anything for granted though, and if you hear anything, or suspect anything, you got my number, give a call, pronto."

16

"Murdered? That's not what you first told me." Jim Morrissey scaled another flat stone across a broad band of water created by the low tide. The flattened pebble reached a sand bar separated from the sandy beach by the wide pool of water. "What makes you think it was murder?"

Sue avoided his question for a moment and instead enjoyed the mild sea breeze skimming over her face. "Boy that feels good. Just what's needed on a day like this." She was referring to the humid overcast day designed by nature and made to order for the producers and sellers of air conditioners and fans. The rounded slightly serrated outline of the noonday sun in the misty sky was barely discernable high above the beach. Except for a few playful and omnipresent seagulls foraging for food and bantering occasionally in shrill voices among themselves concerning something only they had privy to, the beach was quiet and seemingly isolated. Although very close to one of the most populated areas in the world, Sue was certain the deserted beach in front of her had rarely been used by humans.

"What do you think? Were all of them murdered?" Jim persisted while cocking his arm like a catcher and preparing to scale yet another flat stone across the water. He released a slight grunt as he let the stone fly.

Sue remained pensive and appeared to be focusing her attention on the spot where the stone plopped into the water.

Having received no response to his question, Jim continued his monologue. "When I first talked to you about it, you mentioned over the phone that the Stockton guy and his partner were HIV's and still could have committed suicide with the help of someone else. Murder is pretty serious business, involving a whole lot of worrisome things. But suicide is stupid for HIV's, especially if those guys did it on account of having HIV. Latest stuff I read says that people live many years. Matter of fact, some who got it fifteen years ago are still alive and still don't have AIDS and certainly no PCP. We've got a lot to learn about the cause of AIDS and its connection to HIV. Just because the establishment has decided this or that . . . Hey I was listening to this doctor who has a large clinic in Maine, practices homeopathic medicine, I believe." Jim reached down and picked up a flat stone to scale across another pond on the beach created by the low tide.

"Sure are a lot of stones around here."

"Even some with two feet that might be dangerous to one's health, what with all this HIV stuff going around and who knows, he might even be the one who gave it to the others." Again Jim released a grunt as he sent another flat stone sailing and skipping across the beach broadened by the low tide.

"Not Stone," Sue grumbled. "He's too healthy looking. Incidentally, I read some of the same stuff as you. That homeopathic practitioner? He's a best seller in the university bookstore. Almost picked up a copy."

"My guy and some of his cronies, other homeopathic practitioners on his show, were saying that the currently used drugs for AIDS aren't the answer and may do a lot of harm. Mainly because we don't know both the actual and causal relationships between AIDS and HIV; no matter what the establishment of so-called experts say." He reached down to pick up another flattened pebble to sling across one of the many large pools of water created by the receding ocean.

"Getting back to your original question, I'm not so sure we're dealing with a murderer here, even though it appears that they were murdered."

Jim looked confused. "Huh?"

"It's hard to explain. Except that I have a theory that maybe someone killed them to put them out of their misery."

"Mercy killing? Kevorkian-like?"

Sue's attention was temporarily distracted when a heron moved from its frozen position in the middle of a shallow pool to make a lightning strike at the prey it had been stalking. When the long-legged bird straightened up, it was holding a small sea urchin. Sue studied it and made it out to be a crab.

"Sue, wake up. What makes you so sure they were all killed like that?"

"Just a theory. That's not what this detective Marone has concluded."

"What does he think?"

"I really don't know what he thinks." Sue pointed

in the direction of the heron. "Look at that bird. It just committed murder. Only it's okay when nature does it, I guess."

"Same way a person like Doctor Kevorkian who performs mercy killings feels."

"No way. I wish you Catholics would stop picking on him. Instead of a hero, he's treated like a psychopathic killer by you guys."

Jim joined Sue in watching the bird fly off with its seafood catch of the day. Then he laughed. "Like Stone should be, maybe?"

Sue said, "Byron's no psychopath. Although I have to admit that I've wondered about him, especially because of the mercy killing angle. Whoever is doing the killings, and I have only a gut feeling about it, that person may feel a lot like that bird."

"The heron? It doesn't have any feelings."

"No, not the heron. Kevorkian. That it's okay, because there is no other way." She joined her hands together over her head. "Not that I support it one hundred percent, mercy killing. But if the Carters and Stockton were looking for a way out of their dilemmas, there is the possibility still that it may be aided suicide in spite of what that detective Marone says." She shook her head, her confusion obvious.

"I thought I read where the Carters were strangled. And it's funny that this guy Marone talks to you about it." Jim spoke with a smug expression locked onto his beet-colored, sunburned face.

Sue said smugly, "Don't let it get to you. Marone's the friendly type and according to him, they all had illegal drugs in their bodies that are used to fight AIDS."

"Almost sounds like Marone's confided in you."

Sue shrugged.

"I'm still confused about the whole thing."

"Nah. Let's face it, they were all homicides." Sue shook her head. "The only thing left to figure is the motive and that may be forthcoming real soon."

"And a special kind of psychopathic killer is on the loose and you don't seem to be too concerned." Jim laughed. "One that resembles a heron. And he could be someone within your new social circle. Living very close to you."

"Byron Stone?" Sue released a long scoffing laugh. "You don't give up, do you?"

"Okay. Believe what you want to believe."

"You're so jealous of the guy. And it shows."

Jim's head swayed backed and forth. "Y'know, it was nice of you to invite me out here today—to pick on me. And this whole place makes me feel very, very uncomfortable, like a fish out of water. I guess I'm a city slicker at heart, just as you're a country girl at heart. This American brand of the Taj Mahal? That's not me, either of us. I really don't feel comfortable at all on these hundreds of acres of robber baron acquired land, maybe one could even say confiscated territory." He snickered and added, "Still, I must admit, some great bedrooms in that place you now call home."

Sue snuggled up close to him and put her arms around his waist, which she felt could have been slimmer and would have been if he hadn't indulged in as much beer as he did. She made what sounded like a purring sound, before saying, "What? You want more?"

"All kidding aside, Sue, there are other things we could have done on your day off. Some time I'd love to go to the race track with you."

"Horse racing? You'd go?"

"Funny we never discussed horses much and here you are training horses at Belmont. This is one crazy world. I never would have guessed. You've talked about your small farm ranch in California. Didn't figure you knew so much about training them nags at Belmont. Big time stuff." He appeared overwhelmed.

"You'll have to come to our next big race."

"Love to. Haven't been to the races in ages. Used to love it when Dad and my uncle Dan used to take me to Aqueduct or Belmont when I was a kid. Loved looking at the big animals in the walking ring before a big race. Even saw some great horses. So maybe one of these days I will meet you there."

Appearing delighted, Sue released her hold on him, stopped dead in her tracks and stood back chiding, "It's funny. You never once indicated an interest in horses or the racetrack, so it never occurred to me. And most men don't seem to like horses as much as women do, except to bet on them at the track or with bookies. I wish you'd told me sooner. We could have gone to the track today. Still can." She looked at her watch. "Plenty of time left. We could still make the second race, maybe the first at Belmont and even have lunch there. And later I can look after some business there." She made a funny face. "No, I just never thought you were in the least bit interested. You've never given a clue until now."

"Well now you know. Not today though. I'm a bit short on cash and I've committed myself to going back to the university this afternoon. My advisor is willing to go over some stuff that I researched the other day, and you know how Kirby is when it comes to giving any of us some of his precious time."

"I know. By the way, didn't Kirby collaborate with

Doctor Sobel on some demographic study having to do with AIDS in Africa?"

"Now that you mention it, he did. And it was funded by none other than Byron Stone's outfit, S and P foundation of all things." Jim sniffed at the brisk sea air. "Since we're here on your favorite beach in the East, let's take a walk toward that lighthouse over there. Seems like an interesting spot to explore." He pointed in the direction of a peculiar square-shaped, tapered building, surrounded by a dark mound of huge granite slabs and rocks being buffeted by the dark green waters of the Atlantic.

They followed the beach up to the top of a gradually rising promontory and down the other side into a less flat area of rocky beachfront abutting a field containing fir and pine trees which had been methodically and neatly planted.

Jim said, "That's some tree farm; meticulously maintained." He pointed toward a dirt road leading to and through the broad stand of trees.

Sue said, "That road must go back to the main estate road."

Jim snickered. "Must be how Stone gets to his private Christmas tree reserve."

"You really don't like him."

Jim shrugged. "What's to like? I don't really know him."

Sue marveled, "All his as far as the eye can see. Let's try that pathway." Sue pointed to a small road, which appeared to run parallel to the beachfront through several rows of smaller trees.

"Lead on, Daniella Boone," Jim encouraged. "Let's go traipsing through little Byron Stone's big Christmas tree preserve."

The path cut through coarse patches of Bermuda

grass and took them up to a bluff overlooking a broad
flat area with sand dunes and a sea wall running along
its edge. The path disappeared in the deep wind
blown sandy soil, so they halted momentarily as they
spotted and studied the interesting and imposing
structure just ahead of them. Sue and Jim both were
intrigued by the large two story stone building, which
was built at the edge of the ocean where the large
stone seawall ended abruptly. Jim asked, "Wonder
what that place is used for? What giant toy or toys
does it store for the robber baron of the castle?"

Sue caught her breath and said, "I've been here
before, only we came up another road." She looked
around. "The paved road, over there." She pointed
in the direction of the road. "It's hard to believe. I
knew Byron was taking me to a private yacht club.
Didn't realize just how private at the time."

"His own private yacht club." Again Jim didn't
try to hide his jealousy. "For him and his company's
execs, no doubt."

"That I hadn't figured out then, but I still hadn't
a full realization of just how enormously rich he really
is."

"Him and Bill Gates."

"Marone mentioned that." As they got closer to
the imposing structure, they were forced to move
slowly. The sandy soil seemed finer and deeper the
closer they got to the gray granite building whose
long rectangular windows gave it the appearance of
an armory or fortress. They paused briefly to catch
their breaths before trudging another forty or fifty
yards to a cement and stone walkway in front of the
building. The walkway led to some stairs where Jim
put his hand up and said, "Whoa. Look there."

Sue had already started down a wide granite stairway and was just about to step onto a thick-planked wooden pier. She stopped and studied a motor launch in the water next to the wooden dock.

"Hold on, Jim." Sue recognized the man sitting in the operator's seat of the sleek launch. He was one of the crewmen of the Zenith. She whispered, "Let's not be too hasty." She studied the large yacht at anchor in the tiny inlet. The Zenith was like the flagship among a flotilla of several smaller yet impressive sail and powerboats at anchor on either side of it.

When Jim spotted the Zenith he said cynically, "Bet that's Admiral Byron's boat."

"It's the Zenith. The yacht that took us to his summer place in Connecticut."

"Where Stockton got it? Look at that boat will ya, looks like a converted destroyer."

"Sh."

"What in the hell are we whispering for?" Jim asked angrily.

Sue put her index finger over her lips. "I thought I heard some voices coming from the yacht."

The voices grew louder as three men emerged from a cabin onto the broad aft deck of the Zenith.

Jim asked with a stupefied expression on his freckled face, "Why in hell don't we go back to where we belong? Don't really want to see the robber baron again."

Sue put her hand over Jim's mouth. "Nor I. Not today." With her other hand she pulled him down as she knelt and continued to try to make out what the trio were discussing. She said, "I thought I heard one of them say Ruth Stockton's name. Didn't you?"

"Now we're playing junior G-men?" Jim grumbled.

Sue listened intently for several minutes. When the three men went over to the other side of the boat their voices faded and finally became inaudible. Sue whispered, "Did you hear what I thought I heard? I'd swear I heard someone say, Ruth is next."

Jim shook his head. "I'm not sure what I heard. You've always been better at eaves dropping than me. You seem to enjoy doing it in restaurants. I'm not sure, but I think I heard the names Bev and Al, and I believe the other was Ruth and the word replacement."

"I heard Ruth mentioned a couple of times."

"What're we playing, a numbers game or something?" Jim appeared agitated. "I did recognize the robber baron, Stone; who're his cronies?"

"Cameron Blake, a guy who works for Byron. He was on his yacht last week. He's not just a friend. He heads up the S and P Foundation and apparently is involved with Byron in other ways, other projects."

"He's an accomplice in international crime, you mean," Dan said harshly. "Who's the other gee-balky looking guy?"

"I really don't know him that well. His name is Willi Van Woort, a boy friend of Cindy Phillips, Byron's cousin." Sue smiled as she thought she'd discovered something new. Willi never left the dinner table the night of Nick Stockton's demise. She recalled how Blake along with Byron's administrative assistant, Boris, and even Byron had left their lobster dinners to check on something. "Now, I'm more mystified by all that's happened and where I've been and who is involved."

"You are playing detective," Jim emphasized. "What now?"

"I'll tell you later. Let's get back to my place."

"Your place? That's his place, the little dictator's place, you mean." Jim struggled to his feet. "Su casa it isn't, and besides I'm hungry," Jim grumbled and with a disgruntled look on his face, ordered, "Let's get the hell out of here. I can't see spending the rest of the day spying on a bunch of birds I don't even know, nor have any idea why the hell I'm doing it." He turned abruptly. Almost leaping up the granite stairway, he headed in the direction of the tree farm.

Sue checked to see if the operator of the launch had detected her. When she saw his face smiling at her, she forced a smile and waved.

Sue caught up to Jim and said angrily, "I've just a healthy curiosity concerning the murders or possible mercy killings or aided suicides. Aren't you the least bit interested?"

Jim shrugged his broad shoulders. "Not when it doesn't affect me, and you know, I hate to say this, because I'm not too fond of your employer, you could ruin a real good thing from what you've told me. He's paying you more money in a month than you've ever made in a year, and more, if what you told me about the bonuses is true, and I don't doubt it after seeing what this bird owns. This whole thing, it boggles my mind."

Sue said softly, "Mine too." She hooked onto Jim's hand and dragged him along with a sudden burst of energy, as though she were leading a pouting child to a happier place.

17

The fifth race was only a half hour away. The voice over the backstretch loudspeaker was already blaring out, "Get your horses up for the fifth race, amigos. Get them there on time. Get them heading there now, guys."

Sue's face reflected the occasion. Anxiety and butterflies were fluttering around inside of her gut. With wrinkled brow, she watched like an eagle as Jose carefully put the finishing touches on the big gray colt. Royally Sure appeared very alert and aware that something new was about to happen to him. While Jose was brushing him down, though he was a kindly animal, the playful colt attempted an occasional nip at Jose's tee shirt. The colt's large inquisitive eyes rolled right and then left when Jose started placing the headband of his reins over his ears. While Jose slipped the colt's ears through the headband his closed eyelids quavered slightly. He opened his eyes just in time to follow Jose, who gave the colt a tug on the lead line and started leading him toward his primary destination, the saddling enclosure.

"Not much of a crowd today," Sue shouted to Jose who was already leading the smoothly striding colt out the side door of the barn. Sue caught up to Jose.

"Si, small weekday crowd."

"Sort of happy about that even though track management isn't. Sure won't have that old wall of noise to contend with when he moves into the stretch for home. Hopefully he'll be alone when he comes toward the finish line. I'll meet you at the saddling area. I'm going to drive over."

In the parking area reserved for trainers and owners Sue found a parking space. Although attendance was down, there was usually a full contingent of trainers at the track on any given day. At the gate near the paddock area, she showed a stern looking white-capped attendant her trainer's badge and passed through a turnstile. She hastily made her way into the paddock area and looked around for Byron. He wasn't in the small infield area of the walking ring. Disappointed, she took up her position in the paddock saddling area and shaded her eyes as she scanned the spectators gathered around the rail separating them from the walking ring. Then her eye caught a couple of people waving toward her from a park bench. Byron Stone and Joe King were sitting under one of the giant shade trees in the park-like setting of the paddock area.

"Four to one. Generous, really generous," Sue muttered as soon as Byron arrived at her side.

"He looks great," Byron said, nodding toward Jose who was leading the big gray colt into the paddock area. "Look at the way those muscles ripple in his dappled skin."

A. D. RUSSO

Jose led Royally Sure onto the finely graveled area
in front of them. "He seems to have grown overnight," Byron said in awe as he watched Jose walk
the gracefully striding colt around the walking ring
before taking him into his paddock stall.

Joe King had strolled over to Sue's side. "Ain't
ever seen a colt with such stunnin' good looks; he's
not your typical young horse. Appears made of steel.
Look at them other colts; ain't none look like him."
Joe motioned toward two other colts in the race,
which were being walked around the finely graveled
walking area in front of them.

Turning to Sue, Byron remarked, "Hey trainer,
look at them odds." He pointed at the tote board.
"Three to one."

Sue watched the new odds blinking onto the
board. "Nope. Five to two. Probably be even money
by race time. Can fool some of the people some of
the time, as Barnum said, or something like that,
but you can't fool them at good old Belmont, or
Aqueduct. This New York crowd, the betters at least,
are a canny bunch. Sophisticated bunch of betters, I
guess the term is. Hard to find an overlay or under-
lay here. There's an occasional long shot, usually they
know exactly what to bet."

Joe King appeared pleased, especially after Royally Sure was led calmly around the walking ring while
one of the other two year olds in the race was showing his immaturity by acting somewhat rank. His han-
dler was doing all that he could to keep the dark bay
colt from getting away from him.

Watching the hard to control colt for several minutes, Sue was happy that she had become the recipient of a well-trained potential super star. She looked
at her watch and motioned for Jose to bring the colt

back to his saddling stall. Several owners began to appear in front of the stalls. The men were neatly dressed in expensive sport clothes, while the women wore fashionable designer dresses. Some of the women had on the latest in hats as well. Even Sue wore a new pleated denim skirt and frilly blouse, as she wanted to be dressed properly for the expected winner's photo.

Byron noticed her neat new outfit, and teased, "See you're all done up for the picture. That's confidence, isn't it folks?" He beamed an impish smile and started walking toward the tunnel under the Belmont Clubhouse. "I'll meet you in my box, Sue," he said over his shoulder.

Sue nodded, having already begun the saddling procedure. "Okay." She had to push against the now suddenly fidgety colt to help Jose steady him. She wondered how much the rank appearing colt in the walking ring had to do with the way Sure was behaving. She helped Jose hold the colt in place while the track valet assigned to her horse put the saddle clothe and small racing saddle on Royally Sure's back.

"He must be close to sixteen and half hands," the diminutive valet said admiringly, as he had more than a little difficulty reaching up and over the colt's high withers. "Hope he runs like his sister." He smiled with the confidence of one who was really in the know.

"Hope so, or even better," Sue said approvingly, adding cautiously, "Should do okay."

"It's his first time out and he's a baby to boot, never know what they're going to do first time out." The valet again smiled knowingly and left as soon as Sue gave the saddle strap another tug for insurance sake.

"You can take him around the walking area again, Jose. May as well keep him well oiled."

The groom smiled and took the colt back to the walking area. Sue watched them until the jockey she'd chosen to ride the colt appeared. He was the leading apprentice at the meet and appeared on his way to becoming another Angel Cordero. So she felt she was taking very little risk with him and she liked the idea of the young horse gaining a weight advantage. There was a waiting line for the precocious eighteen year old's services, but his clever agent didn't want to lose an opportunity to serve Old Stone Stable and the shrewd agent knew that Royally Sure was the kind of horse which had the potential of becoming a great horse and would be highly sought after later on.

"Hi, Kenny," Sue greeted. "Looks like an easy field."

"Hi, Ma'm," the young Cajun said, smiling shyly.

"I guess you know what to do. As I told your agent and you this morning, he's as good as he looks. Got lots of speed, more than likely classic speed, although we'll know more after today. And he's really fit. So we can take a chance and get him right out there. Actually you'll have to since you're in the seven hole. You know the rest."

The jockey smiled confidently and nodded.

"Ridersss up," a man shouted in back of Sue, so she helped the jockey mount the colt by giving him a leg up. The gray colt was being restrained by Jose who was standing in front of the colt and putting a little pressure on the bit in the colt's mouth for control.

"Bon chance," Sue shouted as horse and rider started toward the tunnel. She followed a short distance behind until they reached the track proper. The horses' entrance onto the main racing surface was being announced by the official track trumpeter, dressed in his bright track finery. He blew so hard on his long French trumpet that his face almost matched the color of his bright red jacket.

The excitement of the moment suddenly caught up with Sue, especially now that her race preparation chores were all out of the way. Her heart raced rapidly. She climbed the stairs to the box seats, but instead of joining Byron and his guests, Sue first went to the betting windows inside the cavernous second level of the clubhouse. She found the fifty-dollar window. "Fifty on Royally . . . number seven." Usually she bet no more than ten dollars on a horse, but she felt so certain of Royally Sure that she decided to splurge. The clerk at the fifty-dollar window smiled as though he recognized her as the trainer of Royally Sure. After he punched in the numbers for Sue's ticket, he said, "Good Luck on your horse, Miss Brown."

Sue smiled as she plucked her ticket coming up through a slit in the counter from the betting machine and wondered how he could possibly know that she was the trainer of Royally Sure. Before she reached the box seat area with the new and strange feeling of having attained instant celebrity status, she nodded knowingly and her face cracked a faint smile, produced by the sudden realization that the track grapevine had to be working overtime.

"He's what I said, even money," Byron told Sue when she joined him in Old Stone Stable's box across from the finish line.

"Everyone knows he's related to Samsona." Sue watched the horses warm up across the track with her compact, newly purchased, state of the art binoculars. "He's doing everything right. Maybe I shouldn't say it."

The familiar "it is now post time" rang out over the track loudspeaker, and as the excitement mounted, so did the crowd noise. Right after the loud announcement of "They're off" by the track announcer, Sue and the others in the boxes around her stood up and started cheering, "C'mon, Sure." But Sue and Byron abruptly stopped their cheering. It was obvious that Royally Sure and the colt next to him in the sixth hole had collided as the two colts emerged from the gate. Sue could discern with her glasses how bad the start had been as almost all the colts came out of the gate in a tangle, bumping into one another. Someone behind her said, "Babies."

After watching to see that Royally Sure had recovered and was starting to run after the other colts, Sue lowered her glasses and groaned. "He, the boy made an error, of judgment, I think. Instead of taking Royally Sure to the right and away from the other green horse, the jock went into the horse coming at him on the left and pulled up on the reins too hard. Reared up as they were coming out."

There had been several other gasps of despair around Sue. The colt's betting backers and well wishers seemed stunned as they watched and heard the track announcer say, "Royally Sure, the favorite in this race, got tangled up with Ray's No Fool coming out of the gate and seems far . . . No he's making up ground even though he trails the rest of the field by four lengths." The track announcer continued with his call. Sue hardly heard a word he was saying as she concentrated on the race and what was currently happening on the far turn now that the horses approached the three-eighths pole.

"C'mon Sure, you can make it up," Sue said. She had dropped her binoculars and was watching without them, feeling she'd miss too much by the time she'd adjusted them to her eyes again. "He's moving good, real strong, making up a ton of ground. He's going by the horse that bumped into him. Urge him Kenny; keep after him. You've got to go all out now." She was calling the race for the others around her as the track announcer's voice was being obliterated by the increasing crowd noise. "They're at the . . . He's catching them . . . quarter pole. C'mon, c'mon, Sure. You can do it." Sue was bobbing her head and rocking her body tensely back and forth as though she were riding the horse. "He's gonna... he's caught 'em." Byron and several others joined her in forming a chorus, shouting, "C'mon Sure, c'mon Sure," as there were now five horses running abreast across the track in a cavalry charge with Royally Sure running on the outside. The furiously contending colts, whose riders were gyrating in their saddles while whipping and urging all the harder, passed the sixteenth pole. Royally Sure's large gray body resembled a giant greyhound as he took enormous leaps forward, his strides seemingly greater and more dynamic than those of his tiring rivals.

"Iii..It's Royally Sure across the finish line first," the race announcer's voice shouted above the din of the crowd. Then he added, "Hold onto your place and show tickets folks. Photo for the rest."

Now that the race had ended, a relieved Byron Stone said, "Who said winning is easy?" Then he smiled, "It sure beats losing though, and it was well earned. I've got to admit I never thought he'd make up that much lost ground. He's a marvel. Let's go take the well deserved picture, Sue." He got up and led the way; he couldn't stop praising his horse until they reached the stairs leading down to the Winner's Circle. There, Byron politely stepped back and allowed Sue to pass in front of him. Sue would have let her owner go first if she were following the usual racetrack protocol, but she was too caught up in the excitement of the moment.

Jose held Royally Sure's reins tightly and was already posing in front of the winning horse and smiling jockey when Sue and Byron arrived in the Winner's Circle. The big gray colt with a smattering of moist sandy soil clinging to his sweaty face and lower legs was blowing and breathing hard through his flared nostrils whose membranes appeared a bright red.

After the photo was taken and the jockey dismounted, Sue took the diminutive man aside and confronted him with, "What happened in the gate? Pretty scary start, if I must say so myself."

The jockey shook his head apologetically and lowered it so that his eyes were completely glued to the ground in front of him. "I don't really know ma'm except that the starter was holdin' onto the colt's tail when the bell rang and the gate opened. It might have caused us to come out slant-wise, sort of crooked, and it didn't help when that totally green horse next to us came veering toward us too, so I ended up having to pull up a little bit to avoid the collision."

"Couldn't you have pulled to the right to avoid it, rather than pull up?" Sue asked sharply, her displeasure written all over her face, as she recalled the alibi used by the jockey for Samsona's last race.

"I dunno, maybe I was to blame, or maybe it was the other horse, but that starter holdin' the colt's tail too long didn't help one bit. Some of those guys, well they get a drink or two in 'em and boffo."

"Luckily it turned out alright. You rode him well as it turned out." Sue smiled and gave him a pat on the shoulder.

"Wasn't me, ma'm," The tiny man said honestly and firmly, his big jaw jutting out from a sinewy neck and body. He raised his head finally and looked Sue squarely in the eye. "That gray colt of yours, he's able to make up all the lost ground easy like, and he sure made up for anyone's mistake." The young man's tapered face was like stone. His voice flavored with a Cajun twang, he said, "He gonna be a good un, huh? I'd say maybe even a great un off'n today's performance. Sure love to ride him agin."

"Thanks again," Sue said with a faint smile, as she knew she wasn't going to have second thoughts about using the young jockey again. Her first choice would always have to be Old Stone Stable's contract rider, Angel Santos, who was recovering quickly. She had even talked to his agent that morning and the jockey's agent had assured her that Santos would be well enough to ride Samsona in the stakes race on Saturday.

18

Sue thought she'd give it one more try. She dialed Ruth's number and waited. She had tried to get her earlier. She glanced at the envelope containing Royally Sure's winning photo. Byron had had an extra photo taken for Ruth. Good excuse to call her.

"Hello."

"Ruth. This is Sue Brown. How are you doing?"

"Sue, good to hear from you. Funny, I was just about to call you. Byron said that he'd had an extra photo taken of his big colt, Royally Sure. I meant to be there for the race, but something came up. Last minute. I really love that colt. Nick had a half interest in his damn."

"In Samsona's dam? Wow."

"Had, originally, but Nick sold his interest. Too soon, even though Byron gave Nick a lot of money for his half interest, which he originally gave Nick and me for peanuts. Byron's so generous."

"He is. When can I come over and drop off the photo? I'm free right now."

There was a slight pause. "Now's okay. Do you know where I live? I'm actually not too far from Byron's."

"I'll need directions."

After giving Sue directions, Ruth stated, "I hope you can stay a while. There's a thing or two I'd like to discuss with you. I understand that you know Doctor Sobel. That you've done some research work for him."

"He's one of my doctoral advisors. The research work I do isn't really for him; it's for my doctorate."

"Advisor? All the more reason why I'd like to see you and talk to you about him and some of his connections. I'll tell you all when you get here."

"See you in a short while."

Sue went into the bathroom to check her face and comb her hair. She wanted to look good for the former model. She grabbed her car keys and the brown envelope containing Royally Sure's photo. She checked her watch. It would take a good ten or twenty minutes to get to Ruth's condo.

Sue noticed several very large limos parked in front of Byron's main house as she turned into the separated two-lane road running out to the main road. Byron must be having another big bash this evening, she thought. Lately there seemed to be a lot of limos and fancy cars parked in the long circular driveway in front of the main house. She hadn't seen Byron in almost a week, not since Royally Sure's race. Even though she had expected to be invited to a small celebration, it never happened. She shrugged her shoulders as she drove down the long tree-lined road to the main gate. She'd be seeing him in a few days when Samsona would be running in the biggest graded stakes race of her life. Sue stopped and waited in front of the massive wrought iron main gate. The uniformed guard recognized her and flashed a friendly smile before pushing a button to make the heavy gate slide open. Sue drove down the county road toward the Parkway. There was little or no traffic on the back roads or even the expressway. Sue checked the speedometer. She was going way over the posted speed limit and the old bucket of bolts was doing it easily. She appreciated the completely remade from scratch vehicle. It had to be more powerful and more efficient than the original. Oh, what money can do. While growing up, she would have resented what money could do. The very rich who had horses with her father seemed spoiled by it. Some of them acted as though wealth gave them power to dictate to others. But Byron's father never acted like the others.

When Sue finally found Ruth Stockton's condo, dusk had fallen over the modern stone-faced structure. She parked in front of the structure, which wasn't joined to any other.

Sue pressed the doorbell button and waited. After a few minutes, she pressed again and waited a few more minutes. Decision time. Leave the photo under the door? As she reached down, her hand nudged the door open.

Sue shouted instinctively, "Ruth, are you there, you okay?" Her heart raced as she waited in the unlighted vestibule, which was an atrium filled with plants and vegetation. She stepped forward cautiously. No sense in getting anxious, she told herself; after all she'd just spoken to Ruth. The Italian marble tiles felt slippery under her leather sandals.

Sue noticed light coming from a room off the main corridor of the condo so she advanced toward it. "Ruth?" She peered into the room, a large master bedroom. When she saw the object on the bed, she froze.

"Not another one?" A gasp came out of her constricted throat as the back of her neck tightened and she felt her stomach heave. Her eyes grew with fright as she looked at Ruth Stockton's body lying flat on her bed with a clear plastic bag over her head.

Sue covered her mouth with her hand and looked all around the room. Her first thought was like that of a horse in danger: flight. Instead she pulled herself together and went over to a phone she spotted on the bureau. She punched in nine one-one. Before she got a response, Sue put the receiver down, fished Frank Marone's business card from her wallet and punched in his phone number with her index finger. She caught her breath and waited. The phone buzzed several times before the abrupt and coarse-sounding New Yorker's voice responded.

"Yeah, Marone here."

"Hi, this is Sue Brown. I, there's been another . . ." She couldn't say the words.

Marone said, "Calm down, Sue. What's up?"

Sue blurted out, "I found Ruth Stockton in her condo. She's been... Please come as fast as you can."

Marone didn't have to say the "m" word. "Don't touch a thing. You called the local cops yet?"

"Not yet. Should I have?"

"You done good. I'll be right there. Don't touch a thing. Matter of fact, wait for me outside. I think I have her address, but run it by me again."

Sue hadn't given him the entire address. Loud click. Marone was on his way. She placed the phone down and hurried out the front door of the condo like a scared animal, almost tripping over herself several times even though the condo complex's streetlights were on.

Sue got into her car, locked the doors and waited. She barely had time to wipe her tears when a car with a flashing light on its roof pulled into the condo parking area. She got out of her car and waved to Marone.

"You must've blown away a few cars to get here so fast. You had to be close by." Sue looked at her watch.

"Car phones come in handy. Just happened to be heading in this direction from Kennedy. Isn't far from where I live."

"I guess," Sue said, hoping Marone wouldn't notice her reddened eyes. She began to regain some of her composure in the cool evening air.

"Let's have a look." The detective acted calmly and forcefully. "We'll have to call the local yokels, but I wanted to see the setup before they did. Sometimes they mess things up. Did she have the same plastic bag thing over her head?"

Sue nodded while following closely behind the detective. "Yes. It's an eerie thing. I didn't know how to deal with it, so I thought about you."

"Especially now that we know where the darn things come from. And they've bagged two more."

"Two more?"

"Yeah, she was pregnant."

"How'd you know that?"

"Your boyfriend Byron told me. That's why he thought her husband had committed suicide—at first. He said Stockton was afraid he made an HIV baby and couldn't live with the idea. You can wait out here," Marone ordered. "I'll be but a minute."

Sue waited. It was many minutes before Marone emerged from the condo building; he was holding a small plastic bag containing a variety of items.

"I called the local guys. They should be here in a few minutes. They'll want a statement from you. I'll wait around too, and I don't think it'll take too long. Then maybe you and me can talk, say over a coffee. I found this note in her hand. Had to pry it loose. Whoever did it must have left in one big hurry to leave it behind. Maybe you and me can figure out what it means."

"I know. I was just talking to her and it couldn't have taken me more than fifteen minutes to get here from my place."

"Hope you haven't got something planned for this evening."

"I'd rather be doing something else. Don't think I've got much choice." Sue's face reflected her frustration and discouragement.

"Unfortunately the local cops will want a full account, a somewhat detailed picture as to the what and why of you being here." He nodded, pushing out his hand in a reassuring gesture. "Don't worry though, I'll help all I can so you won't have to go through the third degree with those jerks. Just let me handle it."

The local police crime squad arrived in a matter of minutes and immediately placed the usual yellow crime scene demarcation ribbon around the front of the condo unit. Sue waited while the chief inspector talked first with Marone and wrote something on a small pad. He entered the condo accompanied by Marone and another policeman. When he came back outside with Marone following him, the police inspector checked what he'd written on the small pad and said politely, "Detective Marone tells me that your name is Sue Brown and that you found . . ." He checked the pad again. "Miz Brown, according to detective Marone, you found the body of Ruth Stockton with the plastic bag over her head and you immediately called him. Is that correct?"

Sue nodded. "Quite correct."

"You didn't touch anything in the condo unit?"

"Nope. Couldn't wait to get out of the place."

"That's understandable. Real gruesome stuff." The police inspector motioned with his head. "Why did you come here in the first place? Mrs. Stockton a close friend of yours?"

Sue explained, "I came here to deliver a photo to her and found her lying there."

"Oh yes, Marone told me that. How come you just walked into the apartment? You a real close friend?"

"The door was open, unlocked I mean. She had been expecting me, so I walked in."

Marone intervened. "If you guys don't mind, I've been working on the case for some time," Marone said assertively, "I can fill you in on all the details later. I want to spend a little time interrogating Miz Brown myself. And I'm sure she'll be available whenever needed, so . . ." He turned to Sue and said, "You can leave your car here for a little while," and escorted her back to his car.

"Where are we going?"

"There's a great diner on the Boulevard. We can talk there." Marone opened the door of his car for her and rushed around to the driver's side.

Sue was happy to escape the clutches of the tough looking precinct head detective.

While driving his cruiser out of the condo parking

area, Marone asked, "Have you heard or uncovered any new info that might be useful? Was there any indication when she asked you to come over that Ruth Stockton might be in any immediate danger? Sounds like you didn't know about her latest circumstance, but did you know that she might be HIV infected like all the other plastic bag victims?"

"I knew, sort of," Sue responded.

"How'd ya know that?"

At first she wanted to say Byron told me. Instead she said, "Actually it was obvious; she was Nick Stockton's wife and he had it. And I might add that Byron may have had good reason to believe what he did about Nick Stockton."

"Maybe at first." Frank Marone's head became tilted. "Nah. And there now appears to be a very strong common thread running through the homicides."

"The HIV thing?"

"That and a little more."

"Sounds like you're closing in on a possible motive and who the perpetrators are."

Marone smiled. "Yeah, perps, plural. It's too big an undertaking for one guy to do."

Marone stopped his car at a traffic light in front of a strip mall. Sue's eyes happened to be focused on clothes in the window of a fancy boutique. Marone noticed and said bluntly, "You'd look nice in one of them dresses there in the window of that store." His slanted, probing eyes seemed to be sizing her up as he snickered, "You must be a farm girl; you always wear them farm clothes." As he drove the car away from the light, he said caustically and as though coming out of a trance, "The HIV is a strong piece of evidence, but there's more. It looks like the same

MO at work even with your friend back there." He motioned back by a lift and jerk of his head.

Sue suddenly recalled the conversation that she and Jim Morrissey had overheard at Byron's private yacht club when they were exploring Stone Henge's beachfront. "There is something I have to tell you about. It may or may not be important. When I went for a walk along the beach with a friend of mine from the university, we thought we heard Byron and two of his friends discussing Bev Carter and Ruth Stockton."

The detective glanced sideways. "Concerning?"

"For what its worth, we, no just I actually, over-heard Byron say to his friends, something like, Ruth . . . I'm not sure of the exact words, but he indicated that she had to . . . Now I remember, at least I thought I heard him say after I heard Bev Carter's name, Ruth is next."

The detective snapped, "Who were the other guys?"

"Willi Van Woort, who works for his cousin's Phillips organization and Cameron Blake."

Marone's smile was a knowing one. "We have a clear line on both of those guys. You're right about that Van warts guy. And Blake, Doctor Blake, you know about. It amazes me that he's such an odd duck and the Stones made him head of their big Foundation which among other things controls pharmaceutical outfits all over in Europe."

"S and P is into pharmaceuticals too?"

"Billie, you know, my counterpart in Connecti-cut, he's come up with the fact that Stone's outfit and The Phillips outfit are sort of intertwined. They support S and P together. Did you know that?"

"It makes sense."

"And this Van Worts guy, he's one of the big execs for the Phillips outfit in Holland where they have their main headquarters. So he and Blake must work together at times." Marone paused and concentrated on his driving for a while.

"Byron Stone's empire is bigger than I thought. I'd sure love to know how and if he's behind these . . ." Sue's face reflected the sad and empty feeling she was experiencing as she thought how really remote her chances were of ever becoming close to Byron.

"So would I. Hey, don't worry we will, in time. There's a lot to work with."

"I'm not so sure. There's so much to it. It seems so complex, so confusing now."

"We're there," Marone grunted. He steered the car slowly up a driveway and into a parking lot in front of a twenty-four hour diner. He parked, turned off the motor and said sourly, "AIDS is causing people to do a lot of strange things. I never thought it would come to this."

"Do you think it's possible that these homicides might all be merely mercy killings?"

"Merely? Now that I found this note in the dead woman's hand back there, I'm not so sure that that might be where it's all at."

"Why? What did it say?"

"Just a few words scribbled on it. Here." Marone produced the note from his lapel pocket and handed it to Sue.

Sue read aloud, "S and P. Sobel. Backfire." She handed it back to the detective.

"What do you make of this?"

"Sobel I know fairly well. He's my advisor and I clued you in about him. We both know what S and P is. And the Backfire part? That's the name of a project Sobel's connected with."

"That's good Sue."

"What do you make of it?"

"Not much. Yet. But I intend to find out what it's all about. With your help since you know this guy Sobel. Professor Sobel, I guess you'd call him."

"I'd like to help. I'll do what I can."

"You know something Sue. This whole thing is weird. I don't, can't believe any of those guys, mostly highly educated men, would be involved in such a weird thing as this. They're too big, especially Stone. Should have more important things to do from what I can see."

"Unless they're having someone else do their dirty work for them."

"All the signs point to them though. Still you have to ask why, and it don't quite fit together yet, the puzzle." Marone shook his head as he let himself out of the car. While escorting Sue to the diner's entrance, the detective appeared very serious. "You know, Sue, I warned you before. Since we don't know what kind of strange people we're really dealin' with, I'd be extra cautious, especially now that you're, you might say, heavily involved in this thing, and not just as Stone's trainer. Those turks ever got wind of what you know . . . no tellin' what they might do."

Sue felt her skin crawl. "It's becoming uncomfortable for me."

Marone hesitated and flashed a knowing look at Sue before he opened the door of the diner for her; then his mood switched quickly to a lighter one once they were seated in a booth. The detective surveyed the entire interior of the nearly empty restaurant. "Oh hell. What am I saying? There's nothing's gonna happen to you if you just mind, or at least give them the impression that you're mindin' your own business. And by the way, I was at the track the other day when that big colt wins. I wanted to see for myself how good a trainer you was, are." He smiled broadly. "You're A okay from what I seen. No, I don't think Stone could afford to lose you."

"I really had very little to do with that win," Sue said. "The big colt did it all on his own. He's an exceptional animal."

"May I help you folks," a waitress asked, standing over them. "Need menus?"

"Nah, at least I don't," Marone said loudly, as he looked over at a blackboard containing a list of specials. "All I want is a coffee, black." He patted a couple of times at his considerable stomach area. "Gotta watch the bonz, but I can't speak for my friend."

"Just coffee. Uh, maybe I'll have a bagel, dry."

"You could easily afford much more. Weight that is, although you seem to have almost enough in just the right places from where I sit." Marone flashed his macho smile. It alone would have been enough to annoy Sue, but his accompanying comment made him doubly repugnant. "You're just right, really, excepting that you're kind of on the muscular side for a woman; at least that's what my mom would say."

"I'm glad she's your mom and not mine."

19

Sue drove the old Buick into the double-lane estate road. The impressive main house of the Stone Henge estate loomed large in front to her. She wondered what Byron might be up to. She hadn't seen him for several days. Good he couldn't see her now. Her bones ached and her clothes felt sticky and damp. She'd had a long hard day at the track. It had been extra muggy and hot and she hoped it wasn't a cold that she was fighting, not this close to the greatest training event of her life. Only three more days to the big one. She was pleased with Samsona's tune-up work for the big feature race for three old fillies on Belmont's outstanding race card.

Sue noticed that there were more limos, some stretch, some black and some white, in the large semi circle in front of the "palazzo." The main house's Renaissance motif made "palazzo" a more appropri-ate label than Jim Morrissey's "Taj Mahal." Several men appeared to be checking and discussing printed materials all of them held in their hands. They were too busy to notice the old Buick passing by them as one of them spoke while holding up what appeared to be a notebook. They were obviously at Stone Henge for another meeting or conference sponsored by the S and P Foundation.

Beyond a sharp curve in the road she could see the guesthouse and was reminded when she saw the Jetta parked by the side of the road that she'd made a date with Jim. Now she wished she'd passed on the date.

Sue parked the Buick in the estate garage and headed for the guesthouse. Muscles she never knew she had ached. She focused on the Jetta. No Jim. When she reached the car, she put her hands on her shapely hips and scanned the horizon. "Where the hell is he?"

She looked inside the Jetta. The back seat contained some books and a baseball cap with Yankees embossed on it. After a short search around the back of the house, she unlocked the front door. Before entering she checked her watch. She was a bit late and he may have decided to take a stroll over to the beach, she thought. As she entered the house, she thought about taking a shower before he returned. But then she wouldn't be able to hear him come in. She turned on the television in the family room and sat on one of the soft leather TV chairs and waited. She had trouble keeping her eyes open. Not fully acclimated to the track routine of going to bed early and getting up long before sunrise, she caught herself dozing off when she heard the loud knock at the front door. She knew it had to be Jim; he never rang a doorbell.

"Come on in." She dragged herself, still half asleep, to the front door, which came ajar before she reached it. "Where the have you been?"

"Came a bit early and you're late; it seemed like I waited an eternity for you before I decided to do some exploring." He brushed by her and plopped himself into one of the cocoa colored soft leather chairs. He appeared as exhausted as she. "Wanted to see what was going on down below in the Taj's main palace. S and P Foundation building. Lots of activity."

"Sorry I'm late," Sue said, her tired voice matching her appearance. She sat on the plush carpeted floor facing him with her back leaning against the bulging front lip of a chair. "Loads of traffic; got caught in one of those juggernaut traffic jams your freeways around these parts are famous for. I tried to leave early, but had to wait for the vet to arrive to take some x-rays of a horse we worked this morning, looks like he'll be going back to the farm for a while."

"Not one of your real good horses, I hope." Jim's sincere interest brought a surprised look to Sue's face.

"All of Byron Stone's horses are pretty good animals and some even great. This one's a two year old. Bucked his shins."

"Sounds serious."

"Isn't very, usually. Though it's the one thing a horse won't tolerate. Stops them cold if they get it in a race. He'll just need some of what my dad calls the Green Vet. Lots of pasture time. We used to pin fire them or put a blister on them."

"Sounds painful, cruel."

"Was, and all it really accomplished was making the horse take time off anyway."

"They seem so injury prone."

"They're all very injury prone. Running as fast as they do, about forty miles an hour, and they're thousand pounds or more on spindly legs." She made a shuddering movement with her shoulders. "Hate to think about it."

"Then don't," Jim scoffed, his mood having changed quickly.

"What'd you discover down below at the Taj Mahal complex as you call it? I thought you might have wandered down to the beach and certainly couldn't imagine you going down toward the main house"

"Where my main adversary the robber baron resides?"

"When I didn't find you waiting out front, I got a bit worried. What with all the things happening these days to people connected to your main adversary."

"I waited a while and then got bored, and as I mentioned, I decided to take a stroll down the road to find out what those limos were all about." Jim slanted his head to one side and gave Sue a queer look. "Them's a weird bunch of guys. Lots of foreigners. Some of them fit right in with the Taj. Indians. Some looked and sounded like them."

"S and P is the sponsor of a lot of international conventions from what Byron told me."

"I believe your friend's hosting a seminar on HIV from what I overheard as I walked around."

"They must have looked at you funny like. The clothes you're wearing had to have caught their eyes."

"Nah. I walked around and pretended I was one of the gardeners. I asked one of them, an Oriental, what was going on."

"Asian is what they want to be called these days."

"Anyway, I asked him what was going on, and he gives me a suspicious look, like mind your own business; although it could've been also, I no speak the English. So I decided to nose around a bit more and kept myself out of sight behind some bushes while these three guys with thick Slavic, maybe Russian, accents had a conversation out on a gazebo in one of the gardens next to the Taj and I heard a lot of bunk about a private war on AIDS. HIV is all they seemed to be interested in. Funny, though, they sounded like they were scientists or doctors. What in hell would doctors be doing meeting here? Stone doesn't run hospitals. They were referring to AIDS patients being treated in hospitals."

"S and P Foundation is funding the research being done by old Doc Sobel."

"They backed Kirby on a big project once."

"Still do maybe."

"Research he was doing had a funny name."

"Do you remember what it was?"

"Back something or other, I believe."

"That's the word I asked you about once," Sue said with ever widening eyes. "Remember?"

"What word?"

"Backfire. The name for the project Sobel's working on."

"Oh yeah, now I remember. At the time it didn't ring a bell. What about it?"

Sue smiled smartly. "Has something to do with the investigation of those murders."

"The deadly Stone bag ones? As in Byron Stone," Jim snickered. "The ones everyone's been reading about in the newspapers? Boy, you're right in the middle of all this. Aren't you scared?"

"A bit, I must admit. Deadly Stone bags." Sue shook her head. "That's a low blow Jimbo."

"Hey, Byron Stone, he's the one who produces them. One of his companies does anyway, according

to the newspapers. And what the hell were you doing there in that woman's apartment? You becoming an amateur sleuth or something? Can be a dangerous hobby, ya know. Maybe I ought to have you
get to know, maybe even hire my Uncle Dan to keep
an eye on you."

"Your Uncle Dan, the one who is interested in
the horses, or should I say horseracing?"

"I've already told him about the whole mess. He's
actually done private investigative work for Stone's
outfit since he retired from the state police."

"State police? Then he must know Marone, the
guy that's handling the case currently."

"More than likely. When I was talking to him
about you, he wanted to know more about, was concerned that you might be in serious danger. He sincerely wanted to help, especially since I told him
about you and me being so close. He'd like to know
more about it."

Sue sprang up from the floor. "After I take a
shower," she teased, "I'll reveal all."

"Hey, you can reveal even more if we take a
shower together." Jim's suggestion was followed by
an impish grin when she nodded her head.

With a resigned look on her face, Sue said softly,
"It may be the only sex we can do tonight. But as you
mentioned over the phone, there's no reason why
you can't spend the night here. Won't be a long night
since I have to leave so early in the morning. Half a
night by your standards, I'd say. But you can leave as
soon as you awaken. Or even stay until you feel like
leaving. I'm sure no one's going to say anything to
you."

Jim followed Sue into the bedroom, an enlarge-
ment already uncomfortably pressuring the zipper

of his slacks. Before they reached the bathroom he put his long arms around her and pulled her back to him. Sue tried to resist and pull him forward into the luxurious bathroom, but could move no more than a couple of inches. She felt his wet tongue already licking her neck and ears, making her stomach feel tingly inside and her body grow supple as she allowed it to relax from the initial response of resistance. She felt his hot breath in her ear.

"It'll be more fun lying down," Sue said as she felt the tension of his bent knees as he tried to lift her up with his ample and now fully extended stiff male organ. He continued to kiss her on the neck and ears and finally released her so that he could unzip his pants. Sue seized the moment to escape into the bedroom. When Jim entered the room, he found Sue standing next to the bathroom entrance. She suggested, "It's either here or on the bed."

"Let's try the bed first, here afterwards. I'll need a shower after we're done." Jim's words came out of his mouth sporadically as he tried to catch his breath.

"Let's go then." Sue took him by the hand and led him to her bed. She said merrily as she looked down at his private parts, "Let the Summer Olympics begin. Who said you couldn't get it to qualify."

Jim ignored her attempt at derision, and stood over her with a serious look for a couple of seconds as though trying to decide on where to begin. He bent over, untied and unzipped her jeans, and started tugging at them to pull them off while she removed her tee shirt.

"Time to get yourself some expensive jodhpurs, I should think." Jim tried to sound very British with a smirk flashing across his freckled and slightly acne scarred face. "Much easier to remove jodhpurs than these things."

"Only if you got some too," Sue said as she watched him continue to struggle with the tight-fitting blue jeans. "Nah, I'm going to go the other route and start dressing in some of the clothes I've lately begun to appreciate, some of the more feminine stuff like an expensive cotton or linen skirt which I saw in a fancy boutique the other day. Might even buy one for the big Stakes race coming up soon; this Saturday to be exact."

Jim responded by tugging harder at her blue jeans while she raised herself up to try to help him. "I'd love to see you and that horse of yours in action, Saturday," he grunted, finally pulling the jeans away and dropping them on the plush carpet.

"If you do a good job here," Sue teased, as she lay nude, "I may hire you permanently."

While undressing, Jim seemed to be salivating as he studied her enlarged red clay colored nipples.

"I may get you a free ticket, maybe even a seat in one of the boxes. You could even come with your uncle Dan who, as you say, likes to bet."

After stripping himself of his sports shirt, Jim lay on his side next to Sue and began the foreplay process, which he and she had learned in the university-sponsored workshop that they had taken together. She relaxed while Jim proceeded to plant kisses all over her body, starting from her lips and working his way all the way down to her vagina, which was already moist and ready for penetration. She responded by kissing him on his neck and ears, and was beginning to feel the sensations preceding a more fully satisfying copulation. Just as she was having visions of them doing C A T together, Jim's impatience showed. The instant he was inside her vagina he ejaculated. The look on his face said too soon. As he withdrew, semen escaped onto Sue's firmly rounded belly as well as onto the sheets of the bed.

Sue lay still and moaned, "Now look at what you've done my primitive friend. And no condom to boot; no pun intended."

He said sheepishly, "Now we do have an excuse for a shower, bath or sauna treatment, or something."

"You're something," Sue said angrily as she eased off the bed and headed toward the bathroom. "Better follow suit."

"Hey," maybe I can do something for you. Orally?" He was still trying to catch his breath.

"Not now," Sue shouted from the oversized bathtub. When Jim joined her, Sue was already covered with soapsuds and preparing to rinse herself, but he started to rub against her with his nude body. "Boy you are pretty hot to trot, tonight," Sue said with a girlish giggle.

"You're not angry at me?"

"What for? For allowing one of my best buddies to have a little fun," Sue said with her eyes closed and beginning to feel stirred up again by the smooth rhythmic motion of his belly against hers.

"But I didn't use a condom."

"I've started taking the pill again," Sue said softly. "Sort of knew I'd be having an affair with someone during the summer break."

"With me?

"Who else?"

"I'm taking the fifth." Jim knew he didn't have to say Byron Stone.

20

"How come you're not wearing that sexy cotton dress you bought when you were with me at that mall?" Jim Morrissey appeared mildly surprised. "Sue, this is my Uncle Dan." Jim got up from the box seat that Sue had reserved for him and his uncle.

Sue smiled and shook the young looking middle-aged man's extended hand. She ignored Jim's remark about the dress, even though she had entertained the idea of wearing the new cotton dress. At the last moment she'd changed her mind, having decided that she'd fit and look the part of trainer better if she dressed in a matching outfit of beige slacks and blouse. The belated decision was made after she'd put on the dress and looked in the mirror. It just didn't seem to be her. "Don't be afraid to come down and be in the picture, if she wins."

"Not if, Sue, when," Jim's uncle said with a confident smile.

Sue put up her hand in a slight waving motion and headed toward Byron's box seat across from the finish line. She had seen him at the barn earlier, but Byron had only taken enough time to see Samsona, pat the filly on the head and have Sue accompany him to his car where his date was waiting for him in his car. When Sue was introduced to the actress, Sue noticed that the sweet young thing had wiped her hand on her dress after shaking Sue's hand. Sue surmised that the sweet young thing hadn't gone into the barn with Byron because she didn't want to get either her shoes or her delicate hands dirty.

The fillies which had been warming up on the far side of the large one and half mile oval main track were turning and starting to slow down into a single file as they turned back toward the starting gate for the six furlong race. Even though they were a long way from the starting gate, the track announcer's voice blurted out over the loudspeakers, "Just one minute to post time."

"The horses are nearing the starting gate." The track announcer's mellifluous voice resounded above the din created by the excited and expectant spectators. "The horses are entering the starting gate. It is now post time," continued the announcer as the last of the fillies was placed in the starting gate. A couple of the three year olds acted up in the starting gate. "They're all in line. They'rrre off." A muffled buzzing sound and the banging of metal gates opening could be heard on the track's loud speakers. The fillies abruptly appeared in the usual melange of darting bodies and long legs out of the front of the starting gate.

"Samsona goes out smartly and is vying for the early lead from the outside. Dink is next on the rail, Becky's Girl and Sunny Bunny are two lengths back with Feeling Good trying to catch up to them.

Samsona is being joined by Dinky and Becky's Girl as they go down the backstretch with Sunny Bunny being taken back a bit; she's being joined by Feeling Good as they approach the far turn. The quarter was run in a fast twenty-one and three. These are fast fillies folks. Samsona and Becky's Girl are running neck and neck already in what looks like a possible duel right down to the finish. Dinky's dropping back to third."

Byron said, "Just what I hoped wouldn't happen. A duel between her and Becky's Girl."

Sue said reassuringly, "Not to worry, Samsona loves to run with another horse. She's different that way."

Byron shrugged. "I hope."

Sue composed a chorus with Byron and the actress shouting and urging intermittently, "C'mon Samsona, c'mon. Move girl, move." Sue paused momentarily and watched intently before saying, "A speed duel."

"Yeah. Still hope they don't pickle each other." Byron nodded with a worried expression but continued cheering. "Keep it up Samsona baby. You can do it, duel or no duel."

"Samsona and Becky's Girl are still going at it neck and neck; no one wants to give an inch. Then it's two lengths back now to Sunny Bunny who's being joined in the chase by Dinky on the rail. Feeling Good's not feeling so good, I guess, as she's falling far back." The announcer's voice, which was being occasionally obliterated by the increasing crowd noise continued, even picked up its cadence as the horses reached the quarter pole. "Looks like Sunny Bunny's really going after the leaders, making a comeback from just off the pace now, a length back. They've run the four furlongs in forty-five flat. They're turning for home and it's still a duel between the leaders, favorites in this race . . . oops Becky's Girl's got a head in front of Samsona. Nope, they're still hard to separate, those two." His voice thundered, "And down the stretch they come. It's, uh, they're neck and neck still, Becky's Girl and Samsona. Can't see who's got what in front. They're even going stride for stride. Becky's Girl's on the rail; won't give an inch. Sunny Bunny's making a quick move on the outside. She's a length back still but in contention for sure. There goes . . . Samsona. She's got a head in front of Becky's . . . Sunny Bunny's moved to . . . Samsona's taken a clear lead. She's spurting ahead . . . And it's Samsona by half a length over Becky's Girl and Sunny Bunny, photo there. Samsona wins the Coaching Club."

Byron, who had been yelling as loud as he could as the two fillies battled neck and neck, shouted "Okay" and grabbed hold of Sue first and hugged her and kissed her, and then turned toward the actress and less enthusiastically kissed her. Sue's heart was still thumping away, but Byron's unexpected reaction to his filly's victory was enough to take Sue's breath away. She stood limp until he nudged her and shouted in a now hoarse voice, "Let's do it folks; let's take the picture. We deserve it. That filly was just too much out there dueling the way she did. That's a champ if I ever saw one."

Sue led the way down the stairs this time, as she didn't want to hold up the picture taking. But she realized when she arrived at the Winner's Circle that she wasn't acting rationally. The usually impatient track photographer would have to wait his turn as the trophy for winning the race, a heavy Waterford

Crystal vase, had first to be presented to the owner of the winning filly.

After the official presentation of the trophy to Byron, as horse, rider, groom, owner and lady friend were lining up to take the picture, Sue looked back at the stairway leading up to the boxes. She was hoping that Jim and his uncle would appear. The photographer was motioning impatiently toward her. She turned and glared at the man and wondered why he always seemed so impatient. His angry look said what he couldn't verbalize to her.

A broadly smiling Byron suggested, "Sue, you can stand here in front." Sue followed his suggestion and moved into position between Byron and the actress, who had already begun to pose. Joe King who was standing nearby came over quickly and stood next to Sue. There was a flash and a smattering of applause from some appreciative fans and betters. "Time to celebrate, and I still don't believe the time of the race. One eight and change on a not so fast track. Almost a record," Byron said happily. "Yep it's time to celebrate. I've made arrangements at the yacht club for a small celebration. And I'm sure Cindy will be there, even though we beat her filly today. But it wasn't easy." He turned to Sue. "You may want to invite your friends. Those two fellas I saw you with. Friends from your grad school program?" Byron seemed to be enjoying his probing.

Sue didn't reply, still savoring the great moment of victory and feeling rather bewildered and finding it a difficult to come down to earth. She finally said gratefully, "I'm sure they've got other plans."

"And they may not."

Sue smiled sheepishly. "I guess you're right. I'll go and see if they're still there." She turned and clambered up the busy stairs to the boxes. The tension began to ease out of her body with her every step and the full impact and thrill of the race were propelling her spirits higher and higher.

21

Sue looked up from her kneeling position in the stall, startled. "Mister Marone. Didn't hear you enter." She hadn't expected the sudden appearance of the detective peering down at her from just outside the stall.

"So this is where you've been hiding."

"What's up?"

"Not much unless you consider another dead body an important item."

"Who this time?" A look of foreboding covered Sue's sweating face.

"Nick Stockton's third partner."

"Third partner?"

"Yeah, the only one left in that firm other than the small fry. We found him dead in his bedroom." Frank Marone's matter of fact behavior contrasted with Sue's reaction. She was clearly shaken. He watched impassively while Sue's face changed from horrified and surprised to sad.

The deep sadness constricted Sue's throat. "Something's got to be done, soon."

"Yep. And it turns out he was also a member of that S and P Foundation's board of directors. That's why I'm going to ask you for a favor."

"What's that?"

"I was hoping you'd search this guy Sobel's files sometime when he's not around. When he goes to wherever he goes in Russia. Me, I'm going to go there when he's there."

Sue stood up. "Sobel's files?"

"Yeah. Ain't you in that building a lot where he has his office?"

"I am." Sue grimaced. "Was a plastic bag used?"

"Yep. Almost same exact MO as the others. In this guy's case we found a note. On his bureau, next to some stuff in a bottle he could've used. I'm having it analyzed."

"What did he say in the note?"

"Wasn't but a few words. Something to the effect that he didn't feel he had much to live for, especially since he had no one to share his life with, probably referring to his lover, whoever that might be."

"Maybe Wilson, Stockton?"

"Who knows?" Marone walked over to Samsona's stall where the filly was eating some of the hay hanging next to her stall opening. "This gal really did it yesterday," Marone said, his mood changing from serious to playful. "I wasn't there but I watched on tv. Some race." He shook his head and took a cautious step toward the filly while admiring her. Samsona looked at the detective with her big curious eyes while occasionally attacking the hay bag, so that some of the hay ended up on the floor in front of her stall. Marone picked up some small strands of hay from the floor, bunched them together and held them timidly toward the curious filly. She hesitated at first but in an instant Samsona's mouth pulled the hay from his hand. "She's really something." Marone resembled a child feeding animals at the zoo as he produced a hearty laugh. He appeared completely fascinated by the robust filly's antics.

Sue enjoyed watching him. "She's really a big pet, like a lot of horses."

Marone's mood swung back to the serious again. "Nice win for your boss, as well as you, but he's in deep doodoo. I heard from Billie the other day that the Feds are working overtime on this case now. Seems they've gone beyond finding out that one of Stone's outfits was flooding the gem market with radioactive diamonds. Have made a connection between one of Stone's outfits that did some insider trading. Also uncovered some sort of connection between some guys who work for Stone and some former Russian bigwigs connected with the Russian Mafia."

"Should you be telling me all this?"

"Hey, I ain't revealing anything that you can't read in the newspapers recently."

"Sounds like it involves the S and P Foundation. Even Doctor Sobel."

"That may be a part of it. They're involved, and your boss may end up being indicted eventually. Article about it in the newspaper, Times I believe. Heck, I asked Stone about it myself and he sounds like he's taking the fifth, and says he don't know himself what it's all about."

"Do you think he's guilty?"

"Who knows what's what when the Feds are involved. All I know is that the former Commies who were big investors in some American and German companies were represented by Nick Stockton and his partners, including John Wilson and this other partner we just found, and that their homicides aren't just my territory and may be leading to a bigger investigation, involving the Feds." Marone started walking toward the exit. "Hey, I've told you enough and only because you've been of some help. I can't tell you any more. As I've told you before, just keep your eyes and ears open wide and don't take any unnecessary chances. And let me know if you discover something in Sobel's files. Make sure, though, that he's away."

"He's away a lot lately. Can't you get a search warrant and look at his files?"

Marone said over his shoulder, "I tried. Judge said I had no good cause or reason. I'll try another angle and you could help." He hesitated before disappearing out the door. "You and me got to get together for dinner some one of these days."

Sue washed her hands in the small sink in the tack room and was drying them with some paper towels when the phone rang. "Yes," she answered.

"Sue, it's me, Byron. I know it's still a bit early, but how about joining me for some lunch? I know you've got a lot of different stuff to do there yet, but I won't be able to pick you up until . . . about one, anyway, by the time I wrap things up here and head your way. One at the latest. Uh, better still, why don't you let Joe take over for the rest of the day and I'll meet you at the guesthouse at twelve or so. If you come this way, we can meet earlier."

"I guess you've heard about the latest death, Jonathan Wainwright, Nick Stockton's partner?"

"I heard." Byron's voice sounded tired and sad. "He did some work for Dad and me just recently.

That's sort of why I wanted to see you, since you're connected with the only real good things that have happened to me lately. And you and your dad, I've always connected good and satisfying things with you guys."

22

Byron entered the guesthouse and shouted, "I hope you don't mind Sue. The door was open so I came in."

Having put the finishing touches on her lipstick, Sue heard Byron's voice and yelled out, "I'm in the bathroom. I'll be right out. Don't have to tell you to make yourself homely, if you know what I mean."

Sue found Byron studying a Monet next to the large stone and Roman brick fireplace of the living room. "This was one of mother's favorites. She loved color and flowers. She selected all the art in the house."

"I love pastels and bright colors too." Sue had lately started appreciating and enjoying the priceless art in the guesthouse. "Your mother really did have good taste. I never got to know her, although I remember her vaguely. I remember that she was a very attractive, though delicate looking woman. She did come to the races with you several times when you first gave Dad your horses, but I really didn't get much chance to talk with her. She must have been too ill to travel much, I guess." Sue's voice reflected uncertainty.

"You're right. She would have liked to accompany Dad and me more, but she just couldn't handle it physically."

Byron seemed visibly moved and on the verge of tears. To divert his attention to something more pleasant, Sue's face brightened up and she said softly, "I'm glad you called. I've been meaning to go over your plans for the colts. There's a race for both of them the first week at Saratoga. I just got a condition book . . ."

"Could we save that for later." Byron's voice was more of a request than a command.

Sue remained gaping at him with her pretty mouth open in mid sentence as she nodded. He appeared helpless as he extended his hand toward her. He seemed to be reaching both for support and help.

Sue took his warm hand into her own and stood studying his large gray blue eyes as though looking for further direction. Her heart was already exceeding its target heart rate and her breathing was increasing as well. She smelled his expensive cologne, which he had luckily not put on excessively or she might not be able to breath at all. Though Byron was a few inches taller than she, his sensuous lips seemed precariously close. For a fleeting moment her work-oriented mind questioned what she was doing here in mid day away from her work. But the conditioned response was dissolved rapidly by the instinctual and cerebral awareness that this person who'd created the work in the first place wanted her to do something else.

Byron's head moved slowly in a circular motion as his eyes appeared to be studying first Sue's hair and smooth forehead, then her beautifully shaped Ava Gardner eyes and slightly raised cheeks and finally her sensuous, slightly opened mouth. His lips seemed to be reaching for her full-bodied lips. It was almost vertigo producing. Sue felt herself move slowly and uncontrollably toward his face. When their lips touched, they both kissed passionately with eyes closed. Byron's strong arms felt like a vise, but she didn't mind. She kissed him hungrily, nearly smothering him with kisses. They continued the barrage of kisses for several minutes with their bodies acting like giant magnets that couldn't be separated. Byron finally released her to catch his breath. "You're really dynamite. No, you're the explosive device that's going to make me explode." Placing his hands on her hips, he separated himself from her for a moment, catching his breath. "This is going to lead to . . ."

"Watch out now. This could get hot." Sue moved toward his broad chest and gripped it on either side with her warm quivering hands. From her training as a sex therapist she knew that the usual drill called for putting a halt to things at this juncture; make the male of the species wait. The magic formula required the female to tease, hold back as long as possible; make the guy chase you. She ignored the little voice saying go slow and brushed his lips with her own. She whispered softly and breathlessly, "Let's enjoy it. Just enjoy it." She tugged at his hand and led him into the bedroom. "Never know when we'll be able to do it again. Take advantage." She was actually thinking out loud when she spoke and was surprised at her own audacity. But now that she'd made the move and he was complying, she realized she'd have to lead the way and not lose the opportunity. If he liked it, he'd be back for more.

Byron sat down on the bed next to her and smiled. "You have no idea how long I've wanted to do this."

"C'mon now." Sue started undressing. "You're only in the mood because of what's been happening to you recently. Losing your best friends and all."

Byron sat stunned. "It has been tough on a lot of people."

"Hope you can undress without too much assistance. All kidding aside Byron, please make your self at home. I've wanted to go to bed with you almost from the first time we met as teenagers. I have to be honest, so just enjoy." She started helping him remove his shirt.

Byron laughed sheepishly. "Funny, the male is usually the sexual aggressor, but you're something else. Whoever would have thought a hayseed like you'd be such a lover. Maybe that stuff you're study-ing is contagious." He kissed her on the forehead as she helped him remove his pants. "You're hot. So am I."

"Can't help it if the good lord made me this way. I admit it. I enjoy sex, especially with someone I really like. I oughtn't sound like I've had a lot of it."

"Ya know, Sue, sometimes you sound so hayseed." When they were completely undressed, Byron seemed to want to devour her as his surprised eyes took in her unblemished silky smooth skin and beau-tifully proportioned body. They fell onto the bed and seemed glued together as their lips began kissing randomly all over each other's neck and face. Sue kissed with unbridled passion. The intensity of her

feelings was greater and totally different from anything she'd experienced before, including her
sexual encounters with Jim. She separated herself
from Byron and worked her way down his body with
her tongue and lips.

Byron noticed that she treated his genitalia as
though they were a very important property both to
her and him. When Byron was about to penetrate,
she suddenly stopped kissing and froze in place,
causing him to pull back.

"What's the matter?" Byron's muscular body
became limp.

"Condom. You'll have to use one," Sue moaned,
sounding apologetic. "AIDS and stuff. Do you have
one on you? I happen to have some." Without waiting for a response, Sue reached over to the small
night table next to the bed and snatched a small box
of condoms out of the top drawer.

"You're like a marine," Byron laughed. "Always
prepared."

"Not always, and I must admit not always as
assertive as I should be. But."

"But you're afraid that since my close friends had
AIDS, I'd have it too. Or might even have it without
knowing it." Byron sat up and stated seriously, "They
and I are two entirely different animals you might
say. I know it's your field of expertise I'm talking about
and I even feel foolish reminding you, and there are
a lot of bisexual guys out there, but I'm not one of
them. Not even close. I do feel for them to some
extent, especially in light of the AIDS epidemic that's
hit us."

Sue smiled and put her hand over his mouth.
"Just playing safe. And I believe you, but . . ."

"That but again. Oh heck, I can't blame you,

keed. Things are being done about it, but until . . .
Even S and P, my family's foundation is involved.
That's small consolation now . . . And, oh yes, I have
had myself checked recently just in case."

"Incidentally, someone I talked to recently be-
lieves that you or someone in your organization may
have had something to do with the killing of Nick
Stockton and all the others because they had AIDS.
Far out theory, but I have to admit that it's one that
keeps buzzing through my own cranium."

Byron nodded, "I can just imagine. No, S and P
has been doing and supporting a lot of research on
AIDS; still, we don't go around killing people." A
sinister smile suddenly came over his face as Byron
jumped up and grabbed Sue by the throat. "Until
now. Now I shall have to kill you too. Now I know
what has to be done with you."

For a split moment Sue became frightened, but
when his grip weakened, she heaved a sigh. "Sorry I
brought the whole thing up, condom that is, not your
private parts."

He chuckled at her attempted humor; then
quickly became serious. "All kidding aside, keed, I
don't know who is doing the killing. Wish I did. We'll
have to talk about it after we get some sex off of our
minds first."

"Whoa. Hold on." Byron had barely finished putting
on a condom, when Sue jumped on top of him and
started doing the first part of C A T. She guided him
to stroke the area around and over her clitoris. He
caught on and continued the exercise for several
seconds before finally slipping into her sexual cavity.

Sue said, "This isn't quite like C A T."

"Cat? As in pussycat?" Byron sounded out of
breath.

"Not really. I'll explain later." Sue enjoyed all of
it even though he finished sooner than she'd have
liked, so she allowed him to stay inside of her as she
remained on top of him and slid back and forth for a
while longer. She enjoyed his wet kisses on her face
and lips and the snake-like action of his tongue in
her mouth even though she could also sense some
of his sticky semen now that he had finished. She
didn't mind as she convinced herself that he was what
he said he was.

She turned over and lay on her back staring up
at the high ceiling. "That was something I've even
dreamed of doing; having sex with you. Now I'm
living the dream."

"Me too," Byron sighed. "From now on, whenever I see you riding a horse, I'm going to develop a
hard-on, I believe the expression is. That was some
nice ride you put us through." He took a deep breath.
"You're not going to believe this because I haven't
treated you as warmly as I should have. Oh hell, Sue."
He rolled over onto his side and looked at her with a
thoroughly fascinated expression on his animated
face. "I've wanted to do this for a long time. You've
got one great face and body and you don't go around
acting as though you do. It's more like you don't even
realize it. That's part, and not all of why I've liked
you, the charm of you. There's an awful lot to you,
unlike that shallow celeb starlette I was with when
Samsona won. Yep, I've liked you from the first time
I saw you, but you seemed so young and innocent,
sort of overprotected then. And you know, you're
different from all the other gals."

"Must have said that a few times before. Sounds
great and coming from you, I just love it. But it sounds
an awful lot like a line I've heard before, although I

like the other stuff you said about me a lot more. Of course, you've had a lot of women to practice on."

"Just a few, really," Byron said modestly. "Maybe a few more than a few. But those were not affairs of the heart as much as just purely affairs."

"Of desire? Which affair did you like the most?"

"I'll never forget my first affair. With an actress that I first saw on the screen. I thought to myself, boy I'd give anything to go to bed with her. Know what? When I met her at a party and did take her to bed, it was the biggest let down I've ever experienced. It seems the reality is always a let down, but not you. This is the best I've ever had, my hayseed friend." He reached over and gently stroked her firm belly and hips, pleasure written all over his face, and then kissed her on her neck and in the ear.

Sue smiled with pleasure and kissed him on the lips and studied his face. "Maybe it's the old expectation thing. If you don't expect too much, or when it, whatever it is, meets your expectations or is a little better than you expect . . . You know what I mean." She lay back completely relaxed. "By the way, Byron, do you know anything about a project called Backfire?"

"Backfire? Where did you hear about that one?"

"From Marone?"

Byron appeared surprised and angry. He looked away from Sue's probing look. "Marone. He's a twerp, a nuisance, actually. I realize he's trying to do his job, but he's been snooping around my company's main office in Manhattan, even questioned my secretary, Harriet, for almost an hour. From what one of my top aides told me the other day, Marone thinks that I'm behind all the killings somehow. I suppose I should be able to see why. Oh hell, I may as well reveal

all. My dad's, our outfit's involved in a power struggle
with a group, the EEG, a cartel made up of Eastern
Europeans, mostly some people around Moscow,
former KGB bigwigs who siphoned off and hoarded
a lot of money from the old USSR. They, as well as a
few other former Eastern Block guys and even some
Germans are trying to gain control of companies in
the West along with a lot of the up for grabs assets of
companies in the emerging new nations from the
old USSR. It's been going on for quite a while and
I'm just starting to get a handle on what's really going
on. There's some stuff going on inside my outfit . . .
The CIA and a couple of other Federal agents were
investigating us as well, but we've begun to cooperate
with them in their investigation."

"Weren't John Wilson, Wainwright and Nick
Stockton representing them, that cartel I mean?"

"Sort of," Byron said, flashing an admiring smile
at Sue, who was gently stroking the muscular arm
that was lying next to her. "And that's also why your
defective detective friend is convinced, I guess, that
I'm behind all this killing stuff. But he's fooling himself. Even though I hardly knew John Wilson, Nick
and I, as everyone knows, were the best of friends. I
must admit, though, that his dealings with the cartel
had put a slight strain on our relationship recently,
but not so much that I or anyone I know . . . well, I
can't go that far. I certainly could never have killed
him."

"There's sort of a hint in what you say that perhaps
you know and may even have more than an inkling,
at least, of who may have committed the homicides."
Sue raised her head and looked inquisitively at him.

"I want to see justice done," Byron responded.
"It's just that this is a complex situation, like a what

you're seeing is not what you're getting type of thing. Yeah, I may as well let you in on a secret. We've got our own people working on this thing. Trying to figure it out. Even hired some private investigators as recently as yesterday, matter of fact."

"You did?"

A faint smile formed on Byron's well-tanned face. In an instant he turned on Sue and grabbed hold of her shoulders as he rolled over on top of her. "How many times must I tell you that you will be murdered if you do not merely comply with my wishes?" He kissed her all over her forehead and tightly closed eyes. Byron's eager lips met Sue's. He kissed them gently before thrusting his wet tongue into her mouth. Though caught somewhat by surprise, Sue began to kiss back as passionately as he.

"I could use some more," he whispered, his breath very hot and his breathing accelerating noticeably. "Of your magic. You're a great lover."

"And a sex therapist worth her salt perhaps."

23

"When I asked you to help me search through Sobel's files, I wanted it to be confined to just you and me, Jim; now I'm glad we've got some professional help." She nodded toward the big man standing next to Jim Morrisey.

"Especially after Marone finally got his search warrant and couldn't get anything from Sobel," Jim scoffed.

Sue said, "Funny he admitted that. He seems to have such a big head." She had her hands on her hips and was standing next to her borrowed Buick in front of her old apartment building.

"Actually, I'm the one who instigated this, Sue," Dan Morrissey said. He loosened his collar from around his thick neck. "Couldn't have picked a hotter day, though."

"Sorry if I sounded so cranky. It has been one long brutally muggy day and I've had one very busy and trying morning and the heat hasn't helped any."

"That should end next week," Jim interjected. "Aren't you moving up to Saratoga then?"

Sue smiled. "That's true. But since you guys are here we may as well concentrate on what's happening today?"

"Before we start Sue, I've got to let both of you in on a secret," Dan said.

"What's that?"

"Actually you may be responsible for it. In a sense I owe you. After I met your friends, Cindy Phillips and Byron Stone at the victory party after Samsona's big win, Mister Stone hired my outfit the very next day after the party at the yacht club. Great people those friends of yours. Anyway, they hired us to do some investigative work for them with respect to their friends' deaths. Seems they can't wait for this plastic bag killing stuff to be cleared up. Sooner the better for everyone."

"You're kidding," Sue said in disbelief. "Although, now that you mention it, I recall what Byron told me just yesterday. That he was launching his own private investigation into the killings. So you're one of the special investigators he hired."

"Small world, eh?" Dan checked his watch as though he were working on an hourly basis. "Time to get started and from what Jim told me, Sue, he says you've got a way of handling the custodial staff; also that your advisor's office and the one which you share is in that building we want to get into. Although Jim may help a little."

Sue said, "He'll probably make a good lookout. I'm just kidding. He's more familiar with that building than I am. His advisor's got his office there too."

Dan grinned and looked all around at the street

full of parked cars, many of which had already been tagged, though not all by meter maids; a few cars were tagged by wise guys using just plain old recycled tickets to keep their cars from getting tagged. "Jim tells me that you have access to the keys of the building you're in and those same keys can be used to gain access to the office of this Doctor Sobel."

"I do." Sue said.

"I could've forced open some locks, but it's much better to just plain old unlock the office doors and the guy's desk with the proper keys."

Jim said, "Funny about Sobel. I always pictured him as just another stodgy, over the hill sort of prof. Now I find out that he's been getting big amounts of money from the S and P Foundation for quite some time. Milking it for all he can get out of it."

Sue said, "Marone told me the other day that Sobel's been playing both sides of the fence. He gets funding from the S and P Foundation, and then uses the info to get more funding from another group in Russia, maybe also some German and Eastern European guys."

Dan said, "Yep Marone told me the same thing when I talked to him, Sobel plays both sides of the street you might say and some of the dough is laundered dollars done through the latest crop of Russian Wise Guys living in and around Brooklyn."

Jim nodded. "A kind of big time Russian Mafia cooperative."

"Russian Mafia and Doc Sobel," Sue chuckled, shaking her head in disbelief.

Jim said, "Yep, and I remember eavesdropping once on one of Sobel's research assistants who went with him to Russia. Sobel took him to some dacha belonging to some former KGB bigwig, just outside of Moscow, and he made it sound like Sobel had been doing this pretty regularly."

Sue said, "Hope Sobel's there now. I couldn't find out anything except that he's been out of town for quite a while."

Dan said, "I checked. He should be in Russia. Let's get started. On the way I'll lay out my little plan and you can fill in the blanks." Dan led the others along an uneven, cracked cement sidewalk. "Jim tells me that you've done some assistant teaching and even a little research with and for this Doctor Sobel."

Sue caught up with Dan Morrissey and walked stride by stride with the heavyset man. "I've done a very small project with him. Actually it was some very, very minor stuff. Jim even helped me with it. Local questionnaire stuff in a few community and neighborhood clinics in and around the city with several other grad students. He paid us a small stipend. He's usually involved in international research, stuff like the AIDS epidemic in the former Soviet Union and Romania and even Africa. My particular job for his local project was to compile data from federally funded outfits in and around New York City which were providing support services to HIV and AIDS victims."

Dan said happily, "Glad you've got a master key for the building Sobel's in. It'll make it easy. May I have it?"

Sue reached into her pocket and suddenly stopped in her tracks, causing Jim to almost trip to avoid going into her.

Jim said, "I hope you haven't forgotten them."

Sue said, "I thought I had my keys."

Jim said, "You're kidding."

"No, I don't have them." Seeing the look of disappointment on Dan's moon-shaped freckled face, Sue said, "No problem. I'm pretty friendly with Jeff Smith, the head custodian."

"His assistant may even have a crush on you." Jim winked over his shoulder at Dan.

"Yuck." Sue's distasteful look said it all. "I'll get us in don't worry. Getting into Sobel's filing cabinets may be a much more challenging undertaking."

"Don't worry about that," Dan said confidently. "Just get us inside his inner sanctum."

"One of his assistants might be there, though," Jim said.

"Then we try to get him to leave somehow or wait until he leaves."

"What if he ain't there and then comes and catches us in the act?" Jim persisted.

Exasperated by his nephew's interrogation, Dan's wide body came to a crunching halt. He said bluntly, "We assassinate him. We'll deal with that problem when and if it arises. Besides, you're going to be our lookout. I'm sure you're up to doing that small job." He shook his frustrated head. "Boy, I'm sure glad you're not working as an investigator for a living."

They entered the nearly vacant social science building with Sue now leading the way. She led them down a flight of stairs to the end of a long and dingy corridor. Sue knocked on the glass panel of a door marked custodian before she opened it and walked in. A bearded man dressed in a blue denim jump suit was filling a metal pail with water.

"Charlie, is Jeff around?"

"He should be in the building somewheres." He turned off the water.

"I want to ask him for a small favor. Maybe you can do it for me. I hate to bother him if he's busy. I just need the master key. Forgot my keys home and these guys have come a long way to see some of the stuff I've been working on lately."

The custodian smiled as he recognized Jim, but he shot a suspicious glance at Dan before saying, "I'll fetch it fer ya." He went over to an old and abused oak desk and found the master key in the top drawer. "Here ya go. Last of the extras. Don't lose it. You lose that and I lose my job, not that I'd be losin' much." He chortled at his attempt at humor.

"Thanks, Charlie, I owe you one. A coffee at least."

"Sort of miss you guys now that most of you've scattered to go on break. Come to think of it, I ain't seen you for some time. Since just before Sobel left for Russia. Where are you off to this summer?"

"I'll be around here, mostly." Sue didn't dare tell the inquisitive man any more than she had to as he usually wanted a full and detailed description and explanation for anything that might provide him with an excuse to take a break from his tedious work.

Charlie nodded and went back to his bucket to put suds into it for his daily mopping chore.

Dan asked, "How'd you know that Sobel's gone to Russia?"

"He told me the day I helped him bring stuff down to his car."

"That was easy," Dan said when they were outside the custodians' room and heading up the dimly lit hallway to a central stairway. They could hear the head custodian whistling inside one of the classrooms while he did his work.

Sue speeded up. "Good. He's occupied with something on this floor. Follow me." She led them upstairs. When they arrived at Sobel's office on the third floor, Sue cupped her hand over her mouth and whispered, "Here we are."

Dan turned to Jim and said softly, "You can stay here to keep watch, while we're in Sobel's office?"

"Will do, although I'd have liked nosing through some of his confidential files." Jim's face beamed as he enjoyed the idea. He looked at the stairs and sat down on the second one. "I'll sit here and pretend I'm fixing one of my shoestrings if someone comes. If you hear me whistling Yankee Doodle it means someone is coming."

"Great song. You're so creative," Dan said as he followed Sue down the corridor to an antique wooden door whose upper panel contained thick-clouded glass. Sue unlocked the door and led Dan to a row of filing cabinets. When she turned around she found Dan shaking his head.

"I'd check the guy's desk first," Dan recommended.

"I'd start there at least. But I'll open the first cabinet for ya and do the desk myself. Have to know what to look for."

"Where'd you work? I mean, what was your job with the state police?"

"Did lots of the usual things when I first started. Highway patrol, et cetera. Started in Connecticut. Left there after a few years and finally ended up in New York as the official forensic lab photographer."

"You must have worked for the famous Doctor Henry Lee." Sue appeared puzzled. "Bugging, surveillance, where'd you learn that?"

"For a couple years, I was on a special squad that did a lot of bugging, all kinds of surveillance work. We were sent to a special training school run by the FBI. For this new outfit, now that I'm doing private stuff, that's really what I've been doing mostly, surveillance and security work. Since my so-called retirement. That's why Cindy Phillips recognized me at the party at the yacht club; I've done some security work for her. First through this security agency I worked for. I even took some pictures for her once. But the company I work for now is essentially a partnership and I'm one of the partners, and it's been hired by her several times, mostly to keep an eye on some jewels she wears at big soirees."

"And she enjoys wearing the real thing, of course."

"Of course."

"Looks to me like she might enjoy wearing very little for a chosen few, sometimes," Sue teased, but she could only imagine Dan's reaction in the darkened room.

"Hey, enough small talk, let's get busy. Gonna be dark soon and we don't have all night." Dan unlocked one of the file cabinets by working on the master lock at the top of the cabinet. He left Sue at the files while he tackled Sobel's large metal desk. A partially shaded window provided some of the light from a disappearing late afternoon sun.

Dan grumbled, "Where's the light switch? Nah. Don't want to put on the lights." He reached into his pocket and produced a small flashlight. "Here use this. I'll use my lighter."

With a jackknife containing a special tool that resembled a thin carpet knife blade, Dan pried open the top drawer of the desk. A manila folder marked correspondence brought a gleam to his eyes. He held it up closer to the window. "Bingo," he muttered to himself, but just loud enough for Sue to hear. She stopped fingering through the top drawer of the file cabinet and watched Dan's frenetic motions as he rummaged through the letters. He extricated one large white envelope and dropped the folder on the desk. After he'd taken a letter out of the envelope and laid it on the desk, Dan pulled out his lighter and started reading the contents of the letter. Sue watched as he nodded several times. When she heard him say, "Pay dirt," she became curious. She started for the desk. Dan motioned her off and pointed toward the file cabinet. He whispered, "I'll take care of this. I'll show you later. Keep at it there. We've got to find more. All we can. Keep digging."

Sue continued to rummage through the file cabinet, but began to realize that she really didn't know what she was looking for and just hoped that Dan would find enough material to make this minor Watergate worthwhile.

"I'd feel more comfortable and confident if I really knew what to look for," Sue said as she searched through several folders. "This top drawer is full mostly of reports from seminars and conferences."

"Just keep searching. You'll know when you've spotted something unusual, something that'll link this guy to those birds connected formerly to the old power elite guys in the old Soviet Union."

Sue started looking through the second drawer, which was full of outstanding grad student's completed projects in which the professor was obviously still interested and which Sue knew Sobel might consider exploiting at some time in the future. She pulled open the third drawer. Her eyes lighted up. She thumbed through several folders marked S and P Foundation before pulling them out. She motioned to Dan, but he was too busy with his own search to notice her. Sue pulled the folders and carried them over to the desk. With Dan's flashlight, she examined the papers in the folder.

"What ya got there, partner?"

Sue handed Dan the folder. "Here."

After thumbing through the folder, Dan smiled. "Sobel's laid out how S and P is organized. And what its latest project is all about." The smile disappeared. "Did you read this?"

"What?"

Dan's voice cracked as he said, "They actually wiped out half of an entire village. Sounds like it's African."

"Why would they do that?"

"To save it, says here. From AIDS. Half the people had AIDS."

"Sounds like the village of Mai Lai in the Viet Nam era. Had to destroy it to save it." Sue looked hurt. "I can't believe that any outfit of Byron's or his cousin Cindy could do such a thing."

"Maybe they don't know what's going on. That's why they hired me, no?"

Sue whispered, "Could anyone get away with such an atrocity in this day and age without the media finding out?"

"How does doctor Kevorkian get away with it?"

"He's a humanitarian."

"They may think their humanitarians. Besides they did get him eventually." Dan started gathering the contents of the folder together. "Let's begin to wrap things up. We can always come back if we need more info. We'd better take only a few things. The important stuff. We can make copies and then return same. These folders of the organizational stuff and letters in this folder may be all we'll need for now. Yeah, why don't we wrap this up. Just look fast through the rest of that cabinet. I'm almost done here." He put up his hand. "Isn't that Jim whistling."

"Yankee Doodle."

"Let's get out of here," Dan ordered. "We've got enough stuff for now."

"We can go down the hall to my office where I keep some books and come back," Sue suggested.

Dan waved her off as he stuffed the folder containing two letters into the front part of his slacks. "Got enough for today."

Sue started back toward the file cabinet to return the folders, but in a hardly audible whisper Dan said, "Take those things with you and shut that cabinet tight. C'mon we got to get out of here. Can't leave any sign that we were here."

Dan was relieved when he and Sue started back down the long corridor with no one walking toward them. They found Jim halfway up the stairs engaged in a discussion with the head custodian.

Sue thought she heard the words "New York Yankees baseball team."

"So this is where you are?" Sue said with a genial smile beamed toward the custodian. "Baseball again. I'll bet you and Jeff could discuss baseball all night. Hi Jeff. How're you doing? Long time no see."

"Doing great. Getting ready to go to Maine next week." The smiling obese individual was enjoying the brief respite from his tedious work as well as the attention he was getting.

"Jeff this is my Uncle Dan," Jim introduced. "Sue and I were showing my uncle around the campus."

"Nice to meet you, Jeff." Dan remembered that Sue had told the other custodian about showing him and Jim her research project. He shook the custodian's clammy hand and maintained his composure. "This a real nice campus considering where it's located."

"Has its pluses and minuses, but the students are a big plus, especially the grad assistants like these two."

Sue nudged Jim toward the stairs. "We'd better get a move on. Jeff's got his work to do."

"Nice meeting ya," Dan said over his shoulder as he led the way down the stairs, taking each step more rapidly as he approached the bottom. When they were outside, Dan heaved a sigh and said, "Nothing like good old fresh air. At least there are a few trees left around here because of your institution of higher learning." He reached into the front of his pants and pulled out the folder containing the two envelopes. Then he eyed the folders Sue was holding firmly under her right arm and said, "Mission accomplished. Now we'll go up to your old apartment and take a good look at the fish we've caught."

They rushed back to Sue's apartment. Dan sat in the lone chair of the one room efficiency apartment. While he perused the two letters, which he felt provided key clues, Sue and Jim started searching through the manila folders.

Jim shattered the silence first. "Listen to this. There's a schematic here of some organization that Sobel and some other guy head up. It's called the S and P AIDS Prevention and Elimination Project. It's a master plan, I guess. There are two major units, the ID or identifier squads which are supposed to compile lists of people with AIDS and the HS or health squads which are further broken down into two more components, preventive squads and mercy killing squads, made up mostly of highly paid medical personnel. Doctor Sobel is the head of the ID unit with this Doctor Cameron Blake heading up the HS unit."

"And the whole works," Sue's voice said sharply. "He's Byron's big cheese at S and P."

Dan nodded. "How close are he and Byron Stone?"

"He was on that boat trip with his wife, Ingrid. They knew Nick and Ruth Stockton pretty well too from the way they acted around one another. Incidentally, they were at the yacht club party the other night. I'm pretty sure you were introduced to them."

"Ingrid?" Dan began to quickly scan one of the letters he held in his hands. "She's here somewhere. Yep, right here. `Please tell Ingrid Blake that her cousin Igor Bachman has set things up for her husband in Saint Petersburg. Things are beginning to fall into place more quickly now that Nick Stockton and his partner John Wilson are no longer in the picture. It is unfortunate the way they were eliminated, and even though I had no idea about the way it was done, it worked out for the better as they were proving more a hindrance than a help. Now we can move forward with our plan to take things over."

"To take things over?" Sue's amazed look was reflected on Jim's gaping face. She gasped, "What the heck have we stumbled onto? Some sort of international plot to take over something? What?"

"More than meets the eye," Dan assured. "And there's a clue here as to who killed those guys and more. Is there any mention of Project Backfire in that organization plan for fighting AIDS?"

"Matter of fact there is," Jim said with a bewildered look on his face. "It's the name used a lot for the entire project. And the guy, our Doctor Sobel even defines it. He says here that as one builds a back fire to stop a raging forest fire, so too, one has got to build a back fire to stop the spread of AIDS, which Sobel claims is about to wipe out some entire nations in Africa. The populations of two African countries are forty percent infected."

Sue appeared sad. "What do you think these guys are going to be able to do to stop this horrible epidemic?"

Dan appeared skeptical. "Make a ton of money off of it. Probably just provide a lot of suicide, maybe even mercy killing stuff for them people. All kidding aside, although I may be on the money with my supposition, that so called Backfire Project, the whole thing for that matter, is being subsidized, financed by the S and P Foundation and a lot of the bread is being siphoned off by Blake and even Sobel, as I read between the lines in these two letters. S and P is the mother lode. According to what this Russian guy, Igor Backman, says to Sobel in this other letter, Nick Stockton's outfit was using and managing money, other moneys provided by a Russian group. John Wilson and Nick Stockton, and even Sobel, may have known what the true source of that money was. Lots of money was being smuggled out of Russia by some of the former power elite of the old Communist Party. More than likely the guts of that Red Star group I've read about, the Russian Mafia. With the money, some of which is now, incidentally, being managed and invested by Bachman, Nick and his partner John Wilson were gradually buying up controlling interests in corporations in the West, including some corporations in which the Stone and Phillips families have an interest. Tied into S and P. Those guys are actually positioning themselves to take a big part in the free enterprise system of the new Capitalist

Order as this guy calls it." Dan looked down at the letter.

Jim said, "Eventually they're hoping to have and control the biggest economic cartel in the world, I'll bet. Russia's loaded with natural resources and they'd eventually have control of those resources and the means to exploit them throughout the world."

Dan looked up. "It's ironic, if I read this thing correctly, that Bachman and his crew with the help of guys like Blake are going to head up this new order they're building with the money they're siphoning off from the old so called evil empire. And Blake and Sobel are doing the same thing with S and P money in addition to the hoarded Russian money."

Sue said, "I can't imagine avuncular old Sobel being as evil as the others."

"Maybe not Sobel, who is more than likely unwittingly involved; certainly Blake is. A lot of it must be in gold and diamonds."

"Radio active ones," Sue said.

"This whole thing needs an awful lot of sorting out." Dan shook his head in disbelief. "It's a lot like what people used to say about the Japanese for a while, until they fell upon bad economic times. They didn't have to bomb Pearl Harbor. All they had to do was wait until they beat us out trade-wise and then bought it. Nah, it's not quite the same thing."

"Who knows," Sue conjectured, "until it's all played out." She returned to her task of looking through a folder.

"They'll be a big economic and political force in the world if they grab the right companies. Key companies. Look at Microsoft and Intel," Jim interjected. "Those former Communist bosses who couldn't retain power through their old totalitarian system will exploit the very system they purportedly opposed and now they're using these guys and who knows how many more like them as their stooges. Ironic though, a college prof and this guy Blake."

Dan said, "The big guys in Eastern Europe, Russia, must think of these guys as their stooges. Does anyone know what Doctor Blake's background is?"

Sue said, "We know a lot about him now. He's got a Russian background."

"Changed his name?"

"Yep. Born in Russia. Did his research for his doctorate in the area of chemistry and medicine. Ironic that he's in charge of this whole project we're investigating."

Dan produced a hearty laugh. "And our Doc Sobel is just another one of his pawns. Stuff we found in his office is going to bust this whole thing wide open."

Sue said, "And to think it was Jim who first made me suspicious."

Jim interjected, "Nah, that's not entirely true. You knew about Sobel already. All I did was remind you that I knew that Sobel was doing research for S and P in Russia and you already knew about that."

Sue said, "Actually, even though I hate to admit it, it was this state police investigator Marone who put me up to this."

Jim said, "Funny we didn't catch on sooner like when you and I volunteered to help Sobel with his local project and passed out those questionnaires. I recall now that it had a lot of the ingredients of this HIV stuff. And I should have suspected my own advisor, Doc Kirby. He's been involved in some of Sobel's stuff. Funny, I once considered using it toward my dissertation."

Dan asserted, "Never know when or where you're going to find a good lead."

"Or exploiter in the wood pile." Sue said angrily. "Where do we go next?"

Dan studied Sue's hazel eyes. He nodded and said soberly, "As soon as I get this stuff assimilated, I'll get together a full report for Byron Stone."

"What about Marone? The cops?" Sue asked.

"Marone may not like our doing what we've done. Feel he's been outdone. He wasn't able to find a thing with his court order." Dan grinned knowingly. "Nah, I know Frank. I'm sure he'll accept what we've done."

Sue appeared mystified. "What if he can't do anything with it? There have been an awful lot of murders and no real movement toward apprehending the ones who did them. This whole thing gives me the creeps."

Dan shrugged. "Marone's working hard on it. He mentioned something about the Russian Mafia to me. And what we've uncovered will help."

"Russian Mafia." Sue shuddered. "Crew members on Byron's yacht had Slavic accents. Boris what's his name, Byron's administrative assistant, he's a Russian." She shook her head. "It all seems so bizarre. All these Russians. Now that I think of it, I should have known from the get-go. On the trip to Byron's summer place, Ingrid Blake did say something that sounded like Russian. Funny how I had jumped to the conclusion she was German because of her first name."

"A lot of former Germans live around the Baltic part of what used to be the old USSR," Jim informed. "Lots of old German names in that area.

"Like Danzig for Gdansk?"

Dan shrugged. "My work's pretty well done. For

now at least. Yours definitely. You're not policemen. It's up to the local cops or Feds or whoever else Marone and or Byron Stone may want to contact to do more. For us to do more could be very dangerous. This Blake guy, especially, he sounds like he's got clout. Who knows, maybe even as much as Stone does. So we've got to be careful. Real careful. Same old story, you know. Once a guy kills, it's a lot easier for him the second time. And this guy sounds like he's becoming an old hand at it, either doing it himself or hiring someone to do it for him. Let's be cautious. This guy not only has a lot of pull, he's no dumbbell, although I'm beginning to wonder if he and even this Sobel character are all there. It has occurred to me that their, maybe Sobel's, master plan, sounds a lot like some egomaniac's plan to save mankind, wiping out whole populations of people who may be HIV infected in order to stop the worldwide epidemic."

"Backfire? Hope it doesn't." Jim laughed. "Maybe those guys are just using the scheme to get tons of easy money from Stone's Foundation so they can accomplish their bigger goals which includes, I'm sure, becoming extremely wealthy. It's only a smoke screen for their other stuff, pure and simple."

Sue said, "Here's something." So that she could read the scribbled handwriting, Sue held up to the light what appeared to be a memo pad. "It says here that Blake will be using Stone Henge as his headquarters for the S and P Foundation projects once Byron Stone dies, at which time Stone Henge will be turned over to S and P. I assume it's referring to Byron's father, although it doesn't say junior or senior." She handed the memo pad to Dan. "Since Blake is head of S and P, he'd get the whole thing."

Dan took the pad from Sue and said angrily, "This guy Blake is a very ambitious and dangerous exploiter type from the looks of things he's done so far. I hope it's Byron Stone Senior that's talked about here." He shook his head apprehensively. "If not, who knows what this guy is up to."

Sue said, "I wouldn't put anything past him."

"You're right. Looks like we can't rule out anything." Dan appeared deeply concerned. "Especially if he's Red Star."

"Who knows, maybe we're reading this guy and this thing all wrong. Maybe Blake and Doc Sobel only want to take over the Taj Mahal as giant research center to benefit mankind," Jim ridiculed.

"I don't think so," Dan said dryly.

Sue studied some more material in a folder. After thumbing through a detailed plan for a new preventive medicine center, she said, "In one way I'm glad we discovered this stuff, but now that we have all this material what do we do with it?"

Dan nodded. "As I said, Our work is done for now. And there's nothing for us to fear as long as we play our cards right. Certainly, as long as the killers don't know that we know about them, after I copy this stuff, we return it without being detected."

When Dan reached over to pick up the small pile of material Sue said, "There's a copier in the faculty lounge on the fourth floor in Sobel's building. Can kill two birds."

Jim said, "No one should bother you there since you're there most of the time during the school year."

Sue smiled at Dan, "Jim's right. It's like a private joke between me and the custodians. They know I've sneaked in and used the copier when no one's around but them. I can run up there and get the stuff done and then return the stuff back to Sobel's office. There really isn't much to run off, while you guys sneak a six-pack of beer over to the custodians and discuss baseball or whatever. I've caught those guys sneaking in a beer or two after doing their afternoon chores."

"Sounds like fun," Jim said as his mood shifted from light to silly. "I'm sort of beginning to enjoy this international intrigue stuff."

Dan liked the idea. "Yeah, let's wrap it up."

24

Byron's fingers played a drum roll over the fat manila envelope on the desk in front of him. Although he appeared to be looking out at the other buildings on the banks of the Hudson, all he saw were a myriad of inner thoughts.

Byron's large office jutted out like a glass-enclosed cliff-house. The designer of the penthouse office had incorporated this feature so that both the sky and the Hudson River could be seen from anywhere in the room. Inscribed on a heavily lacquered wooden strip over a coat of arms on the wall in back of a very large teak desk were the words Le Fils Stone. When the suite of offices were constructed by the elder Stone, he wanted to share them with his son; now there was only one Stone occupying the premises.

Byron's fingers stopped their drum roll. He knew that he had to make a decision about the material in the thick manila envelope, which Dan Morrissey had just delivered. Morrissey and he had discussed the manila envelope's more intricate and revealing contents.

Byron pondered. Although he appeared mesmerized by the river traffic thirty stories below, he pressed the intercom button on his desk. "Harriet, please send Boris Kleptokoff in."

"Right away Mister Stone."

The administrative assistant arrived in a couple of minutes from his office down the hall. Boris hardly looked the part of an executive type. He had the appearance more of a nightclub bouncer with his broad shoulders, thick neck and bulging chest. His arms, and belly expanded his tight fitting navy business suit to its fullest limits. His large rounded and sweating bucolic face gave one the feeling that his comfort zone would be much improved if he could unbutton his stiff collar and remove his tight fitting jacket and red tie. Byron had always sized him up as one who had worked diligently and faithfully for Stone Holdings almost from the time he was allowed to leave the former USSR, when the first Russian emigres were given visas under Gorbachev's glastnost policy. Boris Kleptokoff had mastered the English language before his release from the gulag and he had rapidly mastered the intricacies of tax accounting, a big help for working his way up the Stone corporate ladder.

"Boris, contact Cameron Blake and set up an appointment for him to have lunch with me and you at Stone Henge today." Byron checked his watch. "Tell him I'll meet him there and that you'll pick him up to make things easier for him." Byron resumed tapping his fingers nervously on the report he'd received from Dan Morrissey. He studied the Russian's face.

Boris Kleptokoff eyed the manila envelope with guarded interest. "What time Mister Stone? And may I ask? For what is meeting about, if Cameron want to know."

Byron said, "One-ish. Just received this latest report about S and P."

Boris's eyes became fixed on the manila envelope. "About S and P?" Boris asked. Then he nodded respectfully and left.

Byron looked at his watch again. He had originally planned on going over to Belmont to see Sue for lunch and to discuss plans for the Saratoga meet. He pressed the intercom button. "Harriet, get me Sue Brown over at Belmont Park, please." He glanced at the manila envelope and then up at the ceiling while he waited.

There was a faint buzz. "Sir, Sue Brown's on the phone. Line one please."

"Sue, Byron. I won't be able to make it for lunch today. Some real pressing business. I'll tell you more when I see you. How about dinner tonight? I'll pick you up at six or so. We can go over to the Polo Club. I don't think you've ever been there. Got a string of horses there . . . Yeah, should be a lot of fun . . . See you then."

Like someone who'd experienced a back problem recently, Byron got up slowly from his desk, his mind filing through some of the new information he'd received. The S and P Foundation was being used for someone else's personal gain and certainly wasn't being run the way his father would have liked. The thought hurt him deeply. Cameron Blake had been given too much power. He shook his head in disbelief. He couldn't quite fathom how their tight fisted control over it could have slipped so much.

Yes, he had given Cameron Blake too much power and little by little had allowed himself to be diverted to doing too many other things. There had been too many trips, too many actresses, too many smoke screens and he had come to rely too heavily on people like his administrative assistant, Boris. He suddenly realized that one of Stone Corporation's strengths had contributed to the erosion of control. The fact that Stone Corporation paid so well and knew how to delegate responsibility had a lot to do with attracting capable people to it like Boris Kleptokoff and Cameron Blake. Men and women who were competent and efficient and who made the most difficult of tasks appear simple and easy to accomplish were heavily recruited even from overseas. He recalled how Kleptokoff had been hired on the recommendation of Cameron Blake.

Byron eyed the manila envelope on his desk. The thought of using the information as bait popped into his head. He smiled. Why not? Let him look at it. Good way to flush him out, too, hopefully. He buzzed his secretary.

"Has Boris left?"

"I'll check, sir."

25

Byron sat at the head of the long dining room table and looked about him as though discovering for the first time the tall triple columns of alabaster that supported and embellished each corner of the dining hall, which had served as a ballroom for some of his mother's most lavish dining and dancing parties. Many a stuffy Lester Lannon orchestra had filled the small bandstand abutting and jutting out from the wall to his left. He looked up at the massive genuine Baccarat crystal chandelier high over the rosewood dining table, which had been designed to seat more than forty guests comfortably. His mother had expensive taste. His mind was speculating about what his mother's taste might be in today's world when Stone Henge's head butler escorted Boris Kleptokoff and Cameron Blake into the room. After showing them to seats on either side of Byron, the Englishman bowed stiffly and departed.

"That's quite a ritual and no one does it better than the English," Blake said, referring to the butler and trying to appear lighthearted and upbeat. "By the way did you get a chance to think about my new proposal?"

"About replacing the S and P board members who have been dying on us?" Byron's stony stare gave Blake the immediate notion that there was going to be trouble ahead.

Blake's mood switched gears. He grumbled, "I thought that was a definite."

"Nothing's that definite lately. Instead things have been indefinite, even deadly for a lot of people formerly connected with S and P's board and I'm beginning to have big doubts about the way things have been going at S and P."

A servant entered the room pushing a cart laden with bottles of wine and liquor. He stopped just in back of Cameron Blake whose face became a grim mask with the twisted hint of a bitter smile on it.

"What're you fellows drinking? Byron asked politely.

"Vodka on the rocks for me." Blake added dryly, "Double. Could really use one today."

"Tough day in the trenches?" Byron asked.

"Calls from all over the place about a new project."

Byron studied Blake's face. Was he trying the upbeat approach to avoid the issue? Byron smiled suspiciously and as though he'd swallowed something sour. Then he turned to give Boris a knowing look, causing Boris's face to become flushed before saying something in Russian to Blake who responded with a nervous laugh.

Byron said, "I know very little Russian, but I caught the words Backfire Project. Your pet project."

Blake's face became redder than Boris's. "My pet project?"

"I'll have some vodka on ice. Double like Cameron," Boris said to a servant who had a bottle of vodka on his tray. "I love all offspring from potato, even alcoholic offspring. I still love much stuff which comes originally from my native homeland, even though I'm glad I left much of other stuff behind."

The servant poured Boris his drink and handed it to him. Then he turned to Byron. "Would you like more white wine sir?"

"Not right now, thank you. Just leave the bottle in front of me." Byron addressed Blake assertively: "Cameron, I've decided, now that I'm suddenly beginning to get a better handle on how S and P is being run, to change the plans for converting our main house here at Stone Henge into a conference and research center for S and P. The building next door is more than adequate. Especially since I've been considering downsizing."

"Downsizing? Now? Just when we're beginning to get a good program underway. A most humanitarian program." Cameron Blake's face twisted angrily. "Your father promised."

"I know, but I'm in charge now," Byron said decisively. "Gentlemen, Cameron, I may as well get right down to the heart of the matter. A lot of interesting information crossed my desk this morning, the result of work done by my special investigative outfit."

Blake appeared perplexed. "You have been doing some clandestine investigating. Sounds like the KGB, or should I say the NKVD in the old, old Soviet."

Byron smiled with a nod. "The outfit your father worked for. And y'know what, it does, but it is necessary in light of what my investigators have uncovered and revealed to me about what's been going on behind my back."

Blake resembled a boxer facing his adversary in the ring before a bout. He raised his head and cast a menacing look at Byron. "What kind of game are we playing here, cat and mouse?"

"I won't go into detail here over lunch, but I want to put you on notice, Cameron, that there will be big changes made soon as to the way things will be handled from now on concerning any and all of my business interests, especially S and P."

Blake fidgeted. "That doesn't include the S and P board, I hope."

"I'm glad you brought up the board thing again. I'm dissolving the board at S and P and am going to be the only one making any major decisions from now on." He glanced menacingly at both men. "No one will make any more decisions without first discussing them with me. Also, I've hired a new accounting firm to do a complete audit of all of my books." Byron emphasized the word "my".

"Why all this nonsense all of a sudden?" Blake's fist came down on the table harder than he'd wanted it to, causing both Byron and Boris to look at him queerly.

Byron said, "It's been brought to my attention that large sums of money have been siphoned off from the companies under S and P. Real large sums." He glared at Blake. "And oh yes, your friend, Doctor Sobel, whom you wanted on the board of S and P, will be removed from any further involvement with S and P. And there will be a criminal investigation as well." Byron paused and waited for a reaction. He was surprised that both men sat in stunned silence.

Byron laughed. "You both look too serious. You

still have jobs. For now at least. Enjoy your drinks,"
he prodded, even though he liked what he saw.
Blake's face gradually reverted to its customary scowl
which Byron always thought reflected the man's true
persona, whereas Boris Kleptokoff's appeared not
surprisingly contrite.

Blake took Byron's suggestion. He sipped his
drink while shooting a depressed look at Boris. Then
he nodded solemnly and said, "You're the boss,
Byron, especially now that your father is on those life
support machines and barely alive. There's not much
else I can say except... except yes you are the boss."

"Yes I am," Byron said. "I'm just putting you on
notice so that you'll have time to get your affairs in
order."

"I thought I heard you say we still have jobs?"
Blake placed his drink on the table, almost smashing
his glass. "You're not implying that I'm going to be
replaced?" Blake's dark penetrating eyes suddenly
became red with rage, resembling two chunks of
lighted charcoal.

Byron laughed. He was enjoying the squirming
exercise. "Relax, Cameron," Byron said, holding up
his right hand like a traffic cop. "I didn't say that.
Not yet, anyway. There will be big changes, however.
Big, big changes. I can't blame Dad for letting things
slide. He's not here to defend himself. I have to take
all of the blame, or certainly most of it. Now that it
looks as though I'm the only one in charge, mostly in
charge except for S and P which I share with my
cousin Cindy, of course, even though she's always left
things up to me . . . I've merely decided to get things
changed for the better. Everyone who works for me
will get his or her day in court, however."

"What does . . . that mean?" Blake had wanted

to shout his question but restrained himself when he saw the look on Boris Kleptokoff's face urging caution He looked threateningly at Byron as though he could do him some bodily harm. Then he glanced at the two waiters standing nearby prepared to serve the main meal. "Day in court? We're not criminals."

"Maybe yes, maybe no," Byron said calmly. "That too remains to be seen." Byron nodded toward the two servants who had been in his father's employ from the first day they started work. "May as well try some of those delicious mouth watering filets that my cook prepared especially for us."

Even though they hadn't eaten yet, Blake looked like he already had indigestion. His dark eyes stared down at his plate, his face maintaining its scowl while the filet mignon wrapped in bacon was being served. He said, "I hope you're not going to cut back on all the wonderful humanitarian projects at S and P."

Byron ignored him and said to his administrative assistant, "Y'know, Boris, I never did get your background straight. I know about how Doctor Blake got you for us; where in the old Soviet Union did you come from originally? I know you lived around Moscow, but is that where you were born?"

Even though Boris Kleptokoff's mouth had started salivating as each filet of meat was being placed on his plate, he said, "I came from near Doctor Blake's region in Georgia. My family moved to Moscow when I was little boy. My father was minor official in Communist Party who was promoted to bureaucratic position. Not unlike Doctor Blake's. When he died, my mother and I were left to live in Moscow, as she got job teaching in big university there just before my father died."

"Your family was fairly well off then." Byron

glanced at Blake who had started to carve up his meat. "Cameron, how long have you known Doctor Sobel?"

Cameron Blake hesitated with his hands clutching hard at fork and knife as though he wanted to use them on something other than his filet mignon. "Several years. He has been one of the first researchers ever to apply for grants from S and P, and some of his research, as you must know, is highly regarded, and he is highly respected internationally among people in his field."

Byron turned toward Boris. "Have you been aware that Ingrid, Cameron's wife, came from the Baltic region? Quite far from where you guys come from."

Boris forced a subservient smile and looked directly across at Blake who was staring down at his plate and chewing his food like a big bulldog. Even though Boris would have preferred to chew the piece of steak he was balancing on his fork, he responded frankly, "Yes, I knew this. She and I had, and even Cameron, have had quite a few conversations at your many parties. And even before that. We have been in contact for such long time now. I thought you knew this when you hired me as I gave you letter, or was it your father, a letter of recommendation through friend of Cameron. Cameron knew my father well and some of his close associates."

"I remember, although I don't know everything that's been going on lately, inside or outside of S and P." Byron flashed a wry smile at Boris. "Obviously. Or I'd have had a better handle on what was going on with Nick Stockton and his partner Wilson and all the other stuff." Byron turned to Blake to catch his reaction. A sullen Cameron Blake continued to stare down at his plate as he chewed his food. Byron

laughed as though he were toying with his top em-
ployee. "Y'know, Cameron, maybe we could
reconfigure S and P."

Cameron's face brightened slightly. He looked
up and said, "Reconfigure?" as though he liked the
word.

"Yeah, get you an assistant."

Blake appeared interested. With some food still
in his mouth he said, "Assistant? Sounds like a good
idea. Boris, perhaps?"

Byron shook his head. "Nope, not Boris. Sue
Brown. Of course, after she gets her doctorate from
the university."

26

"This evening was one of the most fun times of my life. I had no idea how good a horseman you are. Too bad your polo team lost, in spite of your good play."

Byron laughed good-naturedly. "Can't win them all."

"When you showed me your polo horses, I began for the first time to see the real Byron Stone." Sue held her hand out the window of Byron's sports car as though about to grab at the crisp evening air. There was a slight thumping against the windshield as the occasional large June bug collided with it. "You seem to love your horses, almost as much as you love giving to good causes."

"Right now you're my best cause."

"I've benefited from the Stone's benevolence for some time. By the way, I really love S and P's slogan: Preventive medicine is the best medicine. Whose idea was it to use Stone Henge and S and P for international seminars to share preventive medical technology and research?"

"Believe it or not, Cameron Blake is the one who sold us on the idea. That's why it's going to be hard to dump him. He is a talented medical technologist and chemist."

"Too bad he's got his own agenda."

Byron cleared his throat. "True. And I shouldn't tell you this, but I shook him up when I told him I was going to make you his assistant. Come to think of it, it's not a bad idea."

"Me?"

"You could keep an eye on him until we decide what to do with him."

"You're not serious?"

"Not really." Byron laughed. "We're home."

Byron steered the car off the town road and stopped before the heavy metal gate which slid open. After he waved toward the gate keeper and drove on, Byron said, "As I was about to say, Cameron Blake and a few of his other highly paid cohorts who infiltrated our organizations spent a lot of their time making us believe that they were competent and trustworthy. Not to change the subject, I'm glad you liked my polo ponies."

"I really did. Now I can't wait to see you in another match."

"Hey keed, you may even want to invade the world of polo and become one of our stars the way you can ride."

"Yeah, I really liked the way they looked and behaved. So smart and yet kindly."

"My polo ponies I can trust. Too bad I can't trust some of the people who work for me. A lot of damage has been done because I didn't have a handle on things as I should have. I was too trusting, I guess."

"One builds trust. You can't blame yourself for

something that was being done sub rosa," Sue said while eyeing Byron for his reaction. "Life would be a lot simpler and much easier to deal with if there wasn't so much hidden agenda."

Byron nodded. "I really misread Cameron. To think, this thing's been going on a long, long time, and under our very noses, my dad's and mine. We should have detected, should have known."

"What's going to happen now? To Blake and the others?"

"The first thing I'm going to have to do is fire the bastards and after we develop enough of a case against them, have them indicted on criminal charges. Nah. I should deal with them the way, Cameron Blake at least, the way he dealt with Nick Stockton and the others."

"Wilson I can understand, certainly, and Nick and their other partner as well; there's motive there. They were all involved in trying to cut in on Blake's territory, but why Bev and Al Carter, or Ruth for that matter? Doesn't make sense unless he's a psychopath."

"A serial type killer of some sort?" Byron paused. "I thought I knew him, but now, certainly Blake is dangerous. A psychopathic type? You'd know more about that than I. Now we find that he always knew what Nick and his partners were up to. But they were safe as long as Cameron felt safe and in control. Lately, though, that changed and Blake must have felt that Nick and the others were going to blow the whistle on the whole thing and as I've just recently discovered, Nick and even Wilson were being pressured to do so by the Feds. Even an investigative team of television reporters came to me and was digging deep and getting ready to do a television expose of this power elitist group of former Communist officials. I really don't know much about how they operate, but through Blake they may have started establishing some kind of contact with Wilson and Nick." He paused. "Blake played things close to the vest. Like most people, though, he got greedy. Wanted complete control by setting up his own board." Byron shook his head. "I can't believe it-eliminating all those people including Al, Bev."

"Yet you knew Blake well."

"Not that well as it turns out. And he isn't going to get away with anything, especially when it comes to the skimming of funds from S and P and the other business of playing both sides of the street."

Sue had never seen Byron this determined. She said, "From what Jim told me, and he did a lot of research on the subject, those power elite guys in their fancy dachas around Moscow are very clever. They must have been having one big laugh at your expense, especially since they were using both Nick and his partners as well as Blake and S and P and guys like Doctor Sobel."

"You're right. We were talking to some of them as recently as last month about investing S and P money in the former Soviet Republics. With Blake, of course, as our chief negotiator. And I was trying to get a handle on the radioactive diamonds debacle, which triggered the Fed investigation. Those guys in Russia are the big money and influence guys, somewhat like the Morgans, Vanderbilts and Rockefellers were years ago in the U.S. They still have a lot of good connections here in the States with many influential former bigwigs of our government."

"So they were merely using, manipulating Blake and whoever else was working for him."

"And vice versa."

"By the way, who else besides Sobel was working with Blake?"

Byron said angrily, "I've got a pretty good idea now." Byron drove on quietly. He took a turn to the right just before the main house and drove up the narrow street to the guesthouse. "We're the good guys," Byron said breaking his silence and attempting to sound humorously self-righteous. "And since they're the bad guys, we'll nail those guys and win in the end."

"Sounds like you have a plan."

"Not yet for dealing with those guys overseas, but even they may be in trouble before we're done. We may pull the same stuff on them that they've been pulling on us. Eventually, buy the companies out from under them, as in pulling the rug." Byron drove the sports car to a halt in front of the large ultra modern guesthouse.

Sue got out of the car first. "Thanks a lot, guy." She sounded genuinely grateful, but tired. "I really enjoyed the evening. The dinner, the horses were just great. Love to do it again."

"Horses? What about me?" Byron cocked his head to look at Sue from an angle. "Do you think we could relax together and even enjoy something stupid like say a movie on the movie channel? Must sound like a funny request, but I have no other plans for this evening and I must admit I just can't seem to get enough of you lately."

Sue blushed. "I never thought I'd hear you say something like that. By all means, lover. Hey, that doesn't sound right. Too much like a hayseed or country bumpkin." She extended her arm toward him. "C'mon in, please, do come in. Su casa es mi casa, literally."

Byron made a funny face and said, "Thanks."

Sue laughed lightheartedly. After she switched on the lights, she said, "You seriously want to watch some TV?" Before she could make a move, she felt Byron's strong hands on her shoulders. She tensed up and said, "I thought you wanted to watch some TV."

"I do eventually." Byron released her and allowed her to turn her lithe body around to face him. "After I take care of some unfinished business first."

They moved toward each other, simultaneously wrapping their arms around each other, their lips meeting. After a minute of heated kissing and hugging, both began to expand their lovemaking, she with her hands first on his firm buns and back, he with his hands on her hips and along her buttocks.

Sue suggested finally, "We'd be more comfortable if we got out of our sticky clothes."

"Great idea."

Sue led the way into the downstairs master bedroom. She had the sensation of wanting to devour Byron. She wanted to rip his clothes off, but instead tried to hold still while Byron began undressing her. He seemed to be enjoying his task until he had difficulty with her bra clasp. She helped by slipping it over her head. "Can't wait," she whispered.

"You're one hot . . ."

"Not really. Just doing what a good sex therapist should do."

"That's some new twist, a real gift, and I'm glad I'm the recipient." Byron unzipped his trousers and let them fall to the floor. He stepped out and over them and sat on the bed while unbuttoning his shirt. Before he was done, Sue, who was already completely nude, helped him. As soon as his hairy chest was bared, she placed her hands on it and pushed him backward. She wet kissed his face, using her tongue like a brush. She went all the way down his chest and was kissing his belly button while he kissed her on the ears and neck. Then she got him to roll over onto her so she could get him into a modified version of C A T. By rocking forward and back with her belly rubbing against his, he soon got the idea.

"This is the way, oh, oh . . ." She released several loud moans.

They were on the bed making hot love in the unlighted room when the lights of the hallway outside the bedroom flickered. A minute later the lights went out completely. Byron, who had just ejaculated, withdrew and lay on his back exhausted. But Sue sat up on the bed in the completely darkened room and speculated, "Must be a blown circuit."

"Yeah, mine," Byron joked. Then he abruptly sat up next to her and listened carefully. "The air conditioning unit is still working. That's funny." He listened alertly for other sounds.

"Wonder what . . ."

"Ssh, I thought I heard someone outside." Byron sounded cautious. "Lots of animals out there, but those lights going out like that . . ." He shook his head.

"Human animals, I'm worried about," Sue whispered nervously.

"Me too." Byron reached over to the lamp next to the bed. The lamp was visible because of the moonlight coming into the room through large skylights. He tried to switch on the lamp. "No juice here. I'd better find a flashlight. Must be one in the kitchen." As soon as he got up from the bed, Sue joined him. They groped their way into the kitchen and started looking for a flashlight in the upper drawers of the multitude of kitchen cabinets. "Think there'd be some matches even."

Byron felt his way carefully over to the sink and used some paper towels to wash his genitalia. "Let's get us cleaned up a bit and get dressed. I'll have to call maintenance and get someone up here to deal with this dumb thing."

"Dumb is a good way to describe it," Sue chuckled.

They returned to the bedroom and were putting on their clothing, when Byron put up his hand. "Hold it. Did you hear the front door, some door . . . sound of a door opening and closing?"

"I didn't . . ."

They continued to put on their clothes. "I love the way you make love and I really enjoyed it, Byron, but have you ever heard of C A T, the coital alignment technique?" Sue was hoping that he had at least heard of it.

"You mentioned that the last time we had sex."

"I know. It's pretty esoteric stuff. I'll have to get you some literature describing it."

"Sounds like something from one of your sex manuals." Byron appeared mildly interested. "No, I honestly can't say that I've even heard about it. Is it something I should know?"

"Perhaps. Maybe the next time we have coitus, we can try it. It works; that I know for sure."

"Coitus?" Byron appeared puzzled for a moment. "Oh yeah, fancy Latin word for the good old Anglo Saxon word fucking. Sounds like you've tried it, this CAT I mean. Whatever we did, I enjoyed it. Did you?"

"I really did," Sue emphasized. "And someday, I'll explain the C A T stuff."

"Sh." Byron put his hand over her mouth. After a few seconds he removed his hand and said apologetically. "Sorry about that. Must be imagining things. Jumpy for nothing."

"Not for nothing." Cameron Blake's voice was loud and abrasive, his wide body appearing ominously in the doorway, as he instantaneously snapped on a flashlight. He shined it into Byron's eyes, blinding him.

Sue gasped. Alarm covered her face. Her bra dangling from her hands, she placed it over her bare breasts.

"What the hell." Byron couldn't finish his sentence. He had all he could handle trying to regain his vision. When the flashlight was turned aside, he could see the semi automatic pistol pointed toward him and Sue.

Cameron Blake motioned for someone behind him to come into the room. "In here, Boris," Blake ordered, "You too, Ivan." Blake looked squarely at Sue and said, "You may not get hurt, if you do as you're told."

Sue's face said she didn't believe him.

Byron rubbed his eyes. When he reopened them, he said with a strained voice, "What's going on Cameron? When I told you there would be changes at S and P, I thought we had worked things out. Can't we work something out?"

"It's not the most appropriate time to be negotiating. Bit late for that."

"Some sort of accommodation?"

Cameron Blake appeared ruthlessly confident. "We'll see. Right now, though, I want you two to complete dressing yourselves." Blake waved the gun toward them.

Sue secured her bra and zipped her blue jeans. "I'll have to get my tee shirt."

Blake growled, "Boris will get it." He looked at Byron who had on only his boxer shorts. "No, we will all get them, your clothes."

Byron got into his slacks. Sue was fully dressed before he was. He seemed to be taking an extra long time to complete his task. When he had finally slipped on his expensive leather boots, Byron shrugged his broad shoulders and said nonchalantly, "I guess we're going to be taking a ride. Not that I haven't been taken for one by you guys before."

"Cut the comedy, chief," Blake threatened. "You've been spoiled long enough by your position and wealth. Time someone else enjoyed it. Someone who worked as hard as anyone for a business empire so that it could be expanded to where it's one of the largest on the planet."

"Like you guys and your other friends, of course," Byron sneered. Sue watched admiringly but nervously as Byron coolly challenged Blake even with the barrel of a gun pointed at him. There was even a swagger in Byron's walk as Blake motioned for Byron to go ahead of Sue.

Boris had grabbed Sue by the shoulder and was prodding her along. They were preceded out of the house by Ivan. Sue recognized the pasty-faced man, a member of the Zenith's crew. He appeared unaffected by what was going on; just another hired renegade who had been through a similar drill before, Sue surmised.

Blake ordered, "We can use the tree nursery road through the woods to the yacht club, so no one will see us."

Blake pushed Byron into the back seat of a large Mercedes sedan where he was sandwiched in between Blake and Ivan, while Sue was seated in front next to Boris who was the designated driver. The car pulled slowly away from the curb and headed toward the main house; just before the estate garage Boris turned into a gravel road.

"Why, Cameron? You've been very well paid, even well thought of, although now I'm beginning to wonder why." Byron's voice reflected his obvious feelings of hurt and betrayal. "You've moved up to one of the top positions in our organization as head of S and P and were even being considered to replace Bill Lacey as head of our entire international operation when Bill retires next year."

Blake grunted a terse, "I've got my reasons."

Byron asked, "What were your reasons for killing Nick Stockton, Ruth, the others? My own, the Fed investigators too, found out that Nick's outfit represented your EEG's interests well."

"You don't know the half of it," Blake interrupted angrily. "The truth of the matter is oh formerly almighty and trusting Mister Bryon Stone that your most trusted and worthy friend, Nick Stockton, was a liar who had completely pulled the wool over your eyes. We, I did you a favor when I took care of him and his partners, those two conniving crooks. They were playing both sides of the street, good guy—bad guy kind of game. Nick was playing the good guy in front of you, while the other twerps were using Nick's inside dope to do you in. But you won't have to worry about that any more."

Byron sat stunned. He couldn't believe his best friend could do what Blake said he did. "I know you didn't act on my behalf. What was your actual motive for killing Nick, Wilson, the others? It wasn't merely because you wanted to have your own board at S and P. That's too simplistic."

Blake shrugged his heavy shoulders. "That's one of the reasons, however. I shouldn't tell you, but what the hell, where you're going it won't matter anyway. Those pimps were using the Baxters deal. It all started there. You remember the Baxters-Marins debacle? You must, even though you didn't gain that much from it. Nick and his buddies on Wall Street were using that deal to try and blackmail my real clients, the guys I really work for."

Byron's face lighted up. "The EEG, the guys in Eastern Europe? I still can't see why you did it, had to kill them. That Marins deal was actually small potatoes even though Baxters collapsed."

Blake interrupted impatiently, "Nick and his main consort, Wilson… those pimps were holding the Baxters deal like a club over our heads, black-mail. Everything would've been fine if they didn't get greedy. They would have gotten a lot of business from us, my clients. But it began to look to us that they, Wilson and the others, with Wilson being the chief instigator, eventually wanted complete control of the cartel I'd worked so hard to organize and de-velop during and even before perestroika. And when I discovered they were both HIV, I decided to make it look like a suicide."

"Too bad no one was fooled," Byron scoffed.

"You were."

Byron shrugged. "For a while. Mercy killings of a sort, I thought."

"Would've worked if your hired investigators didn't start snooping. Anyway, when we discovered what you were up to, especially after you decided to dissolve the S and P board, we had to make a quick decision about you."

Byron said, "Those other deaths, Al Carter's and his wife Bev, Ruth's, done so that you could replace them with your own people? Boris, Sobel? And even some of your other Russian stooges?"

"You're really not such a dumb guy after all," Blake said with a sneer. "Although, like Nick, they're ultimately better off dead than alive with that AIDS thing."

Byron started saying what was on his mind, "No reason to . . ." but decided that antagonizing his vicious captor would accomplish nothing. Instead he asked, "What would you take to let us go free? I could turn S and P over to you with all its assets."

Blake merely made a sniffling sound and remained tight lipped for the remainder of the ride.

Boris drove the Mercedes down the graveled road between rows of neatly planted trees and shrubs. When they arrived at a paved road, Boris took a sharp left turn onto it. In less than a minute, against the clear moonlit night, the large granite yacht club building loomed ahead. Boris parked the car in the yacht club's paved parking lot. Except for a few scavenging birds, large floodlights revealed a deserted yacht club and beach area. Even the Zenith, anchored among a small flotilla of smaller boats, appeared deserted.

"Let's get them out to my boat, pronto," Blake said in a half whisper. "It's just about high-tide now. We can take it from there." Ivan who never spoke a word and appeared to be more robot than human got out first. For the first time, as he adjusted his clothes, Sue saw the butt of an automatic weapon protruding from his pants just over his belt buckle.

Sue grimaced as she pictured what might happen if the gun went off accidentally.

When they were all out of the car, Blake barked at Boris, "The launch? Kirk is waiting at the end of the dock with it, I hope?"

"He be there," Boris replied. "I talk to him just before I met you. He be here and he assure me that the captain of the Zenith will not be around tonight. He is at his home in upper state."

Blake nodded and shot a sullen glance at Byron who was standing next to Blake but eyeing the weapon stuffed inside Ivan's belt. Blake pointed at Byron with his semi-automatic, "Let's move, and don't try anything stupid, you two. Believe me. I know how to use this thing."

With Ivan leading the way, all five marched along the dock abutting the broad front lawn of the very private yacht club. Against the backdrop of a relatively calm night, their footsteps resounded on the heavy planking. Only the element of high tide was causing the slightest of wind bursts and even these seemed to be subsiding temporarily. The tide had almost reached its highest point, making it very easy to see the elevated launch at the end of the dock. When they reached the launch, Boris and Ivan stepped gingerly aboard and then helped Sue climb down into the boat's front cockpit. Boris extended his hand for Byron to take hold of it, but Byron just stepped heavily down into the empty rear cockpit of the launch, causing the boat to bounce and sway precariously. It was obvious he was trying to capsize it.

"Hey, no funny stuff," an angered Blake shouted. Then he blinked and grew sullen and silent as he realized how far his voice had carried. He looked over at the flotilla of boats before stepping into the launch. After he felt comfortably and securely seated, Blake gave the signal with his hand for the launch to proceed toward its destination.

Kirk, whom Sue recognized as another one of the crew of the Zenith when she had gone on the trip to Byron's summer place, revved up the motor and aimed the launch toward the Zenith. After a couple of minutes, he throttled down the engine and started steering the boat around the Zenith toward a luxury motor yacht which, though dwarfed by the Zenith, had to be at least sixty feet long with a very broad beam. The launch slowed down and was eased up to a platform extending just above sea level from the rear of the large luxury cabin cruiser. As soon as the launch was held securely in place by Kirk and Ivan, Boris stood up and stepped onto the rear platform of Blake's yacht and helped Byron and Sue get off the launch onto the platform and then up a small metal ladder onto the aft deck of the yacht.

"Take them to my stateroom and lock them in it." Blake barked his orders like a commanding officer. "I want to talk to Kirk. I'll be right up."

Ivan took up the rear and followed Sue and Byron who were escorted by Boris into the yacht's main stateroom.

Boris said apologetically, "Sorry for all this, folks, but I have work for Mister Blake and the EEG, the cartel. A long time. He has done much for my family and me. Please cooperate so that no hurt will come to . . ." He turned and left the room with Byron and Sue standing in the middle of it at the foot of a neatly made queen-sized bed.

While examining the lavishly furnished room whose walls were constructed of oriental teak, Sue remarked, "He, Boris obviously isn't totally, completely in sync with Blake."

Byron appeared skeptical as he shook his head. "Being treated with respect can often give one a false sense of hope or security. Boris has been treating me with respect for an awful long time and now look at him."

"Until just a short while ago, I thought that you were one of them . . . the killers."

Byron looked hurt and astonished. "You actually thought I could do such a thing? Although I must admit, I was surprised to learn that Boris and Blake were involved. And that report I got from Dan Morrisey about all the killings in those out of the way places in Africa... HIV or no, that was too much."

"Man the predator by nature. Good label, title. I've often thought of writing such a book. Any of us is capable of killing and exploiting. Many men have been known to do it on dates. But all kidding aside, I didn't know what to think and I didn't know that Dan Morrissey worked for you until we moved to uncover Doctor Sobel's involvement in Blake's bilking of your S and P Foundation?"

Byron laughed. "Until Dan went to work for me, I was sort of in the dark. Yet how you could believe that I could have been involved in such a bizarre thing hurts." He shook his head. "That I was behind it all? It didn't surprise me, though, when I discovered the truth of this whole thing. That the EEG cartel, as Blake and his friends call their outfit, was using Nick Stockton's outfit to invest money and gold they had diverted and misappropriated from the old USSR's coffers for years . . . placed it in their own accounts in places overseas, mostly Switzerland of course. And the way money was being siphoned from S and P..."

"I know all that now, but what about . . . Jim and I overheard you talking on your yacht with Blake and that other guy, Willi what's his name . . . It was something about Ruth Stockton. Ruth is next. Or at least that's what I thought I heard you say."

Byron laughed harder than before. "So you and Jim were playing snooper . . . When it comes to you, I can believe almost anything. You're something else. Ruth is next?" He shook his head and smiled. "I don't think so."

"I must've been hearing things."

"Heard what you wanted to hear."

"Yep. In psych we call that selective attention." Sue slumped down onto the queen-sized bed.

"Don't remember that, even though I took psych 101 at Yale. Ages ago." Byron sat down next to her.

Appearing both dejected and helpless, Sue asked, "Now what?"

Byron stood up abruptly and moved around the room as though he were searching for something. He stood motionless finally and stared up at the ceiling with a frustrated look on his face. "I was hoping he'd slipped up. He's thought of everything. No phone. I'm sure he has one somewhere on this tub. There's got to be a way out of this. If we can't escape, we could at least try to get a message out. I actually was hoping that Boris would stay with us so that I could try to talk him out of this thing he's doing with Blake. He may still be reachable. And I really can't understand his doing this sort of thing. He's always treated me and my dad with such great respect. He seemed so genuine, so morally sound."

"Do you think Boris would cooperate in a murd . . . I hate to use the word."

"Murder?" Byron said grimly. "I'm pretty sure now

that he helped with the others. He and Blake come from the same side of the street, same neighborhood gang as it were. No time now to discuss that, though." Byron shrugged his shoulders and went over to a small closet. After rummaging around in it for a short while, he whispered, "What's this?"

Sue stood up and rushed over to Byron's side. "The plastic bags." Her heart leaped. "That dirty animal must have put them there for future use."

"The deadly Stone bags? On us, no doubt." Byron put his finger to his mouth and studied the situation for a moment; then he pressed down hard on the package of heavy duty plastic bags with his knee and one hand while pulling at a couple of them with the other. After he had succeeded in freeing up two of the bags, Byron handed one of them to Sue. "Here, fold it up and stow it in your jeans, sort of flat like against your belly so they can't see it there. Here take another."

"Sure makes me hipper."

"Byron ignored the pun as he pulled out another bag and stuffed it into his own slacks. As he was about to turn around, he nudged a small object with his toe. "And what's this?" He bent over to examine the object. "Of course. Twine to hold the bags on more securely. We may need some too. The small cord at the outer rim of these things may not be enough." He reached into his pants pocket and pulled out a small golden implement.

Sue studied the tiny pocketknife containing a blade and nail clipper. She watched as Byron cut several strands of twine of various lengths from the spool of twine. "What will we need them for?" Sue whispered after they returned to the bed and sat down on it.

"If they use the same M O, and it's only an if, we've got to be prepared—for anything; lets say they place the plastic bags over our heads and drop us overboard, it's going to be a ways out from shore; with these bags we'll be able to make a makeshift flotation of sorts, hopefully, that will keep us from drowning until help comes from somewhere or other."

Sue shrugged her shoulders and sighed.

Byron snapped his fingers as his face brightened into a look of discovery. "It might be a good idea." He stood up and walked over to the closet again and with Sue watching his every move, Byron took the small golden object from his pants pocket again and seemed to be busy counting or doing something to the bags.

When Byron completed the task and was seated next to her again on the bed, Sue asked curiously, "What was that all about?"

"You'll see, although I hope you won't have to."

"See what?"

Byron shrugged his shoulders. "Nothing really. Just made the tiniest of holes in each of those remaining bags. Undetectable I hope. Allow us to breath easier if they use them on us." He looked up at the low ceiling. "What else?" He appeared to be talking to himself. He started removing his expensive leather boots. "Good idea to remove these. Got to get rid of as much extra baggage as possible. Don't want to frighten you any more than you already are, but the thought of what Blake has in store for us has made a lot of my imagination juices flow. We'll have to be ready." He placed his boots completely out of sight under the bed." You may want to remove your Nikes or whatever those things are that you're wear-

ing. Although they're light and your feet will be pro-
tected with them on." Byron grew pensive as he again
mulled over what the Burke scenario might consist
of and what more could and should be done. "Hope
you can swim, though. Can you?" He tried to sound
casual as he asked, not wanting to alarm Sue.

Sue replied with a reassuring smile. "I'm a pretty
good swimmer. Was even a lifeguard one summer
when I was in high school, before I went to work at
the track for my dad. I guess you've forgotten that
our horse farm is almost on the ocean."

"That's right too. Although I remember being
on a tuna fishing trip off Prince Edward Island up in
Atlantic Canada once with my dad and, believe it or
not—I couldn't at the time—the captain of the tuna
fishing boat said he couldn't swim. Can you believe
that? Only on Prince Edward Island. I'll have to take
us up there on the Zenith some day." Byron shook
his head good-naturedly.

Sue was just beginning to enjoy Byron's idea when
the twin diesel engines of the motor yacht started
sputtering. In a few minutes the boat, which had
remained relatively still, started moving and buck-
ing the waves as it was obviously being pointed out to
the open sea. They could feel the impact of the bow
smashing through the waves as the swiftly moving boat
rammed and sliced through the ocean water.

"We're going for a ride," Sue said bitterly. "I hope
your idea works. Pretty good one, though. I realize
that these bags must be used all over your place, Stone
Henge, mostly for garbage collection. Whose idea
was that? Aren't they meant for heavy duty
commercial use?"

"Dad's idea. He's always been a frugal type. Once
when he was visiting our chemical plant that pro-

duces them, he thought it'd be a good idea to use them at home and I must admit they have helped keep the grounds and place pretty clean." He laughed derisively. "Every litter bit helps and all that sort of stuff. Whoops, I think someone's outside."

The door of the stateroom was unlocked. It opened wide. "Okay folks, even though the ride's just beginning, it's nearing the end of the line for you two." Blake pointed his gun toward Sue and Byron and with a smirk ordered, "Get on the bed and lie down. You two should know a little bit about laying and being in bed together by now." After they complied with his order, Blake said harshly, his gun aimed at them like a cobra poised to strike, "Now turn over on your stomachs and lie still." He motioned with his head toward Boris who was standing in back of him to come into the room. "Hand it to me."

Byron felt the needle and winced slightly as it was skillfully applied to his arm by Blake. "Now that didn't hurt did it?" Blake sounded like a medical professional merely doing a routine inoculation. "Next." Sue tried to resist but Boris proved too strong as he held her face down with one hand and pressed firmly down on her back with the other while Blake stuck the needle into her. "That's all there is to it. You folks'll feel absolutely no pain now." He left the stateroom with Boris standing guard over Byron and Sue. Byron wanted to say something to Kleptokoff but the sedative had started taking effect almost immediately.

The noise of the boat's large engines began to diminish and sputter as they were throttled down until they could hardly be heard. The yacht seemed to stop moving except for a slight bouncing motion caused by the ocean's waves.

Cameron Blake returned, went over to the closet and got two plastic bags and a small spool of twine, which he waved at Boris Kleptokoff. "The finishing touches." He stuffed the bags and twine into his pants pockets. "Let's take them out of here." For Sue and Byron, Blake's voice echoed almost inaudibly as the sedatives had already taken effect.

Boris, appearing like a weightlifter, grabbed at Byron with both hands, rolled Byron's body onto his short thick arms and carried him out the open door onto the aft deck. Cameron Blake followed, carrying Sally's completely limp body.

After Sue and Byron were dumped onto the carpeted aft deck, Blake took the plastic bags and twine out of his pockets and placed them on the deck. A gust of wind forced Burke to reach out and grab the bags just as they were about to be blown away. "Boris," he ordered. "Here. Give me a hand." Blake handed one of the plastic bags to the Russian. "You do the first one. Her. I'll hold her steady while you place the bag over her head."

Boris promptly took the bag and said, "Yes Doctor Blake," but his grimacing face showed how distasteful the task was for him. He took the bag and placed it over Sue's head. Then in spite of the tipping and rolling motion of the boat, Boris held Sue firmly while Blake first pulled the built-in nylon cord which secured the giant bag around Sue's waist before he tied some twine around the part of the bag covering her arms and chest.

Boris released his hold on Sue and was about to lay her down gently on the deck when Blake barked, "Let's put some more twine around her to make certain it doesn't come loose." Blake proceeded to wind some more twine around Sue to insure that the plastic bag stay in place. After they finished with Sue, Boris and Blake went through the same procedure with Byron. When they were done, Blake stood back to examine what he and his accomplice had done. As he did so, a satisfied and sinister smile crossed his face. "That's good. Those specially made plastic bags are perfect for the kind of garbage we're disposing of today. Just what the doctor ordered. Now we'll complete the job. Dump them and head back before anyone spots us."

Boris reluctantly grabbed Byron by the shoulders while Blake took hold of his feet. They took Byron's completely limp body over to the boat rail. "We'll swing back on one and on two just let him go," Blake commanded.

When they flung Byron's body over the side, the splashing water came back and caught Boris in the face. He swore in Russian as he spit out some salty water and then said in English, "I did not need that."

Blake, who got but a small sprinkling of water, said derisively, "You'll get a lot more than you need once we get this last thorn out of our sides." He motioned for Boris to pick up Sue with him. "Same thing with this one, on two." They flung Sue over the side. Rubbing his large stubby hands together, Blake said, "All in a day's work." He waved up at Ivan in his perch above him on the forward deck at the boat's controls and shouted, "Take her back."

The boat's powerful engines roared, causing the boat to lurch and within minutes Ivan had the yacht turned and heading toward shore. Even before the noises from the large boat's engines had subsided into a murmur, Byron, who had been revived by the cold ocean water, freed his hands, found one of the small holes he'd made in the bag earlier and started ripping a bigger hole in the plastic bag. The waters, which had been churned up in the wake of the boat, had long since subsided.

Once he had cleared enough plastic from the front of his face, Byron started searching the murky waters around him. "Whoops." He bumped into Sue's body and grabbed onto her. Her head was still enclosed in the expanded plastic bag, giving her the bizarre appearance of someone usually found only in a movie about outer space. "Good I made those tiny holes. At least you can breath. Here, I'll make the hole a little bigger. If I can find it. Nah, I'll cut the twine. We may need the extra floatation stuff." He reached into his pocket and found the small pen knife and made one cut of the twine; fearing that he was taking too long and that he might even cut her neck, he pulled some of the bag away and used the knife instead to make a large tear in the plastic bag. After making an even larger rip into the bag, Byron placed the knife in his pocket and started tearing at the remainder of the plastic bag with his hands until Sue's face was completely exposed. She had already freed her hands and started to dogpaddle.

"How're you doing? That stuff he gave us must have really worked on you more. Probably gave us the same amount. You've a smaller body."

"Not so good," Sue replied, still a bit groggy and trying to keep her head above water by dog paddling. "But I'll make it, thanks to you, and your resourcefulness. Punching small holes in each of those bags was a good idea."

"Only the ones near the top," Byron said as he struggled to keep buoyant while reaching inside of his slacks for the plastic bag he'd hidden there. "Luckily they took the bags from near the top, but I

punctured very small holes into a goodly number of
them. Thank goodness he didn't give us a larger dose
of that sedative. That was my main worry when he
injected us. Wonder why he didn't give us a larger
dose."

"Maybe Boris…"

"Don't know. Possible." Byron pulled open one
end of the plastic bag and blew into it to get it to
open. He had difficulty keeping his head above water as he struggled with the plastic bag. Even though
it was a calm night, he was bounced around by the
waves and disappeared below the surface of the water several times. Finally he held the bag over his
head as air naturally filled it when he grabbed it by
its opening and pulled on the specially made bag's
nylon cord. "I guess I wont need the twine. They
used it to make doubly sure the bags would stay on
us. Nah, on second thought, I'll wrap a little piece of
the twine around the end of it just to make doubly
sure. Here hold onto it."

Sue, who appeared to be handling the water like
a sea otter, did as he suggested, while Byron pulled a
strand of twine from one of the pockets of his slacks
and tied the twine around the bag with the other
hand, all the while using the bag and Sue to steady
himself. When he was done and was using the
floatation device, Byron said facetiously, "I knew these
things would come in handy again. It's your turn.
Grab yours. You've got two of them. Probably only
need one."

While Byron helped keep her buoyant, Sue
reached down into her jeans and produced one of
the plastic bags. Byron again went through the same
procedure as before for creating the second homemade floatation device. It took less time and was

easier to produce as he received more help from Sue, who showed above average aquatic ability now that she appeared to be completely revived. As soon as the task was completed she reached into her jeans and extricated the other bag. "Guess I won't be needing this. As much as I hate polluting the ocean with it." She was about to release it.

"Don't." Byron took it from her.

"It's only extra baggage."

"May need all the buoyancy we can muster if sea gets choppier. Although you do seem to be quite at home on the high seas here."

Sue scanned the murky water around them. The moonlight danced off the bouncing baby waves of a relatively calm ocean. "We're quite a ways out," Sue said grimly. "And it's quite a ways till dawn."

"And to shore, but we'll just have to wait until then. No sense in heading in any direction until we know where we're heading. We can use these homemade floats and wait a few hours until sun-up, when we can make use of the sun for direction."

Sue looked up at the moonlit, almost cloudless sky. "I think I can use the stars, especially the North Star, to give us some direction. Let me see." She started to swim. "Follow me."

They had dogpaddled for an hour or more when Byron shouted, "I'm not going to make it at this rate. Seems we've been out here an eternity and we're going nowhere fast."

"We're closer to shore than you realize."

"If we were close to shore we'd be able to see one of the lighted buoys."

"I thought I saw a light a few minutes ago," Sue lied. "I never told you this, no reason to, I was the California state swimming champ in high school."

"You never cease to amaze me, keed," Byron shouted enthusiastically.

"I'll get us going in the right direction if you promise not to call me keed."

Byron sputtered and managed a laugh. "So it does bother you, my calling you that. I kind of suspected as much. I won't, any more. Just get us pointed in the right direction."

Sue looked up at the sky clearly dotted with stars. After a short study, she began paddling to her right and making like a swimming dog. Byron followed but couldn't move through the dancing ocean waters as quickly as she.

Sue smiled and said calmly and reassuringly, "Take your time, we've got all night. I'll wait for you to keep up."

With Sue showing the way, they dog paddled while holding onto Byron's homemade floatation devices. They had not gone very far when she could hear Byron gasping for air again. "I don't think I can make it. I guess I could be in better shape."

Sue wanted to say: Here you are one of the richest guys in the world and you sound like a pathetic wretch. Instead she said, "Here, grab hold." She reached back and took hold of his free hand. "First, we'll take a short break to catch our breaths. We really do have all night and all day. The weather forecast I saw yesterday predicted good weather for the next two days."

After a few minutes of hanging onto the homemade floatation devices and Sue, Byron said gratefully, "I needed that. Let's get a move on. The sooner I reach terra firma, the better . . . the sooner I can start getting revenge, sweet revenge . . . I hope."

"What's that noise?" Sue asked, just as she was

about to break away from Byron to start dog paddling again.

They listened intently. The barely audible intermittent murmur of a boat's engine began to compete with the swishing sound of the waves around them. A sudden gust of wind bounced the two of them about as though they were large fishing corks.

"Hope those birds aren't coming back," Byron said cautiously as he struggled to keep his head above the water made suddenly more turbulent by small gusts of wind. "Nah, why would they do that? Just hope it's not a large ocean going critter which could go right over us."

"Let's think positively," Sue suggested. "We've had enough adversity for one day. Besides, big boats, freighters and ocean liners don't make that kind of sound. It's probably a fishing boat. Sometimes, guys that are really into fishing, fish at night. I've heard that you can do your best fishing at night."

"Hope so, although I've never heard that. Whoops, they're moving away from us."

They continued paddling with one hand while holding onto each other with their free hands and allowing their floatation devises to keep them in place. They listened intently. The whirring sound of the boat's motor grew softer. It could barely be heard, except in diminishing spurts. Byron shouted loudly, "Hey," out of frustration; then he added, "damn it all, they're heading away from us." He and Sue bobbed in place and continued to listen intently.

Sue said hopefully, "Seems they're coming back this way." The motor's sound became dimly audible again. As the motor's murmur grew louder, she and Byron started shouting at the top of their voices,

"Help. Hey, over here. Help." Exhausted, they stopped yelling for a moment.

"We ought to keep on shouting." Breathing heavily, a very tired Bryon spoke his words in spurts. "Voices carry much farther out here than on land."

Sounding very frustrated, Sue said, "It's no use. Their engine's too loud. We're no better off than two twigs out here in this big pond."

The motor's whirring sound became much louder as the outline of a small boat began to appear like a blur on the moonlit horizon. As they clung onto each other and their makeshift floats, even though the boat seemed to be heading directly at them, Byron first, then Sue decided to shout for help again. "Help, help." They repeated their cries over and over. In the moonlight they could discern the outline of the rounded bow of a lobster fishing boat. It was heading slantwise in their direction. A large searchlight on the boat was scanning and skimming the murky water not too far from them. Within minutes the searchlight was fracturing the darkness around the now frantically yelling duo. As the boat came closer, its attached searchlight as well as several handheld ones flooded the area around Sue and Byron, nearly blinding them. The fishing boat began to slow down and float closer to Byron and Sue until it was almost on top of them.

"Had a feeling you'd be lucky for me," Byron said happily.

"And you for me, especially after Samsona's win. But let's wait and see who it is. Hope it's not one of his people, Blake's men, that guy Kirk, sent out here to check on things."

"I doubt it. Not with a fishing boat. Though it'll be interesting to see who it is," Byron said confidently.

"More than likely just some guys doing some night fishing."

"Sue, Byron. It's me," Dan Morrissey's voice boomed out across choppy waves suddenly being churned by small gusts of wind.

The hand held searchlight was turned off. With the help of the bright moon, Sue could make out Dan Morrissey's broad body. The fishing boat's engine was cut back a notch more. Sue and Byron could hear the voices of the other people on the boat. Even while being rocked and knocked about by the suddenly whipped up waves, the rolling lobster boat floated slowly but surely in Sue's direction. There was a splash.

"Anchor, I hope," Sue sputtered. She raised her head and caught her breath before shouting, "I can't understand how you fellas could do this. Find us out in the middle of the deep here.

Dan shouted, "We did, though, and that's all that counts right now."

Sue was able to make out the vague images of three other men on the boat. One of them looked familiar. Sue identified him as soon as the boat's engine sputtered while being throttled down and finally choked off. The boat bounced and floated just above her and Byron. "I see Marone's with you," Sue said happily. "Glad to see that the state police are doing their job."

Marone grunted as he kneeled and reached down next to Dan to help pull Sue out of the water. After she was lifted into the fishing boat, Byron released his homemade floatation devices and reached up. With a helping hand from Dan Morrissey, he pulled himself slowly but surely up onto the boat. "Man that feels good, almost as good as being on terra firma. Next best thing." Byron sat on the deck and swept back his hair, which the seawater had turned into a messy mop.

After Sue and Byron wiped their faces with some paper towels, they were helped to their feet.

"Let's go down to the cabin. Much more comfortable there," the designated captain of the boat suggested.

Byron followed Sue down a couple of steps into the small cabin of the commercial fishing boat. There was hardly enough room to accommodate everyone in the sparsely and roughly furnished cabin area. Byron seated himself on one side of a small galley table while Sue sat on the other. Dan Morrissey and Frank Marone hovered over them and braced themselves against the walls of the boat as it swerved to turn gradually toward shore.

"How about some coffee?" A man who was dressed in a state trooper's uniform with corporal stripes on his upper sleeve entered the cabin with a large thermos bottle in one hand. From a couple of fingers of his other hand, he dangled a couple of mugs. He reached over to the table and placed the mugs in front of Sue and Byron and then poured the coffee from the thermos into the coffee mugs.

"Man, that's good coffee. How did you guys find us?" Byron insisted after he'd taken a long sip of coffee.

Marone's raspy sounding voice replied, "Wasn't easy. Long story. Dan'll fill you in. He did most of the work. Your private secretary, Harriet, found this and gave it to me when I went to your office to see if you was there. She's a nice gal Harriet." Marone smiled broadly. He took a folded piece of notepaper from his shirt pocket. He unfolded the notepaper and started reading from it in his best New Yorkese. "To whom it may concern. By the time you find this and me, I'm going to be dead from the very thing that I used on Nick Stockton and the others, a plastic bag, just as Detective Marone had suspected. I thought I was killing those people for humanitarian purposes as they were all suffering from AIDS. After a while I began to realize how wrong I was in doing what I did and couldn't live with it, so I had to do what I had to do, take my own life. Besides I could never make it in a prison. Sincerely, Byron Stone."

"You're kidding; that's so bush," Byron scoffed. "That birdo, Boris, on orders from Blake must have left that on my desk so that Harriet couldn't miss seeing it, although she doesn't miss much. But how in hell did you find us?"

"Boris. He ain't so bad after all. He's the one who made sure Harriet got the note, maybe as you said, on orders from Burke, but he's the one who alerted Dan, indirectly, I guess, as to what Blake was up to." The detective nodded toward Dan Morrissey.

"Boris? I knew it." Byron chuckled. "He must have diluted the sedative Blake gave me, the two of us."

Dan Morrissey explained assertively, "As you suggested, Byron, I bugged Kleptokoff's place, but somehow he found out about it and let me know that he did by tapping SOS on the bug. That's not all. He gambled. Added his name in Morse code. Clever guy, Boris. He calls Blake's other henchmen with Blake's orders so I knew exactly what they were up to, narrowed things down. So I got mobilized. Wanted to warn you, Mister Stone, Byron, so I first tried your home, the main house. They told me you were out with Sue, so then I went up to the guesthouse. I felt I must have just missed you, so I called for help. Marone. State police. I knew you were both in trouble when I saw both your cars where you'd left them, and you guys nowhere to be seen. From there I had to work fast 'cause I knew that Blake would be using his big boat to do his dirty work on, from what Boris said to Blake's men. When we didn't get to your private yacht club on time, luckily we found this thing we're in at that fishing pier in the village down the road from your yacht club."

"The captain of this tub is a paisano of mine," Marone interjected.

"So you haven't had a chance to catch Blake yet?" Sue asked, her face becoming flushed with the anger she felt at the mere thought of Blake's being able to escape. She speculated, "I hope he isn't on some private jet heading for some safe haven, a place where you can't catch him and make him pay for what he's done."

"Hope not," Marone growled good-naturedly. "That would be quite a miscarriage of justice. Nah, we'll catch up to him. We'll even get the Feds working on that. First we got to get you two back and get some statements from ya. Tomorrow, though." He checked his watch. "It is tomorrow. Still you'll be able to get a good night's sleep before then. Everything else can wait after what you two have been through." Marone shook his head. "I don't know how you did it. Got through so much. Survived. It must have been hairy."

Byron nodded. "Took team work. Sue helped keep me going. Swims like a fish. No, a champ."

Sue laughed. "And those deadly Stone bags sure came in handy."

Marone shot an oblique look at Byron.

Byron nodded. "They sure did. Don't know how I could've done without them."